BLOODLINES

**Center Point
Large Print**

**This Large Print Book carries the
Seal of Approval of N.A.V.H.**

BLOODLINES

DINAH McCALL

CENTER POINT PUBLISHING
THORNDIKE, MAINE

For every wanted baby, there is another somewhere else who never feels the love of a mother's touch. I dedicate this story to them, and to Christina Carol, our own little baby who was born with two thumbs on one hand, and who had to learn at a very early age how to live in the world without her mother's love.

And I also dedicate this book to her mother, Diane, who was taken from us too early—before her work on earth was done.

This Center Point Large Print edition
is published in the year 2005 by arrangement with
Harlequin Enterprises, Ltd.

The text of this Large Print edition is unabridged. In other aspects, this book may vary from the original edition. Printed in Thailand. Set in 16-point Times New Roman type.

ISBN 1-58547-630-7

Library of Congress Cataloging-in-Publication Data

McCall, Dinah.
    Bloodlines / Dinah McCall.--Center Point large print ed.
        p. cm.
    ISBN 1-58547-630-7 (lib. bdg. : alk. paper)
     1. Large type books. I. Title.

PS3569.A4565B58 2005
813'.54--dc22

2005005791

Prologue

Lake Texoma—north of Dallas, Texas

Marshall Baldwin was wielding the sledgehammer in his hands with as much delicacy as he moved through life, which was little to none. He had always been a take-charge kind of man, and his recent retirement had not changed that. In truth, retirement had only intensified his natural tendencies, driven as he was by fear someone might think him "too old" to cope. Now sweat poured out from beneath his John Deere gimme cap as studs and Sheetrock yielded to the hammer's blows.

From the appearance of the ancient wiring and lack of insulation in the old cottage he'd recently purchased, renovation was long overdue. Besides that, tearing something down and putting it back together in better order gave him something to do besides dwell on the fact that he'd been put out to pasture like an aging herd bull that was no longer worth its salt. Marshall didn't have a problem with hitting sixty-five, but he resented the hell out of being considered old and was taking his frustration out on the walls he was tearing down.

In the middle of a swing, Pansy, his wife of forty-three years, came into the room, stood for a moment watching her husband's face, then sighed.

"Marshall, do you have to make so much noise?"

He paused, trying not to glare. It wasn't Pansy's fault he'd been forcibly retired.

"Yes," he said, and swung the hammer once more.

"Maaarrrsshhaall!"

Marshall gritted his teeth as gypsum dust from the shattered Sheetrock showered down upon his hat, coating the bright green fabric in a white, powdery substance. He wished to God she would go shopping or something. How was he going to stand the last part of his life with her if she was on his case every minute?

The sledgehammer was on a downward arc again when Pansy grabbed his wrist, stopping the motion.

"Marshall! I'm trying to talk to you."

The sledgehammer slipped out of his hand and landed with a loud thud against the floorboard. Before Marshall could voice his frustration, something shifted inside the wall and fell down between the studs, hitting the floor with a thump. He got a brief glimpse of something rectangular and brown as it disappeared from sight.

"Did you see that?" he asked.

Pansy nodded. "What do you think it was?" Then she grabbed Marshall's arm again, only this time in excitement. "Oh, Marshall, what if we've found some kind of treasure? Would we have to give it back?"

Marshall frowned as he tried to peer through the opening. "Hell, no. We bought this place, lock, stock and barrel. What's here is ours."

"Can you see anything?" Pansy asked.

"Just a shape."

"See if you can reach it!" Pansy cried.

He thrust his arm into the opening that he'd made and

6

then reached down, running his fingers along the edge of the object until he felt metal against the leather.

"I think it's some kind of suitcase."

Pansy squealed, then jumped up and down. It was a girlie thing for a woman in her sixties to pull off, but Pansy managed it just fine. In fact, her enthusiasm was contagious. Marshall grinned back at her.

"Don't get too excited," he said. "It might be empty."

"No way," Pansy said. "If it was, then why would someone go to all the trouble of hiding it behind this wall?"

Marshall had to agree with her, but he kept silent as he felt for something to grab on to. A few moments later he felt what he thought might be a handle, curled his fingers around it and pulled. Resistance was minimal, but the opening in the Sheetrock wasn't large enough to accommodate the object and he was forced to let it go.

"It's too big for the hole," he muttered.

Pansy pointed to the sledgehammer that, only moments ago, she had wanted him to put down.

"Make it bigger," she said.

So he did.

A couple of minutes later he tried again, and this time, when he pulled on the object, he got it out.

"Oh, Marshall! It *is* a suitcase! I wonder what's in it. Open it quick!"

Marshall dropped to his knees as he reached for the latches, but they were stuck fast with rust.

"I can't. The latches are rusted stuck."

"Pry it open!" Pansy said, and handed him a pry bar.

Marshall grinned. Pansy had certainly changed her tune. He took the pry bar and jammed it into the crack beside the lock, then gave it a twist. The lock snapped like a twig.

Pansy giggled. "Oooh, what if it's full of money?"

"We'll know soon enough," he muttered, and jammed the pry bar beside the second latch. It gave way as easily as the first.

He looked up at Pansy, then winked. "Here goes nothing," he said, and lifted the top.

There was a moment of stunned silence; then Pansy moaned, covered her face with her hands and started to cry.

Even though Marshall kept looking, he couldn't wrap his mind around what he was seeing. It was a skeleton—of a child. He wanted to believe it wasn't real—couldn't be real. He heard the sudden and rapid thunder of his heartbeat, and wondered if he was having a heart attack there on the floor. Then a small black beetle suddenly crawled out of a tiny eye socket in the skull. Startled, he let go of the lid and rocked back on his knees. The lid fell backward with a thump, shifting the bones of the tiny skeleton even more than they'd been before.

"Oh, sweet Jesus," he muttered, then dragged Pansy up with him as he stood and pressed her face against his chest. For a moment, neither of them could speak. Then he made himself focus and took her by the shoulders. "Dang it, Pansy, stop crying and go get me the phone," he said, then wiped a shaky hand across his face while

Pansy made a run for her purse.

She handed it to him without speaking. Marshall took a deep breath, trying to calm his racing thoughts, but his hands were shaking as he dialed 911.

Pansy looked at the suitcase as tears ran down her cheeks.

"Dear God, Marshall, who could do such a thing?"

"I don't know, and I thank God I don't have to be the one to find out."

Then he heard a woman's voice in his ear. It was the dispatcher.

"911. What is your emergency?"

Marshall took a deep breath. "My name is Marshall Baldwin. I just bought a property four miles west of the Fish Shack near landing number four at Lake Texoma. You need to send the police out to my house immediately."

"And what is your emergency?"

"I just found a skeleton in a suitcase."

There was a brief moment of silence, then the dispatcher asked, "I'm sorry, sir. Did I understand you to say a skeleton?"

"Yes."

"In a suitcase?"

"Yes."

"How large is the suitcase?" the dispatcher asked.

"Not very large," Marshall muttered, then looked down at the open suitcase at his feet. "And neither is the skeleton. It's a child. The remains . . . they belong to a very small child."

1

Dallas detective Trey Bonney strode into the precinct, nursing his second cup of coffee of the morning while trying not to think about the paperwork stacking up on his desk. He was a crackerjack detective, but when it came to filling out reports, he sucked.

"Morning, Trey."

He nodded a hello to file clerk Lisa Morrow without meeting her gaze. To a single man who'd had his share of one-night stands, her come-hither drawl was unmistakable. Three years ago—even two years ago— he might have taken her up on the invitation. But no more. His transition to a true maturity with an end to one-night stands had finally arrived. It had been gradual, and he still wasn't sure when it had happened, but it was a lot lonelier than he had expected. Even so, Lisa's presence and beckoning voice were nothing more than a small obstacle course on his way to his desk. But when another female called his name, he recognized the voice and looked up.

"Hey, Trey!"

Trey set his coffee cup on his desk as he gave Detective Chia Rodriguez his full attention. If she stretched, she measured an inch over five feet tall, but her size was deceiving. She was bulldog tough and constantly pissed due to the fact that the detectives in the precinct had a habit of referring to her as the office "Chia Pet."

Her short, unruly curls did nothing to deflect the image. Still, he liked her attitude and, on occasion, fished with her husband, Pete Rodriguez, who owned and operated his own landscape business.

"Yeah, what's up?" he asked.

"Lieutenant Warren said for you to come see him as soon as you came in."

Trey eyed the backlog of paperwork and grimaced. "Probably going to chain me to the desk until I finish these files."

Chia grinned and pointed toward their superior's office.

"Yeah, yeah, I'm going," Trey said, then took one more sip of coffee and put down the cup, bracing himself for what he figured would be, at the least, a dressing-down.

He lifted his chin, yanked nervously at the tail of his sports coat, then moved toward the office. He knocked once, then opened the door and leaned inside.

"You wanted to see me, Lieutenant?"

Harold Warren looked up from the paperwork on his desk and waved Trey inside.

"If it's about the files . . ."

"Don't second-guess," Warren muttered. "It'll get you in trouble every time. Come in and shut the door."

"Yes, sir," Trey said.

"Sit," Warren said, pointing to a chair.

Again Trey obeyed, wishing he'd brought the rest of his coffee with him.

"How old are you?" Warren asked.

"I'll be thirty in September," Trey said.

"Too young to remember," Warren muttered, more to himself than to Trey.

"Remember what?" Trey asked.

"The Sealy kidnapping."

Trey flinched. Warren saw it.

"What?"

"Actually, I do know something about it," he said.

"How so?" Warren asked.

"I, uh . . . know Olivia Sealy."

Harold arched an eyebrow. "I wasn't aware that you ran in such exclusive circles."

"I don't," Trey snapped. "We went to the same public high school. Even then she was sort of famous, you know. Parents murdered—raised by a rich-as-sin grandfather who showed up for school plays in a limousine."

"She went to public school?"

Trey shrugged. "Marcus Sealy didn't believe in separation of the classes. He wanted her to grow up as normally as possible." *He just didn't want her anywhere near me.*

"You seem to know a lot about her. Is there anything else you'd like to tell me before I continue?"

He thought about the fight they'd had when she came to break it off with him—remembering the shame in her eyes when she'd told him they couldn't see each other anymore and they both knew it was because his father was a drunk and his mother waited tables for a living.

"No."

"Is there anything between you two that could be construed as a conflict of interest?"

Now Trey was getting curious. "I haven't seen her in years," he muttered. "What's up?"

"Two days ago, while renovating a lake cabin up at Texoma, a man found a suitcase in a wall. They found the skeletal remains of a toddler inside."

"Good God," Trey muttered, then frowned. "But what does this have to do with the Sealy family?"

"Maybe nothing, but I want you to go see the Grayson County sheriff. His name is Blue Jenner. He's a friend of mine, and he's the one who caught the coincidence."

"Yeah, sure, Lieutenant, but what coincidence? What does a baby's skeleton have to do with Olivia Sealy's kidnapping? They found her, remember?"

"Maybe . . . maybe not," Warren said. "The Sealy kidnapping was the department's case. I was a rookie when it happened. Hadn't been on the force more than three months when she was snatched. Half the force was on that case. I was there when one of the kidnappers, Foster Lawrence, took the ransom money. We followed him, hoping to get to the kid, only we lost him. By the time we found him again, the money was missing and the kid was nowhere to be found. We were all down and out, certain that we'd blown any chance of getting that kid back alive, when she up and appears wandering around a shopping center in a pair of pajamas and dragging her blanket behind her. Talk about a high!"

Trey couldn't quit thinking of the Olivia he'd known.

As a teenager, she'd been so pretty and self-assured. Even though they'd all known her history, it had never occurred to him to think of her as a toddler, lost and frightened and wondering what had happened to her world. Had she seen her parents murdered? Did she remember any of that now?

"So what does that skeleton up at Texoma have to do with Olivia Sealy?" Trey asked.

"One of the defining factors in identifying the kidnapped baby was the fact that she'd had two thumbs on her left hand . . . a trait that all the Sealy family supposedly share."

Trey shook his head. "But Olivia didn't have—"

"I understand that they all have the extra digit removed once it's obvious which one is dominant. Even the old man, Marcus Sealy, has a small scar to prove it."

"So . . . ?"

"So after the Grayson county coroner finished his autopsy on the remains and Blue Jenner saw it, he gave me a call."

"Why?"

"The coroner's best estimate is that the remains found at the cabin are of a female about two years old. They're still running tests to determine when they think the baby was murdered, but he's guessing it was twenty to twenty-five years ago."

Trey frowned. "I still don't see what that has to do with—"

"It was twenty-five years ago this year that the Sealy

kidnapping occurred, and . . . it seems that the baby in the suitcase also had two left thumbs."

Trey leaned forward. "Are you saying that Olivia Sealy isn't really—"

"I'm not saying anything," Warren said. "Just go talk to Blue Jenner, question the coroner, check out the cabin, and do what you do best, which is nose around. Find out what you can about the previous owners."

"Yeah, all right," Trey said as he stood. He reached for the doorknob, then stopped and turned around.

"What?" Lieutenant Warren asked.

"The Sealys . . . do they know about this?" Trey asked.

"If they don't, they will soon enough," Warren said.

"How so?" Trey asked.

Warren unfolded the newspaper and pointed to the headline: Sealy Connection To Skeletal Remains?

"We don't know squat and they still print it. How do they get away with that?" Trey muttered.

Warren pointed to the question mark in the headline.

"It's all in the punctuation, but maybe after you talk to Jenner we'll have answers for everyone."

2

Marcus Sealy had his taste buds set for the waffles he could smell cooking in the kitchen down the hall, then smiled to himself at the sound of his grand-daughter's laughter coming from the same place. Best guess would be that she was stealing bacon faster than the house-keeper, Rose, could cook it, just as she'd done for the past twenty-odd years.

After three weeks of a much-needed vacation in Europe, it felt good to be home. Last night he and Olivia had been on the last plane to land at DFW air-port. It was after midnight by the time they arrived at the estate. Exhausted from the long overseas flight, they'd ignored a stack of phone messages, a huge pile of mail and suitcases needing to be unpacked, and headed for the comfort of their beds.

The trip had been Olivia's gift to him for his seven-tieth birthday, and they'd had a ball. They'd laughed and partied all the way across Europe, and made mem-ories he would take to his grave. This morning, as he was dressing, he'd kept thinking of how much fun they'd had and what Olivia meant to him. After his son, Michael, and daughter-in-law, Kay, had been murdered years ago, he'd held his only grandchild far too close to his heart. He knew that he'd sheltered her more than he should have, but it seemed impossible to be any less protective. She was all the family he had left, and if anything ever happened to her, it would be the end of him, too.

His musing ended when he heard footsteps and then saw a flash of yellow. Moments later, Olivia came out of the kitchen.

"Grampy! I didn't know you were already down-stairs. After that flight, I thought surely you'd sleep in."

Marcus smiled and kissed Olivia on the cheek as she threw herself into his arms.

"You didn't," he said.

"I know, but it's so good to be home," she said, then added, "You smell good. Calvin Klein's Obsession, isn't it?"

"Yes, and you smell pretty darn good yourself. Oscar Meyer bacon, right?"

As always, her laughter rocked his world. He slipped an arm over her shoulder as he led her to the breakfast room.

"Did you leave any bacon for me?" he asked as he seated her at the table.

Olivia made a face. "Why, Grampy . . . surely you're not suggesting that I'm a pig?"

"Oh no . . . only that you like eating them."

He grinned as Rose carried in a platter of bacon in one hand and a bowl of scrambled eggs in another. The basket of hot biscuits was already on the table beside a pot of honey and a glass compote of strawberry jam. Even though there were only Marcus and Olivia to share the meal, he always insisted their meals be served in an old-fashioned, home-style manner. Despite the vastness of his wealth, the simple bowls of food reminded him of his own childhood and humble beginnings.

"Rose, as always, it looks marvelous and smells delicious," Marcus said as the housekeeper poured hot coffee into their cups.

Rose Kopecnick smiled and winked at Olivia. "Tastes

good, too, doesn't it, honey girl?"

"I plead the Fifth and please pass the bacon," Olivia said.

"If you don't mind, I'll help myself first," Marcus said. "After that, it's all yours."

"Works for me," Olivia said, and served herself a healthy helping of fluffy scrambled eggs while keeping a watchful eye on the bacon Marcus was putting on his plate.

The meal progressed in silence as the first pangs of hunger were appeased, interspersed with bits of conversation later as it drew to an end.

"What are you going to do today?" Marcus asked as he laid his napkin beside his plate.

Olivia swallowed her last sip of coffee, then leaned back in her chair.

"Unpack."

He smiled. "And after that?"

"Return some phone calls and sleep through jet lag. You should do the same."

"I'll nap in the daytime when I'm too old to do anything else," Marcus said.

Olivia rolled her eyes. "Oh, Grampy, you'll never be old."

He thought of the seventy years that were behind him while refusing to dwell on the dwindling few he had left.

"Maybe not in my head, but we'll see what my body has to say about that."

Olivia leaned forward and threaded her fingers

through Marcus's. Before she could speak, the phone began to ring.

"I'll get it," she said.

Marcus stood up and followed her out of the room. He was in the hall and heading toward the library when he heard Olivia raise her voice to the caller on the other end of the line.

"I don't know what you're talking about," she said, and hung up the phone. There was a frown on her face as she turned around.

"Olivia . . . darling . . . what's wrong?"

"That was weird," she said. "Some reporter wanted to know if I had any comments regarding the headline in the morning paper."

"What headline?" Marcus asked.

Olivia shrugged. "I don't know. I haven't seen a paper, have you?"

Marcus pointed down the hall. "Rose probably put them in the library with the accumulated mail. Let's go see."

Rose had laid the mail on Marcus's desk, with the oldest on the left and the most recent on the right. The newspapers were in a stack with the most recent on top. Marcus saw the headline even before he picked up the paper.

"What the hell? Sealy connection to skeletal remains? What does that mean?" He tried to read the smaller print, then squinted and patted his pockets. "I need my glasses."

"Here, Grampy, let me," Olivia said, and took the

paper out of his hands and scanned the story, frowning as she read.

"What's it about?" Marcus asked.

Olivia's frown deepened as she looked up.

"Some people up at Texoma were renovating a house they just bought. They found a suitcase in a wall, and when they opened it, it contained the skeletal remains of a little girl about two years old."

"Good Lord!" Marcus said, and reached behind him for a chair. He sank into it with a thump. "That's horrible, but why would they link the discovery to us?"

Olivia's hands were shaking as she handed him the paper. "Because the coroner said she was born with two left thumbs."

Marcus let the paper fall to the floor as he reached for Olivia's hand, unconsciously rubbing the tiny scar where her second thumb used to be.

"We're not the only family with such anomalies. Why would they single us out again?"

Olivia pointed to the paper, then had to clear her throat before she could say it.

"They're putting the homicide at about twenty-five years ago . . . which was the time of my kidnapping."

Marcus's hand stilled momentarily; then he clutched Olivia's hand firmly.

"See, that just proves that tragedies happen to all of us," he said gruffly.

There was a long moment of silence between them, and when it was broken, it was Olivia who spoke.

"Grampy?"

He spoke absently, his mind still turning over the facts of what she'd read. "What, darling?"

"Were you sure?"

He started, then looked up. "I'm sorry . . . what were you saying?"

She said it again, this time putting emphasis on the last word.

"Were you *sure?*"

"Sure about what?"

"Me . . . when the kidnappers turned me loose. You knew for sure it was me, didn't you?"

Marcus stood abruptly and took Olivia in his arms.

"Oh, Olivia, of course I was sure. You were my grandchild. Your father and mother ate Sunday dinner with me every week. You and I fed the fish in the goldfish pond every Sunday afternoon. I remember the day I let you pick all the blooms off your mother's prize begonias because you liked the way they felt against your skin. I knew you, darling . . . just as I know you now. Never doubt that we are of the same flesh. Never."

Olivia blinked back tears as she wrapped her arms around his waist.

"I'm sorry for asking. It's just that we never talk about it, and I wasn't sure if—"

Marcus took her by the shoulders and pushed her back until she was forced to meet his gaze.

"Darling, we never talk about it because there's nothing to say. You were so small, barely two years old. Thank the good Lord you have no memory of seeing your parents murdered, or of where you were kept, or who had you. It has been the only blessing to come out of it all. The last thing I would ever do is speak of something that I always feared would cause you emotional damage."

"Oh, Grampy, I'm sorry. I never thought of it like that."

Marcus smiled gently as he cupped her face. "You know who you are. There are pictures of you with your parents all over this house, and at least once a year we get out the old albums and look at them, right?"

She nodded, then managed a smile. "And the old movies . . . don't forget them," she added.

"Yes. Your father was something of a fanatic about you. He filmed you at every stage of your life. I'd venture to say there's more film of you and your first two years of life than many people have of their entire existence. Besides that, there's no mistaking that the baby in those pictures is the same baby I got back."

"When the kidnappers let me go, was I happy to see you?" Olivia asked.

Marcus frowned. "You weren't happy about anything, darling, and the doctors expected it. You cried nonstop for days, begging for your mother. It nearly broke my heart."

Olivia laid her hand against her grandfather's chest, taking comfort from the steady rhythm against her palm.

"How did you cope?"

"I finally hired a nanny, remember? It was Anna Walden who finally settled you in, although, to be honest, by then I think you'd just cried yourself out."

Olivia nodded. "Speaking of Anna, it's been ages since I visited her." Then she frowned. "Do you think the reporters will bother her about this?"

"I don't know, but I'd lay odds that if one of them thinks about it, they will," Marcus said. "I'll try to take some time off and drive out to Arlington to see her, but it'll have to wait a bit. I wouldn't trade a moment of our three weeks in Europe, but I fear there's a lot of business that needs to be tended."

Olivia pointed at the newspaper, which had fallen on the floor. "So what do we do about that?"

"It has nothing to do with us, so we do nothing, okay?"

"Okay," Olivia said, then threw her arms around her grandfather's neck. "I love you, Grampy."

He closed his eyes as he hugged her back. "And I love you, too, my dear." Then he turned her loose with a pat on the back and gave her a handful of phone messages. "I believe these are all yours. Don't overdo yourself with commitments. I'm getting selfish in my old age and want a little of your time to myself."

"I promise," she said, and left with the messages in her hand.

Marcus and Olivia weren't the only ones shocked by the morning paper. Dennis Rawlins, a man with painful secrets, read the same headline, but with a different reaction.

Without delving into details, he made a snap judg-

23

ment, deeming the Sealy family guilty of some deadly indiscretion and decided that they must pay.

It would take a lot of planning, but he was determined to make his presence known.

Trey pulled up to the Grayson County sheriff's office, exiting the comfort of his air-conditioned car for the summer heat of Texas just as a skinny, middle-aged woman walked out. It was all Trey could do not to stare. Between her spiky pink hair and the little dog with a matching pink topknot that she was carrying, she was a sight to behold.

The woman caught him looking and blasted him with a hundred-watt smile. As she did, the dog bared its teeth and growled.

Now he was caught. Both with matching pink hair. Both baring their teeth at him. He couldn't help it. He laughed.

The woman scolded the little dog, but at the same time she gave it a gentle squeeze and kissed it on the nose.

"Now, Cujo, you be nice to the pretty man, you hear?"

The dog continued to growl at Trey as the woman shifted it to her other arm, then grinned and winked as she sauntered past.

Trey tipped his hat and wisely kept on walking. Moments later, he was inside the sheriff's office and back to serious business. Investigating anything that had to do with Olivia Sealy felt wrong—as if he was going behind her back. Feeling guilty about that was stupid because he hadn't seen or talked to her in eleven years, and the last words they'd shared had been in anger. He didn't owe her anything, especially loyalty or allegiance.

Still, his conscience continued to smart as he walked up to the receptionist. She was standing at a file cabinet with her back to the door. When she continued to file papers without turning around, he cleared his throat.

"Excuse me," Trey said.

She jumped, then turned abruptly.

"My stars, you nearly scared the life right out of me. I heard the door chime, but I thought it was just Mama and Cujo leaving."

Before Trey thought about how it might sound, he heard himself asking, "The lady with pink hair was your mother?"

The woman grinned. "Yeah, and that little old rat of a dog is the only sibling I'm ever likely to have."

"I'm sorry, I didn't mean to—"

The woman held up her hand. "Don't apologize. She takes pride in her . . . individuality, as she calls it. However, Cujo hasn't been the same since Mama had the dog groomer dye his hair pink, too."

"I can only imagine."

The woman laughed. "Now, how can I help you?"

Trey managed a shamefaced grin. "Detective Trey Bonney to see Sheriff Jenner. I think he's expecting me."

She glanced down at a desk calendar, then up at Trey.

25

"Yes, Detective Bonney, he is, but he's on the phone. Please have a seat, and as soon as he's finished with his call, I'll let him know you're here."

Trey nodded, but before he could sit down, the door to the sheriff's office opened and a man walked out. The receptionist looked up.

"Sheriff Jenner . . . Detective Bonney is here."

Blue Jenner paused in midstep. Trey saw him shifting mental gears as he held out his hand.

"Detective, I got a call you were coming."

Trey nodded. "After the discovery up at Lake Texoma, my lieutenant was pretty insistent."

Blue shoved a hand through his hair, then scratched absently at the back of his neck.

"I welcome any help I can get on this," he said. "I'm looking at a very cold trail to an old crime. Lord only knows if the people who did this are still alive, but if they're not, I hope they're burning in hell. It's been a while since anything got to me like this has."

Immediately, Trey picked up on the timeline.

"So we know for sure that the remains are old?"

Blue nodded. "Let's talk in my office," he said, closing the door behind them as Trey sat down in a chair opposite the sheriff's desk. Blue sat down, too, then opened a file and shoved it across the desk toward Trey. "It's all in there."

Trey picked up the file and leafed through the papers until he came to the autopsy report. It was difficult to maintain his composure as he scanned the coroner's drawings of the tiny bones, with the clinical notations of age and injuries. Despite his years on the force, he never got used to working cases involving children.

"How firm is the estimated date of when the crime took place?" Trey asked.

"As firm as it can be."

Trey sighed. That meant the death of this child really had occurred at about the same time as the Sealy kidnapping. The odds of two little girls with an extra thumb on their left hands going missing in the Dallas area at the same time without any connection to each other were astronomical to impossible.

"What do you know so far?" Trey asked.

"We're researching past owners of the lake house. There were quite a few during the past twenty-five years."

Trey fingered the pages in the file as he thought through his options, but his instructions from Lieutenant Warren had been clear.

"My lieutenant wants to make sure we cover all the bases on this, so before I go, I'd like to take a look at the site of the discovery."

"No problem," Jenner said. "Ever been to Texoma?"

"Yes, but it's been a few years."

Blue reached for a piece of paper and a pen. "I'll draw you a map."

"I appreciate it," Trey said.

Jenner drew the map, explaining a couple of the landmarks to Trey as he handed it over, then walked him to the door.

"Look, Bonney, if this turns out to be connected to the

old Sealy case, I don't have any problem with your department taking over the lead. Just keep me in the loop."

Trey shrugged. "If it turns out to be connected to the Sealy case, we'll both probably take a back seat to the Feds who ran the show the first time. They were the ones who caught the perp who picked up the ransom. Fisher Lawrence, I think his name was. No, Foster. Foster Lawrence."

Blue's eyes narrowed thoughtfully. "I don't think I knew anything about a ransom being paid." Then he grinned. "This was all a good bit before my time."

"Yeah, mine, too," Trey said. "However, I did go to high school with Olivia Sealy."

"You're kidding! What was she like?"

"Rich," Trey said shortly.

Blue Jenner grinned, then changed the subject. "This Lawrence fellow, did he ever give up any of the others involved?"

Trey shook his head. "According to the old reports I read last night, he didn't tell the Feds anything."

"Then how did they connect him to the crime?"

"He was seen picking up the ransom. They went after him, lost him, then found him again, only he'd stashed the money somewhere in between. All he would say was that he didn't know anything about anyone being killed."

Blue grinned. "They're always innocent, aren't they?"

"As a baby," Trey added, then shook Jenner's hand.

"Thank you for the information and the map. When you get a list of cabin owners, let me know, okay?"

"Will do," Blue said.

A short while later, Trey was on his way to Lake Texoma. The map Jenner had drawn for him was easy to follow, and any doubts about being in the right place vanished when he got to the driveway that led to the house. The For Sale sign and the yellow crime-scene tape were impossible to miss. Originally, it had probably been stretched across the driveway to keep the curious away. But now that the coroner and the men from the sheriff's department had come and gone, what was left of the tape was entwined among the trees and bushes at the entrance. It made Trey think of the yellow ribbons family members often tied around trees as a reminder that someone in the family was missing. Only this time a tiny someone, who nobody even knew had been missing, was now found. All the authorities had to do was figure out her identity and they would be one step closer to finding out who had killed her. He turned off the road and accelerated up the driveway.

As he pulled up to the house, he realized he wasn't alone. A tall, gray-haired man was carrying a box out toward the open doors of a rental moving van. When he saw Trey, he began to frown. Trey killed the engine and got out.

"I'm sorry, mister, but this is private property, and I'm going to have to ask you to leave," the man said.

Trey took out his badge.

"Detective Bonney . . . Dallas PD," Trey said.

The man set the box into the back of the van.

"Marshall Baldwin. I own this property," he said, eyeing Trey suspiciously. "What does the Dallas Police Department have to do with this?"

"Maybe nothing, sir, but I've come to check it out anyway. I understand you're the one who found the suitcase?"

Marshall nodded, then shoved his hands in his pockets.

"Yes, I did, and it was terrible, just terrible. Pansy and I will never get over it." Then he gave the area a slow, agonized look. "This was going to be our dream home, and instead, it's a nightmare." Tears pooled in his eyes, then spilled unashamedly down his cheeks. "Poor, poor, little baby girl."

Trey took a slow breath. This wasn't making the trip any easier.

"Since you're here, would you mind walking me through the discovery?"

Marshall took out a handkerchief and wiped his eyes, then used it to blow his nose.

"I suppose one more time won't kill me," he said, and then rolled his eyes as he realized what he'd said. "I didn't mean——"

"It's okay, Mr. Baldwin. I appreciate anything you can tell me."

Marshall stuffed his handkerchief back into his pocket as he led the way into the house.

"As you can see, we were in the midst of some remodeling," he said, pointing to a stepladder leaning against a wall and a pile of drop cloths near the door. "Pansy was getting ready to repaint the kitchen, and I was knocking out this wall here to make these two small rooms into one big living room. I was using a sledgehammer. Hit a stud, and as the Sheetrock shattered, I saw something drop past the opening I'd already made. Right off we figured it for a suitcase." He tried to smile, but it turned into a grimace. "Pansy thought we'd found a treasure."

"Must have been tough," Trey said.

"You have no idea," Marshall said. "Pansy still cries about it. We've got five grandbabies of our own, you know. Can't imagine anyone doing anything so evil to a baby."

"Unfortunately, Mr. Baldwin, chasing evil is my business, and I've seen a lot of it. But when it involves children, it's rough on all of us."

The old man nodded. "I expect so." Then he pointed to a large hole in the wall. "Well, this is where we found it. If you don't mind, I'll just be loading up the last of our stuff. I don't want to have to come back here again."

"Yes, sir, and I thank you," Trey said as he shook Marshall Baldwin's hand.

Marshall made himself scarce as Trey began to poke through the rubble on the other side of the wall, even though he knew that all the findings from the scene were noted in the duplicate file that Blue Jenner had given him.

He tried to imagine the mind-set of someone who

31

would do this. Had the baby died of an accident and someone panicked—or had it been something uglier? Had the intent been to hide a murder most foul? Whatever the reason, the treatment of this innocent's passing had been as cowardly an act as he'd seen.

He leaned into the opening, eyeing the dust and debris, as well as the area above his head where the suitcase had been shoved. He wrinkled his nose to stifle a sneeze and wondered how much asbestos he was breathing, then frowned at himself. It damn sure wasn't asbestos that had killed that baby.

He pulled back from the opening and then stood for a moment, absorbing the silence. Dust motes highlighted by the sunshine coming through a curtainless window hung motionless within the air. Trey wasn't a man given to flights of fancy, but he felt the burden of this crime in a way he'd never felt before. The system might have let this child down once before, but now he had a chance to put things right.

He took a slow, deep breath as a soft vow left his lips.

"We'll find 'em, baby girl. I promise I won't let them get away with this."

Bile hung at the back of Foster Lawrence's throat as he walked toward the outer gates of Lompoc Federal Prison. He wouldn't draw a good breath until he was standing in free space and the gates had closed behind him. When he finally passed through them, he swallowed the bile and inhaled with a smile. Even the air smelled different outside those walls.

For the first time in twenty-five years, still riding on the high of freedom, he started to shake. It was hard to believe, but it was true. It was over. He was free.

Then he amended the thought. He *was* free, but it *wasn't* over. It would never be over until he got what was owed him. He'd spent all these years behind bars for kidnapping, when the true perpetrator had gone free. And while he admitted he had been a party to acquiring the ransom, he considered he'd been wronged. He hadn't known that murder had already been done, or that revenge had been the reason. Still, when he'd learned of the outcome, it had been too late to amend his participation.

When all was said and done, the way he looked at it, there had been little harm in asking for money from a man rich enough to pay it. He had just needed some money to make a new start.

He'd gotten the money—and the new start. He just hadn't planned on it being in a federal prison. And while he could have turned evidence against the other person involved, it wouldn't have changed the outcome of his sentence. So, out of both spite for the powers that be and a sense of obligation, he had kept the rest of the truth to himself and served the sentence, knowing full well that when he got out, the money he'd hidden would all be his, and to hell with old ties and promises. He was out now, and going to take back what he'd stashed all those years ago. The way he looked at it, he'd more than earned it.

As he moved away from the gate, he saw a taxi

coming toward him. As soon as it pulled up, he jumped in, gave the driver a destination and never looked back.

3

Trey's report to Lieutenant Warren was enough to warrant further investigation but not enough to firmly link the skeletal remains at Lake Texoma to the Sealy kidnapping, although Warren felt in his gut that they were related.

Sheriff Jenner had faxed the Dallas PD an addendum to the report he'd given Trey and shipped it to Dallas along with the suitcase and the remains. They now had a complete list of the different property owners since the man-made lake and the house had been built, and had identified the owner of the property at the time the baby had been killed. It didn't prove that the child had been killed on the property, but the body *had* been hidden there, and it gave them a place to start.

Warren frowned as he continued to read. According to the notation at the bottom of the page, the owner, David Lehrman, had died in a car crash a year before the Sealy kidnapping. In despondency, his wife, Carol Lehrman, had immediately moved back to her hometown of Boston. For the next three years the house sat empty, until Mrs. Lehrman finally sold it at auction, which was two years after the kidnapping. Instead of narrowing the field, that information blasted it wide open. With the house sitting empty during those three years, anyone could have had access to it. As if that wasn't enough grief for Lieutenant Warren, he had the media to contend with, as well.

Stories ran in the newspapers daily, dragging up the old tragedy of the murder of Olivia's parents during her kidnapping, along with reminders of how broken Marcus Sealy had been by the events. Pictures and film clips of Foster Lawrence's arrest, as well as the ensuing trial, came next. Then yesterday, a whole new aspect of this case was revealed. It began when a hotshot reporter did a follow-up on Lawrence, stating that Lawrence had recently been released from prison, it started a whole new shock wave of speculation that Warren was having to deal with.

They couldn't ignore the possibility that he might show up in Dallas to collect the missing ransom money. A million dollars would have been worth the twenty-five years in prison his conviction had cost him.

Coupled with Foster Lawrence's release and the discovery of the baby's remains, Warren had a sense of foreboding. It was past time to talk to Marcus and Olivia Sealy. He set his jaw and picked up the phone.

He hadn't slept worth a damn last night, Trey thought, maneuvering his car through the Dallas traffic. And what sleep he *had* managed to get had been filled with dreams of high school and the girl who'd stolen, then broken, his heart. He hadn't seen her since she'd announced it would be in their best interests to see other people, but at the time, thinking of her with another guy had been enough to bring him to his knees. He hadn't let another female get that far under his skin since. The fact that he was less than ten minutes away from seeing her again should have been secondary to the questioning that would take place, but it wasn't. The knot in his belly twisted ever tighter the closer he got.

Dennis Rawlins was also tense, but from anticipation. Before long, he would make sure the world knew of the Sealy family's involvement in a baby's death. It didn't matter to him that the truth was being bent to his way of thinking. He desperately needed the outlet of protesting to assuage his own soul.

For the first time in Olivia Sealy's memory, she felt threatened. She was at the mercy of something completely out of her control. In her heart, she felt she was where she belonged. She'd seen the family pictures. She'd seen the family resemblances. She had her father's eyes, as well as his smile, not to mention her grandfather's reassurances. But it was difficult to ignore the timing of the other child's death, or the anomaly they had shared. She glanced down at the tiny scar on her left hand, absently rubbing the place where the extra thumb had once been. It seemed impossible to accept the similarities as nothing but coincidence, but she had to believe that was all they were.

And now a detective from the Dallas Police Department would be arriving soon to question them about the kidnapping—a kidnapping she didn't remember.

She glanced at her watch. It was almost ten. Time to finish dressing. She reached down into the bottom of her closet, pulled out a pair of shoes and then glanced at her watch again. She didn't want to keep the man waiting. The sooner they got started, the sooner this nightmare would be over. With a shaky sigh, she stepped into the shoes, then turned toward the full-length mirror and gave herself a final look.

She was taller than her mother. She knew because Marcus told her so, but she wasn't taller than her father. He'd been tall—so tall, and very handsome. When she thought about it, she hurt for all the lost years she should have been able to spend with them, then felt selfish for dwelling on it when she still had her life—and she still had Grampy.

She smoothed her hands down the front of her shirt, absently eyeing the moss-green color against the rust-colored slacks, then wondered why she cared how she was dressed. It wasn't her clothes the detective was coming to see. She swallowed around the lump in her throat, and then lifted her chin and blinked rapidly, dispelling the urge to cry.

As she did, the doorbell chimed.

"Please let this be okay," she muttered, then left her room and started toward the stairs.

Rose was already opening the front door when Olivia reached the landing. The man on the threshold walked inside, and as he did, Olivia felt as if reality began shifting to slow motion.

Oh my God! Trey? Trey Bonney?

From the corner of her eye, she saw her grandfather coming out of the library, then moving toward the man standing in the foyer. Sunshine was beaming through the stained-glass arch above the front door, leaving a Monet-like pattern of color splattered upon the blue-veined marble at his feet. Her heartbeat slowed down and then suddenly sped up as an old memory filled her mind.

"Oh, Trey, I'm scared."

"I'm scared, too, Livvie. I'm afraid that I'll do something wrong, or disappoint you. And I know it's going to hurt you."

She locked her hands behind Trey's neck as she gazed at him with passionate intent. They'd come so close to this moment a dozen times before, but each time they'd stopped. Making love was a big thing. Making love for the first time was even bigger, and Olivia was a virgin and Trey knew it.

"I'll stop, Livvie. Just say the word and I'll stop."

Olivia shivered. "No, Trey. I want this . . . I want you. I love you so much."

She felt Trey shudder as he leaned down and gave her a kiss.

"Olivia Sealy, you are everything to me."

Olivia sighed, then gave herself up to the inevitable.

Rose shut the door behind Trey with a firm thump. The sound broke Olivia's mood. As if in a trance, she moved forward, feeling for the top step with the toe of her shoe. Unable to look away from him for fear he would disappear, she stepped down without caution. It was instinct that got her to the bottom of the stairs, but it was fear that held her there. She had seen those dark eyes and that crooked smile too many nights in too many old dreams, but what did he have to do with the present chaos of their lives?

Trey had caught himself holding his breath as he rang the doorbell. It wasn't until the door was opened and he saw a woman he took to be the housekeeper that he pulled himself together.

"Detective Bonney to see Mr. Sealy."

Rose stepped aside as the policeman walked in. "Yes, Detective. He's expecting you."

"I'm here," Marcus said as he hurried down the hall and quickly shook Trey's hand. Then he turned to Rose.

"Thank you, Rose. Bring some coffee to the library, will you?"

"Yes, sir. Right away."

Marcus was the picture of congeniality as he turned to Trey.

"Detective Bonney?"

Trey nodded as he shook Marcus Sealy's hand and tried not to think of the irony of the situation. This was the man who had ended his relationship with Olivia because he considered neither Trey nor his family to be good enough for a Sealy. Now Trey was here to judge the veracity of Marcus Sealy's past. Marcus obviously didn't recognize Trey or remember the name.

"Yes, I'm Detective Bonney. Thank you for seeing me. I know this must be a difficult time for your family."

Marcus kept a polite smile on his face, but Trey noted that the smile never reached his eyes.

"I'm happy to do what I can to help you find the identity of the child who was murdered."

"Thank you," Trey said. "I'll try not to take up too much of your time."

Marcus eyed the detective, then sighed. There was no getting past the inevitable. "Follow me, Detective Bonney. We can talk more comfortably in the library."

As Marcus turned, he saw Olivia at the foot of the stairs.

"Olivia . . . darling . . . I didn't know you were there. This is Detective Bonney. Detective . . . my grand-daughter, Olivia Sealy."

Olivia was pale and shaking. Concerned that she felt so distressed over having the police in the house, Marcus slipped an arm around her shoulder and led her into the library, not even noticing the fact that the detective and Olivia had said not a word to each other.

The moment Trey saw Olivia Sealy's face, the last eleven years seemed to fade away. He felt the same panic he'd felt the day she walked out of his life. Then, he hadn't been sure he would know how to live without her. Now, he didn't know what he thought, but he did know that he wished this meeting was under different circumstances.

He took no satisfaction in the knowledge that he'd

been right to worry about seeing her again. Age had been kind to Olivia. She'd been a pretty girl. Now she was stunning, and, from the look on her face, none too happy to see him.

Olivia couldn't think. The moment she'd seen Trey on the doorstep, she'd gone numb. Now, to find out that he was the detective they were expecting was overwhelming. She felt sick to her stomach. It had been years since they'd seen each other—teetering on the brink of adulthood, so in love. Sometimes, when she let herself think about those years, she felt guilty that she had lacked the courage to stand up to her grandfather. The fight they'd had over Trey had been one of the worst times of her life. Marcus had insisted she was too young for romance and the boy was unsuitable, besides. She'd argued, but in the end, she'd given in to Marcus and walked out of Trey's life. She knew it had hurt him, but what he would probably never believe was that she'd suffered, too. To this day, she still measured her relationships by the feelings she'd had for him, and so far, they'd all come up lacking.

Now, by a cruel twist of fate, he was here to question her grandfather about a murdered child. Surely he couldn't think that they had anything to do with something so horrible?

She didn't know what to do, what to say, and she was afraid to turn around for fear of the look she might see on his face. If Trey held a grudge, he had the power to make their lives miserable.

Oblivious to the undercurrents, when they entered the library, Marcus seated Olivia, then gestured for Trey to sit nearby.

Trey did so without comment.

The brief moment of silence seemed to swell and lengthen until speaking aloud felt wrong. Still, it was why he'd come. As Marcus fiddled with some papers on his desk, Trey chanced a look at Olivia.

Her face was pale, and she was staring at a spot on the wall over the fireplace. He couldn't tell if she was upset because the discovery of the baby's body threatened her identity, or because he was the cop who'd come to do the questioning. Either way, he had a job to do, and the sooner he got out of here, the better for the both of them. Finally Marcus Sealy moved into place and took a seat on the sofa beside his granddaughter. Trey saw the old man give Olivia's hand a gentle squeeze before he leaned back and faced Trey head-on.

"So, Detective, how can I be of service?"

"I have a couple of questions," Trey said, and removed a notebook from his pocket. They had already decided that the original owners of the lake house had nothing to do with the baby's death, but he had to cover all the bases.

"Did you ever know a couple by the name of David and Carol Lehrman?"

Marcus didn't hesitate. "No. Why? Who are they?"

"You're sure? It would have been years ago."

Anger was evident in Marcus's voice as he answered. "I'm old, but I'm not senile . . . at least not yet. I said

I don't know them, which means, no."

Instantly offended by Trey's doubts, Olivia started to object, but her grandfather silently shook his head, discouraging her from saying what was on her mind. It took all her restraint to remain quiet when she wanted to lash out.

Trey heard Marcus's sarcasm and felt his anger, but he had an anger of his own. He kept thinking of the tiny bones that had been inside that suitcase and couldn't summon any sympathy for a man like Marcus Sealy, whose only indignation at the moment was over the inconvenience of being asked to answer a few questions.

The only outward sign of Trey's anger was a muscle twitching at the corner of his left eye, but when he opened his mouth, his tone was terse, his words short and clipped.

"Look, Mr. Sealy, I'm sorry if this offends you, but I'm more offended by the bones of a two-year-old someone stuffed in a suitcase, plastered behind a wall and as good as forgot for the past twenty-five years than by whether or not my questions might tick you off. Someone thinks they've gotten away with murder, and *that* offends me."

Immediately, Marcus was apologetic.

"You're absolutely correct, Detective Bonney, and it's I who should apologize. It's just that Olivia and I have been bombarded by the media since the story broke, and my patience is running thin. I should not have taken my frustrations out on you. Forgive me."

43

Trey shrugged, then nodded. "I'm a little tense myself, so what do you say we start over?"

Marcus nodded. "Done."

Trey heard Olivia exhale. He wanted to look at her but didn't dare. Instead, he referred to his notebook, then looked back at Marcus.

"You only had the one child, is that right?"

Marcus nodded. "Yes, my son, Michael."

"And he and his wife, Kay, only had one child?"

Marcus looked at Olivia and smiled gently.

"Yes, my granddaughter, Olivia."

Trey's gaze shifted to her. She was sitting on the edge of the chair with her hands folded in her lap and a strained expression on her face. She looked as if she wanted to slap him into the middle of next week. He glanced back at the notebook.

"What about anyone else? Maybe cousins . . . someone who would have had a child about the age of Liv . . . uh, your granddaughter?"

Marcus sighed, then leaned forward, resting his elbows on his knees as he met Trey's gaze.

"Once, the Sealys were many, but three wars and a couple of natural disasters have thinned us down. I have a second cousin who is a nun, so naturally, there were no children from that branch. I had a brother who was gay. He took his own life at the age of twenty-nine, in some pitiful hotel room in Paris after his lover left him, which left only me and my baby sister to continue the family line. My wife and I had just the one son, and my sister never married, although I suspect she left a string of broken hearts during her younger days."

"Where is she now?" Trey asked.

Marcus grinned. "Living in an old lighthouse off the coast of Maine with a dozen cats. She paints pictures of the lighthouse over and over and sells them to tourists. No husbands . . . no children."

"What about Uncle Terrence and Aunt Carolyn?" Olivia asked.

Marcus shook his head. "They never had any children," he said shortly.

Trey paused. The tension in Marcus's voice was there, even if the expression on his face said otherwise.

"Where do they live?" Trey asked.

"They're in Italy. Have been for years."

"How many years?" Trey asked.

"I don't know . . . oh, at least twenty-five. Seems to me they were gone before Olivia was kidnapped. Terrence isn't my brother, he's a cousin."

"Did he share the same genetic trait with the rest of the Sealys?"

"What . . . you mean the second thumb on the left hand?"

Trey nodded.

Marcus frowned. "Yes, I suppose he did."

"Where did they live before they moved to Italy?" Trey asked.

"At his family's home north of Sherman."

Trey wrote down the information while mentally mapping out the distance from Sherman to Lake Texoma. It was easily within an hour's drive, even less depending on which part of the lake one was aiming for.

"Do you have a number or address where they can be reached?" Trey asked.

Marcus's frown deepened.

"I have a number and address, but I don't know how current they are. We haven't communicated in ages."

"And why would that be, sir?" Trey asked.

"We never did care much for each other," Marcus said. "You know what they say, you can choose your friends but not your family. They left after some of Terrence's business deals went sour. Ruined his reputation."

"Why Italy?" Trey asked.

"Carolyn's family had a summer home there. She inherited it when her father died. I suppose it was a good place for them to escape to."

"I'll still need those numbers," Trey said.

"Yes, of course," Marcus said. He shuffled through a Rolodex, finally pulled out a card and handed it to Trey.

Trey made a note of the information, then continued to write as Marcus rambled about his dwindling family. When Marcus stopped, Trey looked up, glanced at Olivia, then back at Marcus, and braced himself for another angry reaction.

"Mr. Sealy, this is personal, but I have to ask. You've been a widower for many years, right?"

"Yes," Marcus said. "But what does that have to do with—"

"During that time, it wouldn't have been out of the

ordinary for you to have had an intimate relationship with another woman."

Marcus's face flushed, but his voice never wavered.

"Be that as it may, I did not."

"You're absolutely positive that you did not father another child?"

Marcus's fingers tightened around the arms of his chair.

"Yes, Detective. I'm certain."

Trey glanced at Olivia. She appeared furious, and what he was going to say wasn't going to make her any happier. He turned back to Marcus.

"When your granddaughter was kidnapped . . ."

"Yes?" Marcus said.

"She was missing for seven days, right?"

Marcus nodded.

Trey made a note in his book, then looked up again.

"And you are one hundred percent certain that the child who was returned to you was the same child who was kidnapped?"

Olivia gasped, then stood abruptly.

Marcus grabbed her wrist and gently pulled her close until she was standing beside his chair. He looked up at her and smiled, then fixed Trey with a cold, angry look.

"I know my own flesh and blood, Detective, and I think we're done now."

Trey flipped the notebook closed, then slipped it into his pocket. He'd pissed them off big-time, and he wasn't done yet.

"Nearly, Mr. Sealy. There's just one more thing I need."

"What's that?" Marcus asked.

"We need DNA samples from both you and Olivia."

Olivia turned until she was facing Trey.

For the first time since he'd walked in the door, they were looking—really looking—at each other, and the pain on her face made him sick.

"Now . . . see here," Marcus sputtered.

Olivia looked at Trey without flinching as she lifted her chin and gave her grandfather's shoulder a gentle squeeze.

"No, Grampy, it's all right. I don't mind. It's a small price to pay to get these people out of our lives."

Trey flinched. He'd gotten the underlying meaning loud and clear.

"We'll see our family doctor tomorrow," Marcus said.

Trey's expression darkened. "I'm sorry, sir, but due to the seriousness of the situation, we need to have the test done in our facilities."

"So, Detective Bonney, where would you like us to go?" Olivia asked.

"I'll take you to the crime lab."

"We can get ourselves there," Marcus said.

"No, sir, if you don't mind, I need to be with you all the way."

"And if we do mind?" Olivia snapped.

Her anger was so vivid he could almost feel the slap of her words. Through no fault of his own, he'd been put in the position of being the bearer of bad news. It was a case of shoot the messenger for the news that he'd brought.

"Look," Trey said, trying to maintain a professional attitude in the face of such personal animosity, "none of this is my idea, or, for that matter, my fault. I'm simply following orders, and that includes proving—or eliminating—any connections you might have to the deceased. I'll pick you up at ten o'clock tomorrow morning, take you to the lab, then bring you back. After that, if we're both lucky, it will mark the end of this brief, acrimonious relationship."

At that moment Rose walked in with a tray of freshly brewed coffee and three cups. Trey turned, then nodded politely at her.

"Ma'am, I'm afraid I'm going to have to forgo the pleasure of your coffee, but thank you for the trouble."

Unaware of the undercurrents in the room, she smiled.

"Maybe another time, sir," she said.

Marcus was getting to his feet as Trey started toward the door.

"Don't bother," Trey muttered. "I'll see myself out."

Marcus frowned. Despite the uncomfortable situation, he wouldn't allow manners to fail him.

"Olivia, darling . . . would you please see Detective Bonney out?"

Olivia flinched, but arguing with her grandfather would set him to wondering about things she didn't want him to remember.

"Yes, of course," she said, and strode past Trey,

pausing once to see if he was going to follow.

She saw him bite his lip and knew he was just as uncomfortable around her as she was around him. The silence between them lengthened and darkened until Olivia felt as threatened by his lack of acknowledgment as she'd felt by his presence. By the time they reached the front door, she was on the verge of tears.

And it was those tears blurring her vision that melted Trey's heart. He sighed in frustration, then shoved his hand through his hair, absently combing the dark strands out of order.

"Livvie . . . wait," he said.

No one had ever called her that but Trey, and the sound of it on his lips brought back too many sad memories. She turned to him then, shaking and shamed.

"Trey . . . I had no idea that—"

He held up his hand. "It's okay. I understand." Then he grimaced. "No. That's too easy. I don't understand. I can only imagine what you and your grandfather must be going through. I'm sorry this is dragging up old and painful memories for him, but if you'd seen that house . . . and the suitcase . . . and the contents . . ." He sighed. "You've got to know that you're not being targeted unfairly, but some bastard murdered a baby, Livvie, and I guess I'll do anything to bring him, or her, to justice."

"I know," Olivia said. "And truthfully, we understand. But this is frightening to me. Everything you ask threatens my existence . . . my identity. And . . . I didn't expect the detective to be someone I knew." Then she took a deep breath and added, "I'm sorry."

Trey shrugged. "You have nothing to apologize for."

"Yes, I do. I wasn't strong enough to say it before, but I'm saying it now, even if it's years overdue."

"Really, Livvie . . . that's all in the past. You don't need to—"

She lifted her chin. "I was a coward. I didn't know how to stand up to my grandfather. I've always felt guilty about being kidnapped."

"Guilty? Why?"

"Because it cost Grampy his only son. I gave in to his demands about you even though I didn't want to, completely unaware of what I would be losing." Then she sighed. "All I can say is . . . I'm sorry. I know that's all in the past, but I would like to think that you don't hold any hard feelings toward me."

Trey wanted to hold her. He settled for a handshake.

"No hard feelings," he said gently. "And I'll pick you up in the morning at ten."

"We'll be ready," she said, and opened the door to see him out.

Trey stepped across the threshold, then stopped and turned.

"You have no need to worry. I have no intention of reminding your grandfather who I am. What you and I were. What's past is past, right?"

Olivia nodded, but she was struggling with the need to argue. Her memories of him were filled with love and passion and the feeling of coming apart in his arms. That would never be wholly in the past for her.

She shrugged. "Part of it is, I suppose, but until we

know the identity of the murdered child and find out who killed her, the past will never be laid to rest."

There was little Trey could say to reassure her, so he erred on the side of caution and left her standing on the doorstep.

A few minutes later, as he was heading down the driveway, he glanced up into the rearview mirror. She was still on the doorstep, and he would have sworn that she was crying.

4

Foster Lawrence had been out of prison for two weeks, but he still wasn't used to being free. No matter where he was, each time he reached for a doorknob, he experienced a brief moment of panic that the door would be locked. After twenty-five years of being incarcerated, he was no longer able to sleep with the lights out, and he ate too fast.

The world he'd known before was all but gone. Now everything was high-tech and computerized. There were cell phones that took pictures and pagers that played Bach. Teenage boys wore layers and layers of clothes that looked three sizes too big, while the girls' outfits were so brief and tight, he was amazed that their parents let them out of the house. Television screens were flatter and larger, and sex was used to sell everything from toothpaste to cake mixes. He felt like a foreigner in his own land. But, with what was waiting for him back in Dallas, he figured he could soon buy his way into comfort. He'd purposefully given himself the past two weeks to make sure he wasn't being followed—that the cops had forgotten about him and the money that had never been recovered. He'd gotten a nondescript job washing dishes in a restaurant, and once he'd been certain he was on his own, he'd quit his job and bought a bus ticket to Dallas.

"Step aside, step aside," the bus driver said as he moved toward the underbelly of the bus to unload the luggage.

Since Foster was carrying his worldly goods in a pack on his back, he was able to bypass this last step of the long, miserable ride. All he needed was to finish what he'd begun years ago in this city. Get the money, then get out.

As he walked out of the bus station, he glanced up at the sky. The sun had already set. Before long, it would be dark, and he had no intention of spending the night on the streets. However, he had almost five hundred dollars in his pocket, and his needs were simple. For the short time he would be here, any room would do.

"Cab, mister?"

Foster turned. A short man with a bald head and a slight paunch was standing beside a cab with the door ajar. Taking a cab would be a luxury, but his million was finally within his reach, and it was getting darker by the moment.

"Yeah, why not?" he said, took the backpack off his

shoulder, tossed it onto the seat, then slid in beside it.

"Where to?" the cabbie asked.

"I need a room for a few days. Somewhere close to downtown. Somewhere cheap."

"Yes, sir," the cabbie said, and the taxi began to move.

As Foster leaned back, he began to relax. It was all going to be okay. He was in Dallas and only hours away from what he'd begun all those years ago. All he'd wanted then was a fresh start, and that still held true. The money he'd stashed was going to make it happen.

A few minutes later, the cabdriver pulled over to the curb. Foster glanced out the window. The hotel was obviously not four-star, but then, neither was he—or his bankroll. He paid the driver, grabbed his backpack and got out.

When he walked in, he saw that the bald man behind the desk was sporting tattoos on both his forearms and a handlebar mustache. He gave Foster a less than cursory glance, then took another toke on the joint he was smoking.

"I need a room," Foster said.

"Twenty-five dollars a night—up front," the clerk said.

"How much for a week?" Foster asked.

The clerk didn't bother to look up. "Hundred dollars . . . in advance."

"I'll take it a night at a time," Foster said, and counted out the money. He started to put the bills back in his pocket, then hesitated and peeled off another five from his roll and slapped it down in front of the clerk.

"What about women?" Foster asked.

The clerk looked up, squinting through the smoke encircling his head, eyed the five, then, for the first time, actually paid attention to what Foster was asking.

"What about 'em?" he asked.

"Any available?"

"What's your top dollar?" the clerk asked.

"This ain't the Taj Mahal," Foster growled. "Just send me a female. As long as she's not sporting a mustache and a dick, I'll be satisfied."

The clerk took Foster's money and handed him a key.

"Room 322, third floor. Elevator's out of order."

Foster took the key without comment. Elevators were a luxury he hadn't had in years. Another night or so of hoofing up the stairs was nothing to complain about. All he wanted was the room and a woman.

The clerk took another drag on his joint, then held in the smoke for a few seconds before exhaling through his nose. Foster's eyes narrowed.

"Don't forget about the woman," he growled.

The clerk nodded. He was reaching for the phone as Foster started up the stairs. A few minutes later, Foster unlocked the door and walked in.

The door locked automatically, but he still turned the dead bolt, then tossed his bag on the bed and dropped the room key in his pocket. He thought about unpacking, but there wasn't enough in his backpack to worry about, so he poked about in the bathroom instead.

The towels were somewhat gray and threadbare, and the bars of soap were the size of credit cards and nearly as thin. Several of the black-and-white tiles on the floor were cracked or chipped. There was a large red rust stain in the bottom of the tub around the drain, but the room was three times the size of the cell that he'd had to share and seemed luxurious.

Immediately, he stripped out of his clothes and stepped into the shower, peeling the thin paper wrapper from the soap as he went. A few minutes later he had soaped from head to toe, shampooed his long hair, and was in the act of rinsing off when he heard a knock at the door. Confident that it would be the whore he'd ordered, he turned off the water and grabbed two towels, wrapping one around his waist and using the other to dry his hair as he strode out of the bathroom, past the bed, and to the door.

"Who is it?" he growled.

"Anyone you want it to be, doll," a female voice answered.

His pulse kicked with anticipation, although he opened the door just a fraction before satisfying himself that she was alone. Then he swung the door completely inward, grabbed her by the wrist and pulled her inside.

For a moment the only sounds were the locks turning. Then the woman smiled.

"Hey, hon . . . how you doin'?" she asked, and ran her finger lightly between his belly and the thin wet towel he'd wrapped around his waist.

Foster flinched. Inside, he'd broken a man's nose for

a lesser familiarity. He had to remind himself that he was no longer in prison, while wondering if he could get still get it up for a woman. It had been a long time since he'd had the chance to find out.

"Good," he said shortly as he gave her a hard look.

She would not have been his first pick out of a crowd, but she wasn't all that bad. Like him, she was just a little past her prime. He barely had time to notice the dark roots against her scalp, or the brushy fall of dish-water-blond hair, before she tossed her handbag aside and put her hands on her hips.

"So, hon . . . you want a blow job or what?"

Her voice was part whine, with an indistinct southern drawl that could have put her from Alabama, but more likely Arkansas.

He reached for her breasts, feeling the firm but yielding texture of flesh, then squeezed. As he did, he felt the first stirrings of an erection and knew a great sense of relief.

"What else will twenty-five get me?" he asked.

"A hand job. Another twenty will get you an ass or pussy fuck, but if you want anything kinky, it'll cost you a flat hundred . . . and I don't kiss no one on the lips."

Foster thought about how long it had been since he'd even had the opportunity to sink his prick into the tight heat of a woman, but the way he was feeling, he wouldn't last long enough to make it worth the price.

"Blow job," he said shortly, then dropped both towels, sat down on the side of the bed and spread his legs.

"Money first," she said as she held out her hand.

He reached behind him, took his money from the pocket of his pants and counted out two tens and a five into her palm.

Water droplets still clung to his body as she folded the money and put it in her fanny pack. After that, she stepped between his outspread legs, then went to her knees.

Foster watched long enough to see her red-painted lips sliding up and down his erection before the dampness of her tongue and the intensity with which she was sucking shifted his focus. Warmth became heat and pressure became pain, but a very pleasurable pain. The woman knew her business. She brought him to a climax so hard and so fast that his semen shot into her hands before he could elicit a groan. Moments later, he fell backward onto the bed, still rocked by the intensity of the spasms.

"Oh damn, that was too fast," he groaned.

The woman got to her feet and headed for the bathroom, carrying her fanny pack as she went. He heard her brushing her teeth but was too spent to move, and he was still on the bed when she came out, drying her hands.

"How long was you in, hon?"

He answered before he thought. "Twenty-five."

She grinned. "It's no wonder you got off so fast. Sometimes the men like you come just lookin' at me." Then her eyes narrowed as she stepped back into her shoes. "If you're interested in an encore, you just let Marvin know."

"Who's Marvin?" he asked.

"The desk clerk who called me," she said.

"Oh yeah . . . him," Foster said.

She hesitated a moment, then grabbed the doorknob.

"So, you take care, hon, and thanks for the business."

Oblivious to his nudity, Foster followed her to the door, let her out, then once again locked himself inside.

With the edge gone from his hard-on, he moved back to the bed, picked up the remote from the top of the television, then hit the power button. His belly growled as he thought about ordering up a pizza, but he let the thought ride as he played with the remote. He knew what the phrase "channel surfing" meant, although the room he'd had in California had been minus a TV and he hadn't had the pleasure. He kept his finger on the up arrow and ran through the brief choices the hotel menu offered, then had started through it again when, to his shock, he saw his own face on the screen and heard a newscaster saying his name.

". . . looking for Foster Lawrence, who was recently released from prison after serving twenty-five years for his involvement in the kidnapping of the granddaughter of Dallas mogul Marcus Sealy. At this time authorities want Lawrence only for questioning regarding the recent discovery of the skeletal remains of a child's body out at Lake Texoma. The Sealy family is also being questioned regarding the similarities between the baby's remains and Olivia Sealy, who, as a child, was kidnapped and then returned to Marcus Sealy after an extended length of time."

Foster's heart skipped a beat as his lips went slack. The knot of hunger in his belly turned into a full-blown ache as the remote slipped from his shaking fingers. It hit the floor with a thump and, as it did, changed the channel.

He found himself tuned to the Discovery Channel, watching a male elephant intently copulating with a female elephant who was in heat. Any other time, watching any kind of sexual act would have turned him on, but the only thing hard now was the bed on which he was sitting.

"Son of a bitch," Foster muttered.

The thought of reliving the hell of a federal prison was impossible. He knew for damn sure that the baby he'd seen had been returned unharmed, because he was the one who'd taken her to the shopping mall and let her go. There were things about his accomplice's past he hadn't liked, but he'd kept his silence, thinking that the million dollars would be worth the wait. However, he hadn't planned on having to deal with murder all over again. He hadn't known about Michael's and Kay Sealy's murders until it had been too late, and he didn't know a damn thing about this one, either.

Suddenly the sanctuary of his room began to seem more like a cell. He thought of the clerk who'd seen his face and the whore who'd just sucked his dick, and figured his days were numbered. He jumped up from the bed and started yanking on his clothes. Panic was pushing him into running until he suddenly stopped. He couldn't go out—not like this. That photo had been a recent one, and he would certainly be spotted immediately. He had learned one thing doing time: patience. He had too much at stake to make a mistake, so instead of running away, he began to run through his options.

It didn't seem possible that this was happening, and, by God, it wasn't fair. He'd paid his debt to society, so what the hell was going on? It seemed as if the state of Texas was out to get him, one way or another. He couldn't let that happen, but he couldn't leave. Not yet. Not until he had what he'd come for. But how? Thanks to the news, he was bound to be seen. He thought for a few minutes, then started with the obvious. The authorities were looking for a gray-haired man with a ponytail and facial hair. It was time to make that man disappear. He grabbed his backpack and headed for the bathroom.

With the aid of a switchblade, a can of shaving cream and a disposable razor, he shaved off his beard and used his knife to cut off his ponytail. His face was pale where the beard had been, and his hair looked as if he'd gotten caught in a lawn mower, but it was enough to assure him a safe trip outside to get another room and the goods he needed to finish his new look. He stared at himself for a few moments, then dressed quickly, stuffed his belongings into the backpack and left, leaving the key to the room on the bed as he went.

As he started down the three flights of stairs, it occurred to him that he might have to change more than his look to get past the desk clerk without notice, but he wasn't sure how. It wasn't until he started down the second flight of stairs and saw an empty pizza box in the stairwell that he knew what to do. He picked it up, holding it as if the food was still inside, and walked the rest of the way down the stairs.

The desk clerk glanced up, saw the man and then the pizza box, and immediately looked away, assuming it was a delivery gone bad, just as Foster hoped.

Once he was out on the street, he discarded the box and lengthened his stride. He stopped once at a corner drugstore, exiting shortly carrying a small sack, then proceeded a few blocks farther before checking into another hotel.

The desk clerk was an obese female of indeterminate age, who eyed Foster curiously. He stared back, morbidly fascinated by the faint green tinge to her hair and the number of fleshy folds in her face as he counted out the money for another room. She took the money without comment and handed him a key. Again, he had only paid by the night. If nothing else went wrong, he should have his money in a couple of days and be long gone.

Trey finished reporting to Lieutenant Warren, but his anger was obvious as he went back to his desk.

Chia Rodriguez was finishing a report when Trey slumped into his chair, then rubbed his face with his hands, as if trying to scrub away something foul.

"Hey, Trey, what's up?"

"Today I hate my job," he said shortly, then got up from the chair as quickly as he'd sat down, grabbing his coffee cup as he went.

Chia followed him to the break room.

"Is it the Sealy case?"

He nodded.

She sighed. "God. I can't imagine something like that happening to one of my kids. I look at them every night and pray that I'll be able to keep them safe long enough to grow up." Then she grimaced. "Then there are the nights when I'm afraid to close my eyes for fear they'll disappear when I'm not looking. On those nights, I sleep on the floor outside their door." Then she laughed weakly. "Pretty crazy, huh?"

Trey put down his cup and turned around.

"Damn, Chia, that's scary. You'd be a good spokesperson for birth control." He turned away again.

She pulled a face, then made a big deal out of leering at his backside to make up for the fact that she'd just shared something personal with him.

"Now, Bonney, you know how women are. PMS and shit like that gets us all crazy sometimes for no reason. Besides, with buns like yours, it would be a crime to the human race not to pass them on."

He grinned because she needed him to, but he didn't feel like smiling. Truth was, he could identify with her fears and had an overwhelming urge to hug her, but she wouldn't like it and everyone else would take it the wrong way, so he let the notion slide.

Thankful that Trey was letting her change the subject without comment, she poured him a cup of coffee, then topped off her cup.

"Here, stud . . . drink up. Caffeine always makes the

world a little easier to bear."

"From your lips to God's ear," Trey muttered, then lifted his cup in a toast before taking a sip, after which he made a face. "This stuff is terrible."

Chia reached in front of him, snagged the last doughnut from a plate, broke it in half and handed one piece to him.

"That's what these are for," she said.

Trey eyed the dried-out pastry, then shrugged and dunked it into the dark, greasy-looking brew as Chia took hers and swaggered back to her desk.

Trey ate the doughnut without tasting it and took the coffee like medicine. He would need all the fortification he could get to make it through the next day and get the Sealys to the lab. Then he thought about the notes he'd taken from Marcus and pulled them out. He didn't know what time it was in Milan, but he was going to try the number that Marcus had given him for Terrence Sealy.

Back at his desk, he dialed, then picked up a pen and began doodling on a notepad as the phone started to ring. He counted the rings up to seven and was about to hang up when a woman answered in a breathless voice.

"Ciao."

Trey frowned, frustrated that he hadn't counted on the language barrier.

"Is this the Terrence Sealy residence?" he asked.

There was a moment of hushed silence, then a surprised lilt to the woman's voice.

"Yes . . . yes, it is. Who's calling, please?"

Trey's heart skipped a beat. Pay dirt!

"This is Detective Trey Bonney with the Dallas, Texas, police department. I want to talk to Terrence Sealy."

"Oh no! Has something happened to Marcus?"

"No, ma'am. Nothing like that. Who am I speaking to, please?"

"Oh, yes, of course. I'm Carolyn, Terry's wife. He's gone for the day and won't be home until evening. Can I be of help to you?"

"I certainly hope so, and I'll get straight to the point. A few days ago, the remains of a small child were found in a house at Lake Texoma. She had been murdered about twenty-five years ago, then put in a suitcase and hidden behind a wall. Early investigations lead us to believe that the child might have been a Sealy."

"Oh my God! How awful! But why would you suspect such a . . . oh! Olivia's kidnapping! But we got her back," Carolyn said.

"Yes, ma'am, but we're still questioning the remaining Sealys."

"Why?"

"The child that was found had been born with two thumbs on her left hand. A pretty distinctive trait."

"Dear Lord . . . well, what would you be wanting with us? We weren't able to have children."

"Ma'am, this is a very personal question, and forgive me for asking, but I have to know. Was it you or your husband who had the infertility problems?"

"It was me, but that doesn't—"

There was a gasp, then a long moment of silence.

"Mrs. Sealy? Are you still there?"

"Yes. Yes, I'm here," she said. "Are you insinuating that my husband had an affair? That he fathered some child that was subsequently murdered?"

"I'm not insinuating anything," Trey said. "What I *am* doing is eliminating all the suspects."

"How do you propose to do that?" Carolyn asked.

"I need a DNA sample from your husband."

"This is horrible," she muttered.

"No, ma'am. What's horrible is what was stuffed in that suitcase."

"Dear Lord . . ."

"Can I count on your cooperation?" Trey asked.

Carolyn answered without hesitation. "What do you want him to do?"

"I don't suppose you would consider coming back to Dallas for the tests and to answer a few more questions?"

"That far? But—"

"It would mean a lot to the department, ma'am."

Carolyn Sealy sighed. "It would mean a lot to me, too," she said. "I mean, coming back to Dallas. I miss living in the States, and it's been ages since we've seen Marcus." There was a moment's pause, and then she said, "Yes, we'll come back."

"This is my number," Trey said, then recited it. "Call me when you get into the city. We'll set up a time and place to meet and get this taken care of."

66

Carolyn sighed, as if anxious to get rid of his call. "We'll be in touch," she said, and hung up.

Trey put the phone back on the receiver, then rubbed the back of his neck. One more possible link in the chain.

Marcus speared a slice of meat from the serving platter and delivered it to his plate, then poured a small helping of mushroom gravy next to it before resuming his meal. At the first bite of meat, he rolled his eyes in satisfaction.

"Oh my, Olivia. Rose has outdone herself tonight. The tenderloin is delicious." Then he noticed that her plate was still empty and frowned. "What's the matter, darling?" He sat up a little straighter as concern tinged his voice. "Are you ill?"

Olivia stifled a sigh, then made herself smile.

"No, Grampy, I'm fine. Just not very hungry."

Marcus put down his fork, then leaned back in his chair, crossing his arms over his stomach as he studied her face. He was so accustomed to her appearance that he never studied her features, but looking at her now, he had a fleeting moment of doubt. What if . . . ? Then he frowned and thrust away the thought.

"You're worried about tomorrow, aren't you?"

Olivia shrugged, then nodded as she looked away.

Marcus's frown deepened.

"I wish I could make you believe that there's no need for concern."

Olivia looked up, her eyes swimming with tears.

"Oh, Grampy, I wish you could, too, but there's a dark feeling inside me, and as hard as I try, I don't believe anything is ever going to be the same again."

Marcus wanted to argue with her, but he knew that she wasn't in a frame of mind to listen. All they could do was wait this out. Only time and truth would tell.

Olivia could tell that she'd upset her grandfather, and while it was the last thing she wanted to do, she had never been able to lie to him. All she could do now was trust that his faith in her was justified.

"I'm sorry for being such a whiner, Grampy. I'll be better, I promise. And for starters, I think I'll try some of Rose's tenderloin, after all."

Marcus smiled as he passed the platter.

"Don't forget the gravy," he added.

Foster Lawrence downed the final bite of his burger, then dunked the last two fries in ketchup, nodding affirmatively when a waitress paused by his table with a pot of coffee.

As she poured, Foster inhaled the fragrance of freshly brewed coffee while considering the luxuries that now abounded. It was almost midnight, and yet he'd walked out of his room and down the street to the all-night diner and ordered food.

Not because he'd been especially hungry, but because he could.

"How about a piece of pie?" the waitress asked. "Still got some apple and some deep-dish peach."

Foster's stomach was full, but his mouth watered.

"Peach?" Foster said.

"Peach it is," she said.

"À la mode?" he added.

"Sure, mister. À la mode."

She gave him a friendly wink and moved on.

He watched the sway of her backside with admiration, but on this day, his bodily hungers had been fully assuaged. He would settle for the peach pie and ice cream and call it a day.

Outside the diner, a police car went speeding by, running with lights and siren. He shuddered, thankful that, for now, he wasn't their prey. As the patrol car disappeared down the street, he caught a glimpse of his reflection in the darkened windows and grinned. The man looking back at him was not only bald, but barefaced. If she'd been living, not even his mother would have recognized him like this.

Then the waitress appeared and slid the pie in front of him. Despite his full belly, the aroma of warm pie and ice cream made him hungry all over again.

"Here it is, mister, ice cream and all. Enjoy."

"You bet I will, babe," Foster said with a smile, then picked up his spoon and dug in.

As he ate, he made plans for tomorrow. He'd looked in the phone book for the Lazy Days restaurant but had come up empty. It didn't surprise him to know that it was no longer in business. Lots of things had changed since he'd last been in Dallas, and although businesses had come and gone, the buildings were still there, which made him confident that the building that hid his money would be, too. It was only a matter of time before he got what he'd come for. For now, pie and ice cream would suffice.

Trey sat on the edge of his bed, fingering through the pages of his high-school yearbook. It had been ages since he'd bothered to drag himself through the memories, but seeing Olivia had brought them all back.

He paused at a page, lightly tracing the shape of her face as she smiled back at him from a picture, then laid his hand on the words she'd written beneath.

Love you forever

"But you didn't, did you, Livvie girl?"

Then, disgusted with himself for being so morbid, he slammed the book shut, tossed it on the floor and rolled over onto the bed. But even after he closed his eyes, he could still see her face smiling up at him from the page. Then the image faded, and another, more unsettling, took its place. It was that handful of tiny bones laid out on the examining table that strengthened his resolve.

He would give a name to the bones and find the devil who had ended her brief life, no matter what it took or who he pissed off along the way.

5

Braced with three cups of coffee and three extra-strength painkillers to dull the headache he'd awakened with, Trey figured he was ready for anything the day presented. But when he got in his car, saw the gum wrappers, the empty disposable coffee cup on the floor and the slight film of dust on the dash, he stopped. A picture flashed in his mind of the elegance of Marcus Sealy's home, and he imagined the looks on their faces when they saw the inside of his car. He sighed. Once again, Marcus Sealy would judge him and find him lacking.

He glanced at his watch. He was going to be late, but it couldn't be helped. He started to get out and get something to clean the car with, then stopped.

His car was dusty because of the dirt roads he'd driven on to get to the lake house where the baby's remains had been found, and the gum and coffee had been all he'd been able to stomach in the way of food after he'd left.

At that point, he came to terms with himself. What the Sealys thought about him no longer mattered. He grabbed the coffee cup and gum wrappers, stuffed them into the open pocket at the bottom of the door, stuck his forefinger on the dash and wrote Clean Me in the dust, then jammed the key into the ignition. Seconds later the engine roared to life. As he was backing out of the driveway, he waved at his eighty-one-year-old neighbor, Ella Sumter, who was doing tai chi in her front yard, and grinned when she blew him a kiss.

He began to feel better as he drove toward the outskirts of Dallas and the Sealy estate. By this time next week, it would all be over, and chances were, he wouldn't have to see them again. All he had to do was put on his game face and remember that he was the one in charge.

Olivia paused in front of her bedroom mirror long enough to get a full view of the dress she was wearing. She frowned, then flung it aside to join the four other outfits she'd already discarded on the bed. She had started toward the closet again when reality hit. It shouldn't matter what she wore. She shouldn't care what Trey Bonney thought. He wasn't coming to take her out. He was coming to take them away—to a crime lab for DNA testing to verify her identity, for God's sake.

She sank onto the side of the bed and covered her face, stifling the urge to cry. She didn't want Grampy to know that she was falling apart, and she certainly didn't want Trey Bonney to see her vulnerability.

Slowly, anger replaced fear as she got up from the bed and moved back to the closet. This time, there was no hesitation as she pulled out an outfit, and when she began to dress, it was with purpose. She buttoned and zipped and tucked and smoothed, and then stepped into shoes that matched, ran a brush through her hair, grabbed her handbag and left the room without giving herself a second look.

Marcus was in his room when he heard Olivia's footsteps going past the door. There was a strong, steady rhythm to her stride that hadn't been there last night when she'd left the dinner table in tears. The sound made him smile. That was his girl. He glanced at himself in the mirror, making sure that his collar was smooth and his tie straight as he moved to the dresser to get his wallet and change; then he followed his grand-daughter down the stairs.

They had no sooner greeted each other in the foyer when the doorbell rang. Rose's footsteps sounded on the marble flooring as she came from another wing of the house, but Olivia wasn't in the mood to stand on formalities.

"I'll get it," she said, then lifted her chin and strode to the door.

Marcus saw the glint in her eye and smiled again. The moment he'd seen the dress she was wearing, he knew she'd gone on the defense. It was a power dress in a power color, and she wore it well.

"I'll be right back," he said shortly. "I want to speak to Rose before we leave." He walked away, leaving Olivia to deal with their caller.

Finding herself suddenly alone did not deter Olivia from her intent. She grabbed the doorknob and swung the door inward, leaving her face-to-face with the man whose current presence in their lives had thrown her world into turmoil.

Her appearance at the door was, for Trey, unexpected and, at the same time, mind-blowing. He knew, as well as he knew his own name, that the only thing she had on under that red dress were her panties. He knew because, as she stood in the doorway, the full sun of morning hit her like a spotlight, revealing the thrust of bare breasts and pouting nipples beneath what appeared to be silk. If that wasn't enough, the slight flare of the body-hugging skirt revealed enough of her long legs to remind him of the intimacy they'd once shared.

It took every ounce of self-restraint he owned to shift his gaze from her body to her face, and when he did, he knew he'd been sideswiped. There was a glint in her eyes and a jut to her chin that he remembered all too well. She'd come prepared for battle and, if he wasn't mistaken, had just declared war.

"Uh . . ."

Olivia stifled a smirk. From the look on his face, the dress was a success.

"Good morning, Detective. Please come in. My grandfather will be here shortly, and then we can leave."

"Uh . . ."

Olivia eyed Trey coolly. "I believe you're repeating yourself."

"Shit," he muttered.

She smiled.

He shoved his hands in his pockets, then surprised the smile off her face.

"You always were a pretty girl, Olivia, and I would have sworn there was no way you could have improved upon perfection, but I would have been wrong." Then his voice softened. "You are so beautiful, and I am sorrier than I can tell you that you and your grandfather have to go through this."

Suddenly her defiance seemed out of place. She had been so stunned, and then so frightened, by the revelations of the past week that she'd been pulling a "kill the messenger" attitude just because of the trip they were going to take.

"Look, Trey . . . I—"

"Sorry I kept you waiting," Marcus said as he came striding back into the foyer.

Olivia sighed, then turned to her grandfather and made herself smile.

"No problem, Grampy. Detective Bonney had only just said hello."

Trey yanked his hands out of his pockets and shook the hand that Marcus was extending.

"And hello to you, too, sir," Trey said. "If you're both ready, we should probably go." Without waiting for them to agree, he led the way out the door.

When Marcus and Olivia reached the curb, Trey was standing at the car with the back door open. Accustomed to being driven, Marcus got in and slid over to the other side, making room for Olivia to sit without acknowledging the courtesy that had been extended.

But Olivia felt the awkwardness of the moment. When she turned to Trey to thank him, she got caught in the fire in his eyes and stumbled. He grabbed for her, and for a moment she was in his arms, being steadied firmly against his chest. She didn't know how reluctant he was to have to let her go, and she couldn't have voiced what she herself was feeling. Thankfully, the moment was brief. Then she slipped in beside her grandfather, crushing a peanut shell beneath her foot as she went.

By the time Trey had buckled himself into the front seat, she was staring at the back of his head and remembering how springy his dark hair felt to the touch. Unintentionally, she sighed aloud, then caught him looking at her in the rearview mirror. Startled, she quickly turned and smiled at Marcus, as if to reassure him that all was well, although it wasn't. Suddenly the shoe was on the other foot, and she felt breathless and out of control.

Trey made himself look away as he put the car in gear and proceeded back down the driveway. At the same time, the sunshine caught on the dash, highlighting the thin film of dust.

When Olivia saw what he'd written on it, she stifled a grin. Her first love had certainly grown into a bona fide hunk, and being a detective with the Dallas PD put him in a very respectable light, but it made her happy to know that the part of him that she'd fallen in love with so long ago had not changed. The fun-loving cutup who'd refused to take her social status seriously and then loved her in spite of it was still there.

But the memory also reminded her that, because of that same social status and her inability to stand up to her grandfather, their relationship had ultimately ended and she'd lost the love of her life.

Unwilling to dwell on what had been, she leaned back and closed her eyes as her grandfather clasped her hand.

"Olivia, darling, it will be okay," he said.

"Oh, I know that, Grampy. Quit worrying about me."

Trey glanced up into the rearview mirror, then quickly looked away before they caught him staring. From the start, Olivia had been out of his reach; he'd just been too young to realize it. But he was no longer the naive teenager he'd been before, and he was too smart to set himself up for another heartache.

"Say, Mr. Sealy, I thought I'd let you know that the phone number you gave me for Terrence was good. I spoke to his wife yesterday afternoon. They will be flying in sometime soon so that Terrence can submit to DNA testing as you two are doing."

He glanced up in the rearview mirror again as he spoke and caught a look of anger on Marcus's face. Being the good detective that he was, he didn't let the opportunity pass.

"Why do I have the feeling that this is not good news for you?"

For a few moments Marcus didn't answer; then, when he did, his words were sharp and clipped.

"There's never been any love lost between Terrence and I. No reason, just a fact of life."

They drove in silence for a few miles until Marcus's cell phone began to ring.

"Excuse me," he muttered. "I meant to turn the thing off," he said, and glanced at the caller ID, then frowned. "It's the office. I'd better take this."

Olivia nodded, then tuned out the conversation by staring through the window at the passing scenery and the constant flow of traffic. Before she knew it, her grandfather was disconnecting.

"Yes. I'll be there as soon as I can," he said, then ended his call and dropped the phone back into his pocket. "Detective Bonney, how long will this test take?"

"Not long," he said. "Do you have a problem?"

"I didn't, but I do now. I'll need to leave for my office as soon as we've finished. I trust you'll see Olivia home?"

Olivia flinched. "Oh, Grampy, I don't need to be treated like a child. I can get a cab."

"No, ma'am," Trey said. "I brought you. I will take you home. It's part of the job."

"That's settled, then," Marcus said. Satisfied that his problems were solved, he leaned back and relaxed.

But Olivia's problems had just escalated. With her grandfather's presence, she'd been able to maintain a mental distance between herself and Trey. The change in plans was unsettling, but she would handle it. Eleven years was a long enough time to get over a mistake—even if she was coming to believe it might have been the biggest one she'd ever made.

She was still struggling with her emotions when they arrived at the crime lab. As they pulled into the parking lot, they quickly realized something was wrong. Two vans from local television stations were waiting, and a half-dozen reporters with cameramen were hovering around the entrance, as well as a man who was standing on the corner carrying a sign that read Baby Killer?

"Oh, hell," Trey muttered. "I'd like to get my hands on the jerk who tipped them off."

"What's going on here?" Marcus demanded.

"Just stay in the car," Trey said tersely. "I'll get rid of them."

From the corner of her eye, Olivia saw Trey reaching toward the police radio, then heard him calling the dispatcher to request assistance. To her horror, the reporters suddenly spied her in the back seat and rushed toward the window. The press of their bodies against the car set it to rocking. Then, in the midst of it all, the man carrying the sign slammed his way through the crowd and shoved it against the window.

All she could see of the man's face were his eyes and their maniacal gleam as he peered over the placard into the car. In sudden panic, she grabbed her grandfather's hand.

Trey turned abruptly. She knew he was talking to her, because his lips were moving, but she couldn't hear what he was saying above the noise outside. She sank back, putting as much distance as she could between herself and the doors. Even though she knew they couldn't get to her, it didn't deter them from aiming their cameras at the windows while pushing and shoving at each other to get a clear view of her face.

She started to shake.

"Trey . . ."

He heard the fear in her voice and silently wished all the head cases and the media a long, slow trip to hell.

"It's okay," he said quickly. "I'll get rid of them."

"Do something," she mumbled.

As Trey was reaching for the door latch, someone shouted her name.

"Trey . . . for God's sake," she begged.

Disgusted, he got out of the car shouting, with his badge in his hand.

"Get back!" he shouted. "Get the hell away from my car, or I will arrest the whole lot of you."

The reporters backed up, but, still wanting to get some kind of sound bite for the evening news, they persisted in shouting out questions. The man with the sign was jostled to the back of the crowd, but Trey could still see the sign waving above their heads.

At the same time, two police cars pulled into the lot and parked beside Trey's car. Four uniformed officers emerged and headed toward the crowd.

Confident that the media was now contained, Trey strode to his car, opened the back door, leaned in and took Olivia's hand.

"Come on, Livvie, it's all right now," he said shortly.

Her fingers curled around his wrist as he helped her out of the car.

"It's not all right," she whispered. "Oh God . . . don't you see? It's never going to be all right again."

Marcus was right behind them. He put his arm around Olivia's shoulders, shielding her from the reporters with his body.

"It's nothing, darling," he said briefly as they hurried toward the door. "They're only reporters doing their job. They can't hurt you."

Trey led them into the building, then seated them in a

hallway, safely away from the prying eyes and long-distance camera lenses of the media.

"Wait here," he said, and pushed through a pair of double doors opposite where they were sitting.

"Oh my God," Olivia mumbled. "That was terrible. Why do they do that?"

Marcus sighed, then laid a hand in the middle of her back.

"Lean back, sweetheart. Relax. That's nothing compared to what they were like before."

"Before? You mean, when Mother and Daddy were murdered? When I disappeared?"

He nodded.

"That was bad," he said. "Today is nothing. They're going to poke a swab in our mouths, gather their precious DNA, and then we'll go on about our business. The rest of this mess will be their problem, not ours."

Olivia looked at him then, taking courage from the glint in his eye.

"You're really sure . . . about me, I mean . . . aren't you?"

"Yes, darling. I'm as sure as a man can be."

At that moment, Trey came back.

"They're ready for us," he said, nodding at Marcus. "This way, sir."

As soon as the police cars arrived, Dennis Rawlins made himself scarce. He couldn't afford to get himself arrested—not this time. This time he was on a mission from God, and he had to succeed. God had told him he would be absolved of guilt if he made an important act of contrition. And only God knew how much guilt Dennis carried with him every waking moment of the day. As for sleep, Dennis couldn't remember the last time he'd slept without reliving the horror of what he'd done. It didn't matter that he hadn't planned for the bomb he'd planted at an abortion clinic to kill seven children.

For weeks afterward he'd lived with thoughts of suicide, wanting relief from the sight of those tiny bloodied bodies every time he closed his eyes. How could he have known that a church bus would break down right in front of the clinic? He'd tried to tell himself that if God hadn't meant for the children to die, he wouldn't have let the bus break down there. But there was still enough rationality in Dennis to admit that God probably didn't bother himself with engine failures. It was Dennis who'd set the stage for the disaster, and now he was living with the consequences.

But that was all going to change. Once he'd heard about the remains of that little baby being found and gathered that the Sealys were suspected of somehow being involved, he'd known what he was supposed to do. Enacting revenge in the baby's name would absolve him of the guilt in the other deaths.

He folded his sign in half, stuffed it under his arm and disappeared into an alley. By the time he got back to his apartment, he was on an adrenaline high. The first blow for vengeance had been struck, but he was by no means through.

• • •

Oddly enough, the actual retrieval of DNA was, as Olivia's grandfather had predicted, quite anticlimactic. They put a swab to the inside of her mouth, aimed a Polaroid camera at her face when she was least expecting it, and caught the wide-eyed stare of her confusion. They repeated the process for Marcus, took names, addresses and dates of birth, then thanked them for coming.

The cab Marcus had called was, at his request, waiting for him at a side door. After a quick goodbye to Olivia, with a promise to see her at home for a late lunch, he left, leaving Olivia and Trey alone.

Trey, preoccupied with getting Olivia out without more problems with the press, didn't have time to consider what being alone with her for the ensuing thirty minutes would mean.

But Olivia *was* thinking about it. In fact, she hadn't been able to think about anything else. In a way, it was ironic that the thing she feared most, which was not being the true Olivia Sealy, had been thrust to the back of her mind by Trey's presence. All she could do was sit in silence, watching with grudging admiration at the way he tore into the people at the crime lab for leaking the news of their presence. Even when the man he was talking to vehemently denied it, Trey gave him no slack.

"I don't give a damn whether you're the one who made the call or not," Trey said. "You're in charge, and someone on your watch doesn't know the meaning of privacy."

83

Larry Flood knew Trey was right, but he didn't like him and wasn't willing to take any blame.

Flood's face was as red as his hair as he pointed a finger in Trey's face.

"Dammit, Bonney, don't take that holier-than-thou attitude with me. Any number of people from your department, as well as mine, knew they were coming," he argued.

"That's where you're wrong, and get your finger out of my face before I shove it up your ass," Trey snapped.

Olivia stifled a grin when the man quickly yanked his hand back and stuffed it in his pocket, but not before she saw him curl the fingers into a fist. She guessed he would love to punch Trey in the nose but obviously didn't have the nerve.

Trey was so angry he would have welcomed an excuse to punch someone. That it might have been Larry Flood would have been a bonus. He knew it was a matter of personalities, but they had never liked each other. Still, right was right, and he wasn't giving Flood an out.

"It's like this, Flood. I know it wasn't me, so unless you're accusing my lieutenant of being the snitch, then it came from in here. And other than helping the PD with the process of elimination, Mr. Sealy and his granddaughter are not a part of our investigation. I won't have them hounded by those damn vultures out-side, so consider this your only warning. You find out who did this and deal with them, or I'll assume you're it and deal with *you* accordingly."

Flood's face was a dark, angry red. The urge to punch Bonney now and suffer the consequences later was huge, but he couldn't ignore the woman sitting in the chair down the hall. The Sealys had pull in this city, and he didn't want to lose his job because of the circus the media had made of their appearance at the crime lab.

"I'm sorry," he muttered. "I'll make sure it doesn't happen again."

Trey pointed down the hall toward Olivia.

"Tell *her* you're sorry—she's the one who got ambushed. Then tell her to sit tight. I'll be right back," Trey snapped, and strode in the opposite direction and disappeared around a corner.

Larry Flood took a deep breath, pasted a smile on his face and moved toward Olivia.

"Miss Sealy . . . I'm Larry Flood, chief investigator here at the crime lab. Please accept my apologies for that fiasco outside. Rest assured that I'll find out who tipped off the media and deal with them accordingly."

Olivia was still rattled, and her voice betrayed it by trembling as she answered. "Yes, well . . . thank you. It was certainly unexpected." Then she glanced down the hall. "Where did Detective Bonney go?"

"Oh . . . sorry. He asked me to tell you he'd be right back."

"All right," Olivia said, and glanced away.

Flood had just been dismissed, and he knew it.

"Well then . . . again, I'm sorry you were upset. If you'll excuse me, I need to get back to my office."

He left quickly, leaving Olivia alone. Moments later,

Trey appeared at the other end of the hall.

"Hey, Livvie."

She turned, saw him motioning for her to come, and gladly obeyed, anxious to be done with this place.

"I borrowed a car," he said. "And we're going out a different door."

"Oh, thank you," she said. "I was dreading another round with that bunch."

Without thinking, he slid an arm across her shoulders as he led her down the hall.

"I'm really sorry about that," he said. "I had no idea that might happen, or we would have done things differently."

Olivia told herself that the way he was holding her was nothing more than a gesture of comfort, but she couldn't help but think how natural it felt to slip back into his arms again.

"It's all right," she said. "It was just unsettling, that's all."

When they got to the door, Trey paused.

"Wait a minute," he said, and stepped outside, giving the side parking lot a careful look. Satisfied, he motioned her forward.

Olivia followed him to a red sports car that had dark-tinted windows and yellow flames painted along the fenders.

"Who did you borrow this from?" she asked.

"There's a guy I know who janitors here at the crime lab during the day so he can afford to pursue his music career at night." Then he grinned. "I believe he refers to this car as the Love Machine."

"Lord have mercy," Olivia muttered. "It's hardly unremarkable. Don't you think it will be noticed, too?"

Trey grinned. "Oh, sure, it will be noticed, but the windows are dark. No one can see in. Come on, Livvie. Hop in."

The sound of the engine was as flashy as the car's appearance. When Trey turned the key, the engine rumbled loudly, and when he pressed down on the accelerator, it actually roared.

Olivia's eyes widened, and then she laughed out loud.

Trey grinned in response, then shifted into gear and headed out of the parking lot. A couple of reporters and one news van were still parked at the end of the street, although the nutcase with the baby-killer sign was nowhere in sight. Trey and Olivia sped past without concern, and within moments, they'd left them behind.

Without the media as a topic of conversation, an uncomfortable silence returned between them. Trey was conscious of the stiff set to her shoulders, of her hands lying awkwardly in her lap. He knew that what had once been between them was gone, but he still hated the emotional distance he was feeling. He wasn't sure what to do to change it, but he knew he wasn't going to drive the thirty-something minutes it took to get her home in total silence.

"Say, Livvie, did I mention how much I like your dress?"

Olivia grinned before she thought, then looked at him and laughed.

"No," she said.

He frowned. "Hey . . . yes, I did."

"No . . . what you said was, *uh*. In fact, you said it twice."

This time it was Trey who laughed.

"Okay, but you can't blame me. Both the dress and the woman in it are dangerous, and you know it."

She managed a small smirk but didn't answer. It was, however, the icebreaker they both needed.

Trey glanced at his watch.

"I know you're meeting your grandfather at home for lunch, but I heard him say it would be a late one, right?"

"Yes."

"So how about a little snack?"

"Oh, I don't know about—"

"Don't worry. We won't have to get out of the car," Trey said.

She relaxed. "Okay, then, that would be nice. I was so nervous this morning that I didn't eat much breakfast."

Trey told himself that none of this meant anything, that he was only helping an acquaintance through a tough time, but some might have called what they were doing a date.

Olivia was expecting a fast-food restaurant, and possibly an order of fries and a drink, when Trey suddenly wheeled off the street and pulled into the drive-through of an ice-cream shop. At that point, he had her attention. Suddenly she remembered how they'd always ended their date before he took her home and felt a swift rush of emotion. She started to say something, then stopped, listening as he ordered one deluxe banana split to go.

"Nix the whipped cream, add extra nuts, and, uh . . . oh yeah, we need two spoons."

A young man's voice said, "That will be three-fifty. Please pull ahead to the first window."

Olivia's mouth was watering before the order appeared. She didn't argue as he took the huge dish of ice cream, then pulled into a parking space. She took the spoon he offered and dug straight into the scoop of ice cream topped with hot fudge before he had the car in Park.

Trey watched her, savoring her eye-rolling ecstasy as she put the first bite in her mouth.

"I knew you'd eat that first," he said softly, then thrust his own spoon into the scoop that had been drizzled with strawberry preserves.

"Mmm . . . oh my God . . . this is sooo good," Olivia said as she took her second big bite. "I can't remember the last time I've eaten one of these."

The car was quiet for a bit as Trey held the narrow plastic bowl and the two of them ate, both remembering without having the guts to tell each other what they were feeling.

It was Olivia who finally tossed in her spoon.

"That was fabulous, but I can't possibly eat another bite." Then she leaned back in the seat, absently licking the last bits of chocolate from the bowl of her plastic spoon as a child would lick a lollipop.

Trey was rendered momentarily speechless by the sight of her tongue on that spoon, and he might have stared longer if a girl in a pickup truck hadn't wheeled into the parking space beside them, then borne down on her horn. Before he knew what was happening, she had exited her truck and was slapping her hands on the hood of the car.

"Donnie Lee! You're a lyin', sneakin' bastard. I know you got another girl in there. You get on out of there right now before I start breakin' things on your precious Love Machine."

Olivia was staring at the ranting female in disbelief. Then she started to grin.

"Would your friend who owns this car happen to be named Donnie Lee?"

"Well, hell," Trey muttered, handed what was left of the banana split to Olivia and bailed out of the car. To add credence to his order, he flashed his badge as he yelled, "Hey! Lady! Get your hands off the car!"

The look on the girl's face was priceless. Olivia couldn't hear what she was saying, but she could tell that she was begging forgiveness in every way she knew how. She could hear enough of what Trey was saying to know he was getting Donnie Lee off the hook. And as she watched, with a bowl of melting ice cream in her lap, she laughed as she hadn't laughed in days.

It felt so good not to be afraid.

Finally the girl shrugged and smiled, then got in her truck and drove off.

Trey opened the door long enough to take the bowl from Olivia and dump it in a nearby trash can, then got back in the car. There was a glower on his face and a slight flush at the back of his neck; then he saw the laughter on Olivia's face and had to grin.

"That was something, wasn't it?"

Olivia chuckled. "You should have seen your face."

"I'm glad it provided you with some amusement," he drawled.

Without thinking, she laid her hand on the back of his hand.

"It was a much-needed laugh," she said softly.

Trey turned his hand palm up and threaded his fingers through hers.

"Livvie, I—"

Olivia gently pulled away.

"I think we'd better go. I wouldn't want Grampy to worry if I wasn't home when he got there."

Trey would have laughed if it hadn't been so painful. Olivia had grown up physically, but it was obvious she was still under Marcus Sealy's thumb.

"Yeah, we can't have him thinking you're spending too much time with someone beneath your class."

He started the car, backed out of the parking space, then drove her the rest of the way home without speaking, although he wished he could have taken back that last bit. It sounded too much like an old grudge, and he didn't want her thinking she still held any kind of power over him.

Olivia knew she was responsible for the uncomfortable silence that lengthened between them, but before she could find a way to explain, she was home.

Trey got out, then stepped around to the passenger

side of the car, opened the door and helped her out. They walked to the front door in silence. On the doorstep, Olivia turned to him.

"Thank you for the ride and the ice cream," she said.

"You're welcome," he said, and smiled politely, but the smile never reached his eyes.

Reluctant now for him to leave, Olivia struggled with bona fide reasons for him to linger.

"Uh, Trey . . . I was wondering. How long will it take to get the results of the tests?"

"At least a week or so, I think, maybe longer. You'll be notified."

Then his cell phone began to ring. He glanced at the caller ID, then backed off the step.

"I've got to take this call."

"Yes . . . of course," Olivia said, and unlocked the door. Even as the tumblers were turning, she felt as if she'd done something wrong. "Thank you, again," she added.

He stopped, and for a moment his gaze softened.

"Livvie."

"Yes?"

"It was good to see you again."

An unexpected film of tears suddenly blurred her vision.

"Yes. It was good to see you again, too," she said.

And then he was gone.

6

Marcus never made it home for lunch after all, which left Olivia sitting at the table alone, picking at her crab-meat salad and wondering what might have happened if she'd stayed longer with Trey. When Marcus called and told her he wouldn't be home, she could have called some of her friends and met them for a late lunch. They were always ready for an afternoon of gossip and margaritas, only she knew that this time, the topic of conversation would have been her. It also occurred to her that not one of her so-called friends had phoned since the media had broken the news of a possible connection between her family and the remains of the murdered child. This led her to consider just how shallow her friendships were, and how true Trey's caustic remark about her relationship with her grandfather was. It was hard to admit that she catered her life to suit Marcus's whims, but she did. What surprised her, and what she'd never considered, was that the female friends in her life were not really friends, just longtime acquaintances. She didn't have one special friend with whom she'd grown up, or with whom she had shared hopes and dreams. On the surface, her life had seemed perfect, but that illusion had shattered quickly when their family became headline news.

Frowning, she shoved the salad away and was getting up from the table when Rose entered with a tiny dish of

lemon sorbet. The minute serving was perfectly pro-
portioned and in the shape of the real thing, right down
to the yellow color and the tiny sprig of mint leaves at
what would have been the stem.

When Rose saw that the salad had hardly been
touched, she frowned.

"Is something wrong with the salad, dear?"

Olivia sighed. "No, it was delicious. I'm just not very
hungry, I guess."

Rose waved the small crystal dish of sorbet beneath
Olivia's nose in a tempting fashion.

"How about a serving of sorbet? It's your favorite."

"Actually, it's Grampy's favorite. But I like it, too,"
she added, anxious not to hurt Rose's feelings.

Rose removed the salad and left the dessert.

Olivia picked up the dish and shoved the mint leaf
aside with the tip of her spoon. Even as she was
scooping up the first bite, she couldn't help but compare this to the extravagant concoction that she and
Trey had shared earlier. When the sorbet hit her tongue,
she grimaced. The spare tartness of the cold treat was
no match for the decadence of the hot fudge she'd had
before. She ate the sorbet, more to satisfy Rose's feelings than from an enjoyment of the taste.

It wasn't until she was on her way up to her room to
change clothes that she realized what she'd just done.
She'd turned down an invitation to spend more time
with Trey because her grandfather had told her he
would see her at lunch; then she'd eaten a tiny dish of
sorbet that she didn't want just to pacify Rose. It would

have been just as simple to have made a call to Marcus and told him she'd made other plans—Lord knows he did it to her often enough—only she hadn't. Then she'd eaten food she didn't want so as not to hurt someone else's feelings.

She sat down on the steps, then thrust her fingers through her hair in frustration. What was wrong with her? When had she become this gutless wonder—and why? Why was she living her life to please everyone except herself?

She sighed. It was times like this that she missed having a mother. She needed another female's reactions to what she was feeling, but the only female of any importance to her was her old nanny, Anna Walden. As she pictured the dear woman's face, she knew what she wanted to do.

She jumped up and ran the rest of the way upstairs to her room. Once inside, she took off the red dress and hung it back in the closet, trading it for a pair of old Levi's and a Dallas Cowboys T-shirt. She abandoned her red heels for sneakers, and the loose hairstyle she'd had earlier was bunched up on her head and secured with an oversize pink clip. This time she was dressing for comfort, not impact.

After telling Rose where she was going, she hurried outside to the garages where the cars were housed. She started to get into her BMW, then, for some reason, changed her mind and took her grandfather's black Chevy Trailblazer. She loved the SUV with its get-up-and-go engine. As she backed out of the garage, she realized it had been weeks since she'd driven herself anywhere—and certainly not since they'd returned from their vacation. It felt good to be in control of something, even if it was only a car.

With an odd feeling of having escaped something threatening, she sped off the grounds. Before long she was on the freeway, aiming for Arlington and the two-bedroom bungalow that was now Anna Walden's home.

Dennis was so excited, he was shaking. Staking out the Sealy estate had been a brilliant idea. He hadn't been there more than thirty minutes when he'd seen the black SUV come down the driveway and pull out onto the street. The windows were too dark for him to tell who was driving, but it really didn't matter. The SEALY1 license tag marked it as belonging to the family, and anyway, he knew Marcus's car when he saw it. Already, his next plan of action was moving into place.

Then, suddenly, he tilted his head to one side, listening to voices that only he could hear.

"Yes, Lord . . . I hear you," he mumbled, and started the engine.

He glanced over his shoulder to make sure there was no traffic behind him, then quickly accelerated away from the curb. He drove without caution in an effort not to lose sight of the SUV, knowing that God was on his side.

Anna Walden's sixtieth birthday had come and gone.

The years had not been kind to her, but she didn't seem to mind. In her youth she'd had a hot body and an attitude to match, but seeing her now, one would never have suspected. She could never have predicted the twists and turns of fate that had taken her to Marcus Sealy's residence to care for a little two-year-old girl, traumatized by the events of her life. But she'd known from the first day that it was where she was meant to be. Anna had needed Olivia as badly as Olivia had needed her.

Anna had raised her to adulthood with a great sense of pride and accomplishment. She'd known that one day her presence at the Sealy estate would no longer be needed, but she'd still been shocked by her termination. Even though Marcus had furnished her with a comfortable retirement income and a nice little bungalow in a good neighborhood, it had not buffered her from the painful sense of loss.

Over the years, she'd learned to cope, satisfying herself with the impromptu visits Olivia occasionally made, looking forward to her own birthday, knowing that Olivia would come and take her out to dine somewhere elegant, and always enjoying the cards and letters that Olivia wrote. Just recently, she'd received at least a half-dozen postcards from both Marcus and Olivia during their trip to Europe, and she had lived vicariously through their trip from the notes and pictures. She was proud of the woman Olivia had become, but had never had aspirations of reinventing herself and moving on.

Today was no exception. She was flat on her back with her feet propped up on the arm of the sofa watching *The Price Is Right*. The loose float dress she was wearing to disguise her extra weight had slipped back toward her belly, revealing white pudgy legs and deep-dimpled knees. The flip-flops she favored were dangling from her big toes. The gray roots in her dyed red hair were a good three inches long, evidence of how many beauty-shop appointments she'd missed. When she heard the doorbell chime, she frowned. Bob Barker had just called for another contestant to "come on down," and she always loved to see the surprised reaction on the new contestant's face. But when she heard a familiar and beloved voice calling her name through the door, she almost fell off the sofa in her haste to get up.

"Nanna . . . Nanna . . . it's me, Olivia!"

Anna flung the door open, her expression mirroring her delight and surprise.

"Olivia . . . it's so good to see you!" she cried, and gave Olivia a hug of welcome. "Come in, come in. If you'd warned me you were coming, I would have baked chocolate crinkles. I know they're your favorites."

Olivia beamed. "Yes, they are," she said as she let herself be engulfed in the familiar comfort of Anna's arms.

She'd been right in coming here, after all. Although Anna was not blood kin, she was the closest thing to a mother figure she would ever have. Anna had helped Olivia learn to braid her hair, gone with her to buy her first bra, and taught Olivia all she knew about what it meant to be a female. And, unlike Rose, Anna knew Olivia's likes and dislikes, including chocolate crinkles, not lemon sorbet.

"So how have you been?" Anna asked as she closed the door and led Olivia to the sofa. "Did you and Mr. Marcus have a good time in Europe? Tell me all about it."

Olivia was a bit startled by the disarray of the room and Anna's unkempt appearance, then shrugged it off. Looks didn't matter. Anna was Anna—her Nanna, the woman who had become her touchstone to security— so she ignored the niggle of concern at the back of her mind.

"Europe was great," Olivia said. "We shot a couple dozen rolls of film, but I haven't had them developed yet. After everything that's been happening, they sort of slipped my mind."

Anna frowned. "What everything, dear? Has something happened to Marcus? Is he ill?"

Olivia was surprised that Anna hadn't keyed in immediately on what she meant.

"No, no, nothing like that," she said. "I was talking about the media . . . you know. You must have seen the papers about that baby's remains."

Anna frowned. "Baby? What baby?" Then before Olivia could answer, she added, "I have to confess, I broke my glasses a week or so ago. I can see the television just fine without them, so I haven't bothered to get them fixed, but it's limited my reading."

"Oh, Lord," Olivia muttered. "I wish I could be so unconcerned." Then she turned sideways on the sofa, kicked off her shoes and folded her legs up beneath her. "I should have called you when it all started," she said.

"When what all started, dear?" Anna said, then jumped up from the sofa. "Wait! Before you start, I'll get us something to drink."

"No, no, thank you," Olivia said. "Maybe later. We need to talk in case the reporters start calling you, although I can't think why they would."

Reporters? Suddenly, Olivia had all of Anna's attention. The old woman sat back down, then folded her hands in her lap.

"Why would reporters be calling me, dear?"

"They shouldn't, but that doesn't mean they won't. Grampy and I both agreed that you should be warned of the possibility."

"Of what?" Anna asked.

"About a week ago, a man found the remains of a small child . . . a girl . . . in a suitcase in the wall of a house up at Texoma. The police are trying to connect it to us because the baby was born with three thumbs."

Anna paled, then reeled, as if she'd been slapped.

"A baby? In a suitcase? Good Lord! That's appalling." Then she added, "But I'm not sure I understand. I know having three thumbs is unusual, but yours can't be the only family where that happens."

"Yes, but there are other complications."

"Like what?" Anna asked.

"The coroner claims that the remains are about

twenty-five years old, which is when I was kidnapped. And with the timeline, the age of the girl and the three thumbs . . . well . . . the long and short of it is, we had to submit to DNA testing to prove that I'm me and not someone else." Then her chin quivered, and her eyes filled with tears. "Oh, Nanna, I know it's silly, but I'm scared. What if I'm not Grampy's real granddaughter? What if that poor dead baby is the real one?"

Anna's chin jutted, and her voice grew rough in anger as she grabbed Olivia's hands.

"Now, you listen to me. That's foolish, and you know it. DNA or not, you're Marcus Sealy's granddaughter. I've seen the pictures. You've seen the pictures. I can't believe you'd think for one minute that you don't belong. Sealy blood runs in your veins. Now straighten up and act like it!"

Olivia had expected sympathy, not a scolding. For a moment she was too taken aback to react, but when she did, she managed a crooked smile.

"Oh, Nanna . . . I miss you. I came because I thought I needed sympathy, but as always, you gave me exactly what I need, which was an attitude adjustment."

As Olivia threw her arms around Anna's neck, Anna shuddered, then held her close.

"It's all right, sweetheart. Your Nanna is here. I didn't mean to sound so angry, but I won't have you doubting yourself. Not ever."

"You're right," Olivia said. "No more doubts. Now, about that cold drink . . ."

Anna leaned back, staring intently into Olivia's face,

as if searching for truth. Whatever she saw in Olivia's eyes seemed to satisfy her. She smiled, then patted Olivia's cheek.

"I have iced tea . . . sweet, like you like it."

"Sounds great," Olivia said. "I'll help."

Anna grunted as she got up, wincing slightly from the pain in her knee as she stood.

Olivia saw the pain on Anna's face and frowned.

"Are you all right?" she asked.

"I'm fine, just fine," Anna said. "It's just my old bones."

Olivia shuddered. The reference to old bones was too vivid a reminder of why she'd come. She shoved the thought out of her mind and put her arm around Anna's shoulders.

"I'm sorry it's been so long since we've last visited," she said. "Let's go get that tea."

Anna grinned as they moved toward her tiny kitchen. It felt good to still be needed.

At Anna's insistence, Olivia sat down at the table while Anna assembled their refreshments. At first Olivia's focus was on the joy of being with her Nanna, so she didn't notice the oddities of Anna's behavior. But when Anna poured tea in two glasses, then put the ice cubes in a bowl and set them on the table, Olivia blinked.

She looked up at Anna and started to laugh, then realized Anna had not meant it as a joke. Breath caught at the back of her throat, leaving her momentarily speechless; then, without comment, she took a couple of ice cubes from the bowl and put them in her glass, before adding some to Anna's. The tinkle and crack of the cold ice as it hit the warm tea was familiar, but the panic in the pit of her stomach was not. Something was wrong here, but she couldn't put her finger on what it was.

As she continued to watch, Anna took a box out of the pantry and set it on the table next to the bowl of melting ice.

"They're not homemade, but they're tasty enough," she said. "I'll get us some napkins and we'll be all set."

Olivia stared in disbelief at the box of steel-wool soap pads and struggled to breathe around the knot in the back of her throat.

"Nanna . . ."

Anna turned. The smile on her face was genuine, but the confusion in her eyes didn't belong.

"Aren't you hungry, dear? If the cookies don't tempt you, I could make us some sandwiches. Yes . . . that would be good. A sandwich. Maybe some chips. You like chips, don't you?"

Olivia got up and put her arms around Anna.

"Don't," she said gently. "It's all right, Nanna. I'm not hungry. Now come sit down and have some tea with me."

At the simple request, the confusion in Anna Walden's expression disappeared.

"Yes . . . tea. And you can tell me about your vacation."

Olivia pulled out a chair and seated Anna at the table, then took the chair next to her. She put the tea in front of Anna, then set the box of steel-wool pads on a chair out of sight. Her fingers were trembling as she laid her hands in her lap. Her heart was hammering inside her chest, but she made herself stay calm.

Anna stared at the glass of tea, then took a tentative sip.

"It's tea . . . isn't it?" she said, then took another sip and smiled. "Yes. It's tea. Good tea. Sweet tea, just like we like it. Thank you, darling. You always were so thoughtful."

Olivia's eyes welled with tears.

"You're welcome, Nanna." Then she took a deep breath. "You know, it's been ages since you've come for a visit. Why don't you pack a bag and come stay with Grampy and me for a few days."

Anna's eyes widened; then the confusion returned.

"Leave? Oh no, dear. I couldn't do that."

"But why, Nanna? You're just here all day by yourself, and Grampy and I would love to have you. Besides . . . there's the possibility that the media will start hounding you about the years you worked for us, and you'd be sheltered from that at our house."

Anna frowned. "I won't talk to them. I wouldn't tell them anything, I promise. I don't want to leave." Then her voice faltered. "It's been too long since I was there. I wouldn't know where anything was."

Olivia could tell that her insistence wasn't doing anything but agitating Anna further, and she couldn't bear to be the one to cause her Nanna any distress. Still, the sadness of what she was seeing overwhelmed her.

Before she could stop herself, she was out of her chair and down on her knees in front of Anna. She wrapped her arms around Anna's waist and laid her head in the old woman's lap.

"It's okay, Nanna. You don't have to do anything you don't want to do. If you want to stay here, then you can stay here. And don't worry about reporters. Grampy and I will take care of that—and you."

The pressure that had been building at the back of Anna's throat began to subside. She looked down at Olivia, then laid her hands on Olivia's hair and started to hum beneath her breath, just as she'd done when Olivia was a little girl.

The sound was so familiar to Olivia, and so comforting, that for a moment she let herself believe everything was all right. But then her gaze fell on the box of scouring pads on the chair next to where she was kneeling, and she closed her eyes against the pain.

How could a world that had been so perfect disintegrate so horribly in such a short span of time? As she knelt at Anna's feet, she realized she wasn't the only one with an identity in crisis. If she wasn't mistaken, her Nanna was coming undone. She didn't want to leave her like this, but she could tell the woman was going to need some backup. She would talk to Grampy about it tonight. He would know what to do.

A short while later, Olivia drove away with the feel of Anna's dry lips still imprinted against her cheek.

Foster Lawrence gave the cabdriver the address he

wanted as he slid into the back seat. The driver put the car into gear and peeled away from the curb before Foster had the door shut.

"Dammit, man, I been waiting a long time for this ride. I don't aim to be killed on the way to my destination, so slow the hell down."

The driver never acknowledged Foster's demand, although he did slow down.

Foster cursed beneath his breath, then made himself relax. A lot was riding on this trip, and there were plans to be made. He was under no misconception that the restaurant where he'd hidden the money was still in business, because he'd checked the phone book the first night without success. In twenty-five years, lots of things were bound to have changed. The actual location of the money was in the basement, and he was hoping that whoever had taken over the building would have done little to no renovation at that level. He just needed to get there, scope out the present business, see what it was going to take to get to his money, then get the hell out of Dallas. At least, since his physical transformation, he was confident that he could move around the city without being recognized.

A short while later, the driver pulled up to the curb.

"That'll be ten-fifty," he said.

Foster peeled off two fives and a one and tossed them over the seat.

"Keep the change," he said, and slammed the door behind him as he got out.

He heard the driver cursing but couldn't have cared

less. He would teach the little bastard to drive like that and then expect to get a good tip. He was still smirking as he turned around. At that point, the smirk died.

"What the hell?" he muttered, looking first up the street, then down, checking the addresses of the adjoining businesses to make sure that the driver had dropped him off at the right place.

When it hit him that the address was correct, his heart skipped a beat. A sick feeling grew in the pit of his stomach as the implications of what he was seeing sank in.

"No . . . it can't be," he mumbled, and then stumbled toward the building.

"Look out, mister," a man said as Foster lurched against him.

"Oh. Sorry," Foster said. "I didn't see—"

"Whatever," the man said, and kept walking.

Ordinarily the man's attitude would have ticked Foster off, but not today. After twenty-five years of dreaming about this moment, his dreams had been dashed. As he'd expected, the restaurant was gone, but the building he'd known was also gone, and another had been built in its place.

He stood in the middle of the sidewalk while his mind kept racing. Even if this business had kept the foundation and made no use of the basement other than to house the heating and cooling equipment—and that was assuming they hadn't gutted the basement and were using it for a vault—there was no way he was getting into it without going through these doors, and there was no way in hell he would be able to get down into the basement from inside this building unless he worked there—and for a man with a criminal record, that would never happen.

He looked up at the massive edifice and the words carved into the stone.

FIRST FEDERAL SAVINGS AND LOAN

If the situation hadn't been so painful, he might have laughed. What better place to stash a million dollars than a fucking bank? Only, the money wasn't in an account in his name. If it was still there, which he was beginning to doubt, it would be behind the north wall of the basement, near the west corner. Ten bricks up from where the boiler connected into the wall and eight bricks over from the corner.

"Son of a bitch." Then he took a deep breath and said it again, slower and louder. "Son. Of. A. Bitch."

"Well, I never!" a woman said.

Foster's focus shifted to the woman who'd just exited the bank. She was glaring at him with disdain. He glared back.

"If you had, then you might be in a better mood," he snapped, then strode past her and into the bank.

She hissed in dismay, but there was no one around to whom she could complain, so she stomped off down the street.

The guard looked at Foster as he entered the bank. Foster nodded pleasantly and kept on walking as if he had a destination in mind. He moved with purpose, and after a few moments of observation, took a seat in a waiting area near the busiest loan officer, which he figured would give him time for a good look around.

There were security cameras everywhere and at least two guards in plain sight, but that didn't mean there weren't others elsewhere in the building. There wasn't one doorway that wasn't blocked off from foot traffic by a desk or a counter. He was feeling sicker by the moment. Then a woman stopped where he was seated and spoke.

"Hello. My name is Pat Hart. Is there something I can do for you?"

He looked up, then blurted out the first thing that came to mind.

"I . . . uh . . . I'm checking into your interest rates for small-business loans."

She smiled. "Come with me. I'll be happy to discuss them with you."

He followed her into a small cubicle, then took a seat across from her desk. She put her elbows on the desktop as she leaned forward, and it occurred to Foster that if she knew who he was, she wouldn't be smiling.

"Now. About your loan. How much were you interested in borrowing?" she asked.

Foster shook his head. "My partners and I are still in the planning stages for the restaurant. We're just checking into interest rates at the moment. We'd like to limit the number of investors by getting the backing ourselves, but it all depends on payback rates, you know."

"Of course," she said, and swiveled her chair toward her computer. "Let me bring up the screen and see what we've got here." As she was waiting for the computer to do its thing, she looked back at Foster. "So you're going to open a restaurant? Are you a local?"

He shrugged. "I used to be, however, I've been on the West Coast for years." He didn't feel the need to mention that it had been in Lompoc Federal Prison. "You know . . . there used to be a good restaurant right here on this very spot. Of course, that was years ago . . . still, I wonder? Do you know what happened to it?"

She shrugged. "I wouldn't know. I grew up in Seattle and have only been here in Dallas for the past five years. But I know someone who would know." She picked up her phone. "Ms. Shaw, would you come into my office for a moment?"

"My secretary," she explained. "She's a native of the city."

Foster caught a glimpse of an older woman getting up from her desk, then coming their way.

"Yes, Ms. Hart?"

"Liz, this gentleman was mentioning that, years ago, there used to be a restaurant in this location. By any chance, do you remember it?"

"Oh yes," the woman said. "The Lazy Days. It burned. Down to the ground and then some. It was such a shame, too."

Foster reeled. He felt the blood leaving his head and

thought for a moment he was going to pass out. Twenty-five years of expectations gone. Just like that.

"Burned?"

She nodded. "Completely."

"Well then," he mumbled. "I suppose that's that." He got up from his chair and stumbled toward the doorway.

The loans officer stood abruptly. "Sir? Wait. We haven't discussed interest rates yet."

"It doesn't matter. Not anymore," he mumbled, and walked away.

7

Olivia was coming up on her exit. Still distraught about Nanna's disturbing behavior, she didn't see the approaching minivan until it suddenly appeared in her side-view mirror. She was thinking to herself that the driver was going too fast when the van accelerated and swerved almost into her lane. She had a brief glimpse of the driver's face, as well as the gun he was aiming at her, before the window glass on her side of the door exploded.

She screamed—and the sound seemed to go on forever.

Before she knew it, she was off the freeway and over the guardrail. She felt the SUV go airborne, then the impact as it hit nose down. Her body lurched against the restraining seat belt as the air bag deployed, while at the same time, a terrible pain exploded in her shoulder. She thought she screamed out Trey's name, and then the car started to roll. After that, everything went black.

It wasn't until Dennis saw the SUV moving into the far right-hand lane that he realized the driver was going to exit. He'd been toying with the idea of abandoning his plan ever since he'd realized that it was Olivia Sealy, not Marcus, who was driving the SUV. Still, in his mind, since she bore the name, so she also bore the shame. Without giving himself time to change his mind, he accelerated, swerved quickly across two lanes of traffic and moved in behind her car. When the traffic cleared ahead of them, he drove out from behind and pulled up until he was almost even, got as close as he dared, picked up his gun from the seat and took aim. He fired rapidly into the front seat, then sped away.

In the rearview mirror, he saw the car swerve sharply, hit a guardrail, then go over the side. His eyes filled with tears of relief. Tonight he would sleep guilt free.

"Yes, Lord, it is done," he said, and never looked back.

Trey was on his way home for the day when he heard the call about an accident with injury go out over the police radio. It made him think of how fragile life really was and how someone's world had suddenly been altered. He said a silent prayer for their well-being, then let it go.

Truth was, he was still reeling from the morning he'd

spent with Livvie. The banana split they'd shared had brought back a world of old memories. Memories of how sweet first love had been, and how painful it had been when it ended. Foolishly, for a time, he'd let himself consider the remote possibility of recapturing what had been between them, but the moment had been brief. It had cost him a lot more than ego to realize how little Livvie's life had changed from when she was in school. She might be a grown woman, but she was still not the one in control of her life. And, as much as he might be attracted to her, he knew better than to go down that road again.

He made himself focus on the mundane and began considering whether to make dinner from what was left over in the refrigerator or to pick up some carry-out on his way home. Just as he was opting for carry-out chicken, his cell phone rang. He saw the caller ID and sighed. It was Lieutenant Warren, and the thought of being called back to work was not a pleasant one. For a few seconds he toyed with the notion of not answering; then he yanked himself in gear and did what he'd been hired to do.

"Hello."

"Trey . . . where are you?"

Trey stifled a groan. This sounded like the buildup to a callback, and it served him right for answering.

"Almost home, sir . . . what's up?"

"We've got trouble. Olivia Sealy was shot at on the bypass. She hit a guardrail, then went over it and rolled down an embankment. They're taking her by ambulance to Dallas Memorial. Get down there fast. I've got Rodriguez and Sheets on the case, but since you're something of a friend of the family, find out as much as you can and let Rodriguez know."

"Shot? You said she'd been shot?"

"Shot at, for sure. First reports indicated she had a bullet wound besides her other injuries, but I can't confirm that."

"Other injuries?"

"Yes . . ."

In shock, Trey pulled over to the curb. He could hear Warren's voice and knew the lieutenant was still talking, but none of the words made sense. All he could hear was the sound of Livvie's laughter as she ate hot fudge off the banana split. For a second he couldn't find the breath to talk. Then, when he did, everything came out in a rush.

"How bad is she hurt? Do they have the shooter in custody? Has Marcus Sealy been notified?"

"I don't know her condition. The shooter's still at large, and yes, Mr. Sealy is en route. Get there. Find out what you can. I have a gut feeling that this is all connected to the discovery of that suitcase and those bones, although for the life of me, I can't imagine how."

"I'm on my way," Trey said, and dropped his cell phone into his pocket. He slapped his red light onto the dash, hit the siren, then made a U-turn and headed for the hospital.

Olivia smelled blood—tasted blood—felt blood. It

had to be hers, but she didn't know why. Fear warred with pain as she struggled to get up, only to discover she couldn't move.

"Olivia? Olivia? Do you know where you are?" someone said, and laid a hand across Olivia's forehead.

No, she thought she said, then realized she hadn't answered aloud when the voice kept talking.

"You're in the hospital. You had an accident on the freeway. Do you remember?"

Gun. Blue van. Screaming . . . someone is screaming . . . Oh, God, it's me. "Help me," she whispered.

"We *are* helping you, dear, but you need to lie still."

"Grampy . . . tell Grampy," she mumbled.

"Your family has been notified. Please, don't move, dear."

Cognizance shifted to a lesser state of being, leaving Olivia hovering in a sort of twilight. She felt pain— heard voices—but from a distance away, as if she were standing outside her body.

"Doctor! Her blood pressure is dropping!"

"The bullet nicked an artery!"

"Type and cross-match . . ."

"Bleeding out . . ."

"Stabilized for now . . ."

"Get her to surgery . . ."

Suddenly she was moving. She knew because she could see the fluorescent lights in the ceilings above her as if they were one long continuous stream of illumination.

Then, over the turmoil, she heard a deep, anxious

voice calling her name, felt a hand against her cheek, heard footsteps running beside the bed to keep up as they wheeled her toward the operating room.

It was Trey.

Acknowledging his presence was, at the same time, a blessing and a pain. He'd come when she needed help most, but she wasn't sure she could make him understand. As she struggled against the approaching darkness, she heard him beg.

"Livvie . . . Livvie . . . it's Trey. You've got to stay strong for me, baby. Stay strong."

Trey . . . I'm here. Need to tell you something. Something about the van. Oh God . . . the gun . . . He had a gun. But all she managed to mumble was, "Shot me."

Trey wouldn't let himself look at the blood on her face or the wide, spreading stain of red across her chest.

"I know, baby . . . I know. Did you see him? Do you know who it was?"

A nurse was pushing Trey aside as they neared the doors to the surgery.

"Detective . . . Sir . . . You need to get back."

Olivia felt Trey's hand on hers. With every ounce of energy she could focus, she curled her fingers around his and pulled.

Trey felt her tug, and when he saw her lips moving, immediately leaned down.

"What is it, Livvie? What are you trying to say?"

"Shooter . . . baby killer."

"I don't understand, honey. What do you mean?"

"That's it," the nurse said. "You have to leave. Now."

The coppery scent of fresh blood was all over her. Trey could see her eyelids fluttering as she struggled to speak. But to delay would be risking her life, and he would willingly give up everything to make sure she survived.

"It's okay, Livvie . . . it's okay. You can tell me later." His voice broke as he kissed the side of her cheek, then whispered softly against her ear, "Stay strong for me, Livvie. Don't leave me again."

Trey had seen plenty of gunshot victims since his career with the police department had begun, but he'd never known one as intimately as he knew Olivia Sealy. Standing on the far side of the doors as they whisked her away was quite possibly the most difficult thing he'd ever done. He felt rooted to the spot, knowing that this was the closest he would be to her until they brought her out of surgery. He wouldn't let himself think about consequences other than catching the bastard responsible for her situation. He took a deep breath, then laid the flat of his hand against the door.

"Don't you die on me, Livvie," he said softly. When he turned around, Marcus Sealy was coming toward him on the run.

"Olivia! Olivia! Where is she?" he asked. "Is she all right?"

Trey saw the panic on Marcus's face, as well as the gray tinge around his mouth. Instinctively, he grabbed the older man's elbow and led him to a nearby chair.

"Mr. Sealy, let's sit down. I'll tell you what I know."

Marcus was shaking so hard he could barely breathe.

"I didn't come home for lunch. If I had, none of this would have happened," he said, then covered his face with his hands. "I can't lose her, too," he moaned. "I just can't."

"First of all," Trey said, "it's not your fault. It's not Livvie's fault, either."

Marcus lifted his head, and for the first time Trey saw past the money and power of Marcus Sealy's world to the truth of what really mattered to him.

"Who did this?" Marcus asked. "Why would someone want to hurt Olivia? She's been the victim in this tragedy from the start. She lost her parents, and now her very identity is being threatened. Why would someone want her dead?"

"I don't know, sir, but I promise you, we will find out."

Marcus shuddered. "God . . . this is a nightmare."

"Yes, sir, and then some," Trey muttered.

Marcus looked up, realizing that the detective seemed as distraught as he felt himself. Then he vaguely remembered Bonney referring to Olivia as Livvie—a nickname that denoted familiarity. But how could that be, when they'd only just met?

"Did Olivia say anything to you about the man who shot her?" Marcus asked.

Trey frowned. "Nothing that made any sense. She said something about a—" Suddenly the expression on his face changed. "I'll be damned."

"What?" Marcus asked.

"I think I know what she was trying to say," Trey said. "I need to make a phone call."

"Wait! I have a right to know what—"

"If I'm right, you'll be the first to know," Trey said, and headed toward an exit. He had to call his lieutenant, and using a cell phone in this part of the hospital was not permitted.

Once outside, he made a call to headquarters and was patched through to Chia, who was still at the site, interviewing witnesses. She answered on the first ring.

"Rodriguez."

"Chia . . . it's Trey. I may have a lead for you."

"I hope it's better than the three witnesses we have. Two saw a black van, one thought it was blue. One said the driver was a man, one said she couldn't tell, and the other was watching Sealy's car go over the embankment. No one got a tag number, so talk to me."

"You still got that friend down at KLPG?"

"Yeah, but what's that got to do with—"

"Stay with me on this," Trey said. "The media was all over the place when I took the Sealys to the crime lab this morning. It was nothing less than a small riot. They were trying to get film on the old man and his granddaughter, which I'm sure they did."

"And this matters because . . . ?"

"There was a man, some head case, waving a sign that said Baby Killer. If they have some footage with him in it, you need to find out who he is and where he lives. When you do, find out what kind of an alibi he has for the past three hours."

"Why?"

"Right before they took Olivia Sealy into surgery, she said three words to me. 'Shooter . . . baby killer.' She was real rattled about the whole mess at the crime lab, so I'm not sure if she was just mixed up in her head from the wreck and being shot, or if she was trying to tell me something about the man who shot her. Either way, we need to find out."

"I'm on it," Chia said. "And thanks."

"You find the bastard who did this to her and I'll be the one saying thanks," Trey said, and disconnected.

He dropped his cell phone into his pocket and headed back into the hospital.

When he got back, Marcus was still sitting where he'd left him. He sat down in a nearby chair, and although he knew it was too soon to know anything, he still asked.

"Any news?"

Marcus shook his head.

"Do you have any news about who did this to her?"

Trey hesitated, but only for a moment.

"We're not sure," he said. "Olivia said something to me just before she went into surgery. It might be nothing, and then again, it might not. I gave the investigating detective the information. We won't know for a while whether it meant anything or not."

Marcus shuddered, then looked away, and after a few moments, Trey leaned back in his chair, sprawling his long legs out in front of him, and closed his eyes. He'd never been on this side of a crime, and he didn't like the helplessness of it all. He tried to put himself in Marcus's place but couldn't wrap his mind around what must be complete devastation. The man had already lost his son and daughter-in-law to an unspeakable crime, and now his granddaughter was fighting for her life because of another.

After a while, he sat up.

"Mr. Sealy?"

Marcus looked up. "Yes?"

"Would you like some coffee?"

Marcus shook his head. "No, but thank you."

A few more minutes passed. The silence between them lengthened before Trey thought to ask, "Is there someone I could call for you? Another family member . . . a close friend?"

"No," Marcus said. "There's no one but—" Then he looked startled. "Oh no . . . I didn't even think. She will have heard it on the news and be beside herself with worry."

"Who?" Trey asked. "I'd be more than happy to—"

"No, no," Marcus said, then added, "But thank you. It's Olivia's old nanny. They're very close. In fact, that's where she'd been when she was . . . when—" Tears spilled down his cheeks. "I can't even bring myself to say it," he said, then slowly got to his feet. "I need to find a phone and call her myself."

Trey took his cell phone from his pocket.

"Please . . . sir . . . use mine," Trey said, and handed it over.

Marcus took it, looking at Trey again, only this time

as if seeing him anew.

"Thank you, son."

"For what?" Trey said. "It's just a phone."

"I mean, for being here . . . for staying with me like this."

Trey swallowed past the knot in his throat.

"Sir, right now I wouldn't be anywhere else."

He watched as Marcus took the same path out of the hospital that he'd taken earlier, then dropped his head and started to pray. He prayed for Livvie's life to be spared in every way he knew how to ask.

A short while later, Marcus came back, handed him the cell phone and sat back down. "Any news?" he asked.

"No, sir," Trey said.

Marcus eyed Trey for a few moments, trying to figure him out. His behavior suggested something more personal than a cop's interest in a crime, which made no sense. They'd only met him two days ago.

"Detective Bonney, may I ask you something?"

"Yes, sir, of course."

"Earlier, I thought I heard you refer to my grand-daughter as Livvie."

Trey's pulse skipped, then settled. It was nothing of which he should be ashamed. In fact, he should have said something on the first day. He leaned forward, resting his elbows on his knees as he met Marcus's curious gaze.

"Did I? I don't remember saying it," Trey said, then added, "but I'm not surprised. When we were in high school, it's all I ever called her."

Marcus's eyes widened in surprise.

"High school? You and Olivia have known each other since high school?" He frowned. "I wonder why she never mentioned it earlier."

"Well, back then, you considered me unsuitable company for her, so I'm thinking she would have assumed you might still feel the same." Trey smiled and shrugged. "But that was years ago. Times and people change, don't they, sir?"

Marcus's thoughts were reeling. He kept trying to remember a time when he'd forbidden her anything.

"I'm sure you must be mistaken," he muttered. "I can't remember ever telling her to—" Memory emerged as he eyed Trey with sudden understanding.

"Bonney! William Bonney the third! Of course . . . Trey. Now I remember. You were the boy who—"

Trey quickly interrupted. "Loved your granddaughter? Yeah, that was me."

Marcus leaned back in his chair in disbelief.

"I hope you don't hold any of that against me," Marcus said. "She was young. I was just trying to protect her."

For a moment Trey held Marcus's gaze without answering. Then he shook his head and managed a cordial smile.

"Of course not, sir. We were kids. Like I said, times and people change. Except I still care for Livvie's . . . I mean, Olivia's well-being. Surely you can allow me that much?"

Suddenly Marcus felt ashamed. He didn't know why, and he wasn't sure what to say, but he knew that in some way he'd overstepped the bounds of propriety. He'd kept Olivia so close to him that he hadn't allowed her any personal life at all. What hurt the most was that, except for that time so long ago, she'd never objected. In trying to protect her, he'd also ruined her chance to make choices—and mistakes—on her own.

His shoulders slumped.

"I'm sorry," he said softly. "Of course you're free to do and say what you wish. I didn't realize . . . I mean, I never meant to . . ." He looked down at the floor, then clasped his hands and swallowed past a knot in his throat. "When this is over, we would be honored to have you as a guest in our home. Anytime."

Trey felt the emotion in the old man's voice and knew what it had cost him to say that.

"Thank you," Trey said, then added, "When this is over."

There were a few awkward moments of silence afterward, then Trey thought to ask about the phone call Marcus had made.

"Sir?"

Marcus looked up, and his expression showed every one of his seventy years.

"Call me Marcus, please."

Trey hesitated, then nodded.

"If you'll call me Trey."

"So, Trey, what did you want to know?" Marcus asked.

"Your phone call . . . were you able to get through?"

"Yes, thank goodness. Of course, Anna was terribly upset, as I expected her to be. Anna Walden was not only Olivia's nanny, she was also the only mother figure my granddaughter has ever had. Olivia is very close to her. In fact, she was on her way home from visiting her when this . . . incident occurred."

"I see."

Marcus glanced down at his watch.

"I sent a car for her. In fact, she should be here soon. If you're still here, you can meet her."

Trey's mouth firmed.

"I'll still be here. I'm not going anywhere until I know Livvie's okay."

"Of course," Marcus muttered. "I didn't mean—" He sighed. "I don't know what I meant. I don't know what I'm saying anymore." His voice was shaking, and then he dropped his head. "Dear God . . . why is this happening? Why is this happening again?"

Foster Lawrence had been walking the streets in a daze ever since he'd learned what had happened to the money. He didn't know where he was, or how to get back to his hotel, and right now, he was too numb to care. The same thoughts kept going around and around in his brain, and there wasn't anything that was going to change the facts. Twenty-five years ago he'd let the idea of a million dollars override his good sense and gotten mixed up in a mess that had landed him in prison. Still, the knowledge that the ransom money was there waiting for him had been enough to make doing the time a whole lot easier. Only now it was over. The only good thing that he could say about his life was that, for the moment, he was free, although that could change at any moment. According to what he'd read and heard, the authorities still wanted him for questioning.

He'd been safer inside Lompoc than he was now. He didn't know a damn thing about a dead baby, but if it was connected to the Sealy kidnapping, he knew who was probably to blame. Problem was, he didn't know where to start looking or if the guilty party was even still alive.

He thought about just turning himself in to the police right now, saying he'd heard they wanted to talk to him and starting to talk. Looking back, he should have spilled his guts from the start, but he'd let his hate for the law and his emotional ties to the killer sway his judgment. It had cost him a million dollars and twenty-five years of his life. Now, through no fault of his own, he was in danger of losing his newly found freedom. Emotional ties aside, he wasn't doing another twenty-five for anyone, no matter how good the reason.

He paused in front of an electronics store, staring blankly at the same television show being broadcast on a window full of television sets—flat screens, big screens, plasma screens, screens he didn't even understand. But when a news bulletin flashed across all thirty screens, he understood that the complications of his life had just been upped.

He watched with his hands in his pockets and a blank expression on his face, listening to the newscaster stationed outside Dallas Memorial Hospital as she broadcast an update on the attempted murder of Olivia Sealy.

When it was over, he turned around and walked away. In the back of his mind, he was aware that night was near, but he couldn't bring himself to care. There was a part of him that wanted to keep on walking— to leave the city of Dallas and the state of Texas so far behind that he would forget they'd ever existed.

But he didn't. He was caught up in this mess whether he liked it or not. Someone had tried to kill Olivia Sealy today. They'd shot at her on the freeway. Her car had rolled end over end down an incline. Since she was still in surgery, it was unclear what the extent of her injuries or her prognosis might be, but his name was, once again, mentioned in conjunction with the case. If he left town, he might find himself running for the rest of his life. On the other hand, if he turned himself in, there was a real good chance he would never see daylight again. He didn't know what the hell to do.

A police car went speeding by with sirens screaming. Out of habit, he ducked into a darkened alley, waiting until the car was well past before coming back out to the street. As he stood, a cab pulled in to the curb a few feet away to let off a passenger. On impulse, he grabbed the ride, gave the driver the address of his hotel and sat back. He still didn't know what to do, but at least for tonight he could be confused in relative comfort and safety.

· · ·

While Foster Lawrence was in his hotel room taking a shower, Trey and Marcus were still waiting for news of Olivia's condition. Added to their worry was the fact that Anna Walden had yet to arrive. Marcus was concerned, but he wasn't leaving again until he had word of Olivia's condition. It had been three hours since they'd taken her into surgery, and the more time passed, the more worried they became.

Just when Trey thought he would go out of his mind, he heard a commotion at the end of the hall. He and Marcus both looked up just as a heavyset woman turned a corner on the run. She was stumbling and crying as she came.

"Oh dear," Marcus said. "It's Anna."

He jumped up from his chair and hurried toward her, and in doing so, missed seeing the doctor appear at the other end of the hall.

But Trey saw him. He stood abruptly, very aware of the sick feeling in the pit of his stomach. As badly as he wanted to know how Olivia was doing, he was almost afraid to hear the verdict.

"Are you a member of Olivia Sealy's family?" the doctor asked.

"Yes," Trey lied without hesitation, "but let me get her grandfather, too." He hurried up the hall to where Marcus was standing. In his haste, he barely noticed the woman. "Marcus! The doctor is out of surgery and waiting to talk to us," he said.

"Oh! Yes, of course," Marcus said. "Come along,

Anna. You'll be wanting to hear this, too."

"Oh Lord, oh Lord . . . my baby . . . my baby," Anna moaned, and suddenly sagged against the wall.

Trey steadied her by one elbow while Marcus held the other, and together they managed to get her down the hall. Trey could see that she was upset and disoriented, then forgot about her behavior entirely as the doctor began to speak.

"Is this all of you?" the doctor asked.

"Yes, yes. Please," Marcus begged, "is Olivia all right?"

"She came through the surgery beautifully. The bullet entered the back of her shoulder and nicked an artery. She must have been turning slightly away when the shot was fired. It exited just below her collarbone, barely missing her spinal cord . . . but it *did* miss it."

Trey's vision blurred. Unashamed of his tears, he listened intently, desperate for every word of her condition.

"Her other injuries are fairly mild. Thanks to her seat belt and the air bag, she didn't suffer any broken bones. She has a mild concussion, but we were given to understand the vehicle she was in rolled several times, and that would be expected. However, she lost a lot of blood and received a transfusion during surgery."

Marcus grimaced. "Will she need more? If so, I'd be happy to donate. We share the same blood type."

"So would I," Trey added, then asked, "What's her blood type?"

"It's a little unusual," the doctor said. "A negative."

Trey frowned. "I'm O positive."

Anna came to herself suddenly, as if she'd only just arrived, and spoke with calm confidence.

"I can donate," she said.

"What's your blood type?" the doctor asked.

Confusion stirred, and Anna's expression shifted.

"I don't know . . . but I'm sure I can help. Olivia is my baby girl. I raised her, you know."

Marcus patted Anna's arm.

"Yes, you did, Anna dear, and I don't know what we would have done without you."

"But I want to donate blood, too," she said.

Before it could become an issue, the doctor intervened.

"All of you are welcome to donate. We're always in need."

Suddenly Anna's emotional confusion disappeared.

"So that's that," she said shortly. "My baby girl will be fine, then, won't she?"

"Barring any unforeseen complications, she should be," the doctor said.

"I want to see her," Marcus said.

"I will go with you," Anna stated, confident of her place in their family.

Trey felt left out. He desperately wanted to see her, too, but figured it wasn't going to happen.

However, Marcus saw the look on Trey's face and surprised himself, as well as Trey, when he said, "Detective Bonney will come, too. He's a childhood friend of Olivia's."

Anna looked startled, and for the first time, eyed Trey curiously.

"You knew my baby?" Anna asked.

"Yes, ma'am, I did. We went to high school together."

Anna frowned thoughtfully, but didn't comment.

"Can we see her now?" Trey asked.

"She's still in recovery," the doctor said. "Why don't we go see about those blood donations. By the time you're all done, she should be in her room."

"I need to make a phone call," Trey said. "I'll catch up with you."

They went one way as Trey went the other. He made a quick call back to Chia.

"Chia, it's Trey. Did you get the tape?"

"Yes. We got a couple of good views of the man's face. No one at the station knew who he was, but I'm running him through the database now."

"If you get a location on him, let me know. I want to be there when you bust him."

Chia frowned. "You got some kind of investment in this case that I don't know about?"

"It's personal," Trey muttered.

"As in . . . woman personal?" she asked.

"Just keep me posted," Trey said, and disconnected.

8

"Olivia! Olivia! Wake up, dear. Your surgery is over. I need you to open your eyes. Can you hear me? I need you to open your eyes."

Olivia moaned.

"Hurts."

"I know it hurts. I'm so sorry. The doctor has given you something for pain. It will kick in soon. Meanwhile, we'll get you some warm blankets. How will that be?"

She moaned again and tried to open her eyes. There was something she needed to remember, but the thought wouldn't come. While she was struggling to concentrate, the warm blankets arrived. She felt their weight, then the heat, and gave in to the comfort of unconsciousness.

"Is she awake? I need to talk to my baby."

Olivia reached toward the sound. *Nanna? That sounded like Nanna.*

"Olivia, darling, it's Grampy. We're here for you, darling. Don't worry about a thing. You're going to be fine."

Grampy. That was Grampy. Why are Nanna and Grampy in my bedroom?

She tried to answer, but her mouth was so dry. She licked her lips, then moaned.

"Hurt . . ."

Someone touched her hand, then her forehead. She felt the warmth of breath near her cheek.

"I know, Livvie. I'm sorry."

Trey . . . is that you?

He answered, almost as if he'd read her mind. "It's me, Trey."

The image of a man pointing a gun at her face jumped into Olivia's mind so quickly that she flinched. The motion caused such pain that tears poured out from beneath her eyelids.

"Trey . . . hurts," she whispered.

Trey had never felt so helpless in his life. He wanted to hold her, protect her, take away the pain— and all he could do was mumble platitudes that solved nothing.

"I know, honey. I'm so sorry, but the doctor said you're going to be fine."

Fine. He said she was going to be fine. The knowledge was comforting. Trey didn't lie. Then she remembered, Trey was a cop. She needed to tell him that she'd been shot.

"Shot me."

Trey frowned. "We know. The police are looking for him now."

She'd always been able to trust Trey. She should have known he would take care of this, too. She sighed.

"Sleep . . ."

Marcus stepped forward and kissed Olivia's cheek.

"Yes, darling, you get some rest. We won't be far."

Anna said her goodbye with a tender touch to Olivia's forehead.

"Darling, it's your Nanna. Don't you worry about a thing. When you get to go home, I'll take care of you, just like I did when you were small."

Nanna? Nanna! Olivia flinched. That's what she'd been trying to remember.

"Grampy? *Grampy.*"

"I'm here, dear."

She licked her lips again, trying to shift her thoughts into words.

"Take care . . . Nanna . . . lost. Losing focus on . . ."

Olivia sighed. There was more she meant to say, but the painkillers made her thoughts as heavy as her limbs. She lost her hold on reality and fell back into the hole in her mind.

Olivia's words made Anna nervous. She scooted sideways without looking at the men, then pushed the hair away from her face. She didn't understand why Olivia had said that, but she didn't like it. Everyone was looking at her, and she didn't want to be looked at. She knew she wasn't pretty anymore. What people didn't know was that she just didn't care. She'd already lived the part of her life that had value. As far as she was concerned, her life now was just a matter of marking time.

"I'm not lost," she muttered. "I'm not lost. I'm right here."

It had been obvious to Marcus that Anna had come to the hospital quite disheveled, but he hadn't thought anything of it. It had been an emergency call. At times like that, her appearance would have been the last thing on her mind. But now he was seeing Anna anew, and for the first time he wondered if the blank expression in her eyes mirrored more than fear for Olivia. Was there a measure of fear for herself in there, as well?

He cupped her elbow. "Anna, why don't you—"

"You see me . . . don't you?" Anna asked.

Trey looked at Marcus, then looked away, as if he'd stumbled on something too private to share.

Marcus frowned. Something *was* wrong with Anna. Olivia had obviously seen it. It had bothered her enough to remember it even in the midst of her own pain and fear.

"Yes, dear, we all see you. Now, here's what I think we should do. Let's get you home so you can pack a bag or two."

"Oh . . . no . . . I can't leave. I already told Olivia I can't leave."

Marcus slid an arm around her shoulder in a gesture of comfort.

"You won't be leaving your home, dear. You'll just be coming home to help take care of Olivia, remember? You said you'd help take care of her."

Anna frowned. "Yes. Yes . . . take care of Olivia. But she's here."

"Yes, she is. But you'll need to get settled in before she gets home, don't you think? Rose is still cooking for us. You remember Rose. She'll love having the company."

"Rose makes good meat loaf," Anna added.

Marcus sighed. Lord. He hadn't known this was happening to her. He didn't know what was wrong, but he suspected she'd either suffered a stroke, which had obviously affected her memory, or possibly had the beginnings of Alzheimer's disease. He would have his doctor take a look at her, but for now, taking her home with him seemed the best thing to do.

"Yes, she does," Marcus said. "So you'll come stay for a while?"

Anna looked down at Olivia, then nodded.

"Yes. Until she's better. Then I have to go home, okay?"

"Okay," Marcus said, then glanced at Trey.

Trey caught the look and understood.

"I'll be here," Trey said. "Go do what you have to do."

"You have my number," Marcus said.

Trey patted his pocket, where he'd put the business card Marcus had given him.

"Yes, and you know how to contact me."

Marcus was reluctant to leave Olivia so soon, but it was obvious Anna couldn't stay.

"Will she be all right?" Marcus asked. "I mean . . . they haven't found the man who shot her yet. What if he—"

"I'll have a guard put on her door," Trey said.

Marcus nodded, then held out his hand.

"I'm sorry that we've met under these circumstances, but it's a pleasure to know you."

Trey shook his hand. "And you, too, sir."

Olivia moaned in her sleep.

Trey turned to the bed as Marcus led Anna from the room.

He pulled up a chair, then sat down. For the time being, he was going to leave chasing the bad guys up to someone else. His first priority was making sure that the bad guys didn't come here.

Dennis Rawlins had crossed a line. He'd become a part of the violence he claimed to abhor and, to his surprise, he'd been quite good at it. Setting bombs was anonymous. There was no one-on-one involved in the procedure. But what he'd just done had been confrontational. He'd made a plan, stared the enemy in the face and destroyed her. It felt good, but there were loose ends that had to be tied up.

After the shooting, he'd taken the next exit off the freeway, driven straight to a junkyard that he knew about, circled around to the back side, slipped in through a gate with a broken lock and parked the van in the midst of a graveyard of rusting metal. The van was old enough not to stand out among the junked vehicles. No one would ever know it was here.

He emptied the van of every scrap of paper with his name on it, wiped it down of prints, pocketed the keys and the gun, and started back the same way he'd come in. On the way out, he passed the hulk of a black 1952 Chevrolet. On impulse, he dropped to the ground, took the gun out of his pocket and shoved it up under what was left of the padding in the back seat, dislodging an old pack-rat nest in the process.

He glanced around as he got up, brushed the dust off his clothes and slipped out of the yard, pushing the rusted gate back into place as he did. Within the hour he was a mile away. He hailed a cab back to his house, locked the door behind him as he went in and stripped out of his clothes on the way to his bedroom.

He had a shower, put on a pair of sweats, and then went into the kitchen and made himself a bologna and cheese sandwich. He poured a glass of milk, humming as he went, then tossed a handful of chips onto the plate next to his sandwich. The cuckoo clock above the phone struck 6:00 p.m. He paused, watching intently as the clock did its thing—smiling fondly as the little man came out of the clock and ran from the woman who chased him from behind. The clock had belonged to his mother. He'd watched the tableau all of his life, and the old familiarity of the moment gave him a false sense of peace, as if his mother was in the other room and might appear at any moment, when in truth, she'd been dead for years. When the chase was over, he carried his food into the living room to eat while he watched the evening news.

He picked up the remote, turned on the television, then sat back to enjoy his meal. Two bites into the second half of his sandwich, he heard Olivia Sealy's name. He quickly upped the sound, anxious to hear the gory details of his success.

"... *this afternoon. Witnesses claim it was a dark older-model van or SUV. The driver was reported to be a Caucasian man from thirty-five to forty years old, possibly wearing a white baseball cap. If you have any information regarding this crime, please call the Dallas Police Department. Calls will be confidential.*

As for Miss Sealy, she is reported to be in serious but stable condition in Dallas Memorial."

Dennis choked.

She wasn't dead? How in hell could that be? He'd been less than five feet away when he'd pulled the trigger. He'd emptied the gun into the car before speeding away. He'd seen the car rolling down the embankment, end over end. It had been a brutal wreck.

And she hadn't died?

What did that mean?

He looked down at his food and set it aside. His guts were rumbling, and his hands were shaking.

"Oh Lord . . . I tried," he mumbled, then dropped to his knees and started to pray.

The moment he closed his eyes, he saw dead children scattered across a lawn, their broken and bleeding bodies a marker to his mistake.

"I tried," he said again. "God forgive me," he moaned, and threw himself facedown upon the floor, lying prostrate before the God who lived in his head. "Give me another chance, Lord, give me another chance. I won't mess up this time, I promise."

Either God wasn't talking, or he just wasn't home, because Dennis heard nothing but the sound of his own sobs. There was little left to do but close his eyes and pray, once again, to be cleansed of his sins.

· · ·

It was sometime after midnight when Trey came out into the hall. He knew without looking at his watch because the nursing shift had changed. He had been banished to the hallway long enough for the nurses to change Olivia's bandages and assess her condition. He'd left reluctantly, but he wouldn't go farther. Marcus had called Trey hourly ever since his departure. Trey felt sorry for the old man. He was obviously torn between his desire to be with Olivia and the responsibility of tending to a woman who was now having difficulties tending to herself.

Trey sympathized with him but was secretly glad that he'd been allowed the freedom to be with her alone. She'd awakened a couple of times, but not enough to know much of what was going on. Still, just seeing the blue of her eyes now and then, and knowing that she was stable and steadily improving, was all he needed.

He'd already made points at the nurses' station when they'd found out that he and Olivia had been childhood sweethearts. The knowledge had elicited a collective sigh and access to the coffee in their break room. But what he wanted was news that the shooter had been identified and taken into custody. Unfortunately, that hadn't come. Knowing that the man who'd tried to kill Livvie was still on the loose made him eye every passing male warily. The only male he allowed in her room was her doctor, and Trey already knew him on sight. For now, it was the best he could do. The rest had to be left up to his peers in the department.

He was standing at a window at the end of the hall that overlooked the parking lot when a nurse called his name.

"Detective Bonney . . . Detective Bonney."

He turned around.

"You can go back inside now," she added.

Trey waved a thanks and turned away from the window just as a cab pulled into the parking lot and let out a fare.

It was past visiting hours, but Dennis knew his way around the hospital. His mother had spent her last eight weeks in this place while the tumor in her belly slowly ate up her life. One night, several weeks before the cancer was diagnosed, in a fit of drunken remorse, Dennis had confessed to his guilt in the botched abortion bombing. His mother had been horrified and refused him access to the house he'd considered his home. In the ensuing days, she'd prayed to God for deliverance from her part in the shame of having given birth to such a creature. When the tumor had appeared in her belly, she'd considered it a sign from God that she was being punished for having given birth to such evil and refused medical treatment or surgery.

When the pain had gotten to the point of maddening, Dennis had overridden her wishes and taken her to the hospital. The doctors had begged her to let them treat her, but without explanation, she'd patently refused— taking death as both punishment for and release from her guilt.

Even though it had been nine years since her death, the skin still crawled on Dennis's back as he walked into the E.R. As he'd expected, the place was teeming. The waiting room was full, and the medical personnel were up to their ears in patients. He sat down near the door, losing himself in the noise and the crowd until he'd discovered a pattern in the movements of the staff.

When an ambulance suddenly wheeled into the lot with two police cars right behind it, he stood. As the EMTs came rushing in with an obviously injured man, he walked right past the door marked Employees Only, took a right into a utility closet he'd noticed from his seat, closed the door, then turned on the lights.

After a quick look around, he saw a pair of coveralls hanging on a peg. He slipped them on, found a wheeled bucket and mop and a handful of cleaning rags, hung a spray bottle of disinfectant on the side of the bucket and wheeled the gear out into the hall.

No one paid any attention to him as he moved through the hospital, then up to the third floor. He knew which floor she would be on because he remembered where surgery patients were sent, and he moved with purpose, pushing the mop bucket along as he went.

The floor was busy with nurses coming and going. He'd counted on the recent shift change to give him some cover, and waited until the nurses' desk was momentarily unattended. It took less than thirty seconds for him to find out what room Olivia Sealy was in, and then he headed for another utility closet.

A nurse passed him with a medicine tray, glancing

142

only briefly at him before hurrying by. He slipped into the closet, grabbed a roll of paper towels from the shelf, pulled part of them loose, wadded them up and then dropped them into the bucket. He struck a match, staying only long enough to make sure that the paper had caught, then stepped out of the closet. Olivia's room was third from the end, and he moved in that direction while keeping an eye on the door.

Within seconds, smoke began seeping from beneath the door. It never occurred to him that he might be setting off another disaster. He wasn't thinking about the fire getting out of control, of more innocent people suffering because of him. His focus was on redeeming himself in the eyes of his God.

A minute passed. He watched a nurse come out into the hall, but she turned in the other direction and missed seeing the smoke. It grew in size and substance, billowing slowly upward. Suddenly the shriek of a smoke alarm sounded, the strident, repetitive squawk bringing everyone who could walk out into the hall.

Someone screamed. Someone else shouted. And the sprinklers began to shower water down onto the floors.

When the door beside Dennis swung inward, he stepped back against the wall. A big man came out of Olivia Sealy's room on the run.

Dennis flinched. The man was unexpected. The thought crossed his mind that this plan might have some flaws, but he was too far in to pull back.

The moment the man cleared the doorway, Dennis slipped in, closing the door behind him. Almost instantly, the peace Dennis felt made him cry. Despite the water coming down on him like rain, he saw her— the conduit that would alleviate his sins. He took a deep breath and moved forward.

Almost instantly, Trey saw the source of the smoke. He yanked the door open, saw the fire in the bucket, and pulled it out of the closet and dragged it into the hall before the cleaning solvents exploded. A nurse appeared from behind him with a fire extinguisher and quickly put out the fire, while Trey stared at the bucket in disbelief.

"Kill the sprinklers," he said quickly. "It's out."

A nurse ran to call maintenance as others began running for mops and towels.

Someone had set fire to a roll of paper towels. But why? The smoke was already dissipating. An orderly was shutting off the alarm as nurses raced from room to room. Trey frowned. What could someone possibly gain by—

His heart stuttered to a stop as he pivoted quickly. The door to Livvie's room was closed, and he distinctly remembered leaving it open.

"Has anyone been in Olivia Sealy's room?" he asked sharply.

The nurses stared at each other, then shook their heads.

"Call security," Trey said, and bolted for the door.

Water rained down on the back of Dennis's head and

hands as he leaned over Olivia Sealy's bed. His fingers were around her throat. He could feel the warmth of her flesh and the throb of her heartbeat against his palms. He shuddered. The power of life and death was, literally, in his hands.

This must be how God feels.

He exhaled softly, his heart pounding as he leaned forward, beating out the rhythm of absolution in his ears.

"In the name of the Father and the—"

Dennis's neck suddenly popped backward, and the water began pounding on his face. His knees buckled as a low, angry voice growled near his ear.

"Take your hands off her or you're dead."

Dennis froze, blinking rapidly to clear his vision, but the water in his eyes made it impossible to see. The thought of resistance never entered his mind. What he did realize was that he'd been waiting for this day for the last nine years. Justice had caught up with him before redemption was gained, and he was vaguely surprised to be feeling relief.

"The Lord told me to do it. I am only doing what he—"

"Shut the hell up and do what you're told!" Trey shouted as he grabbed the man by his shoulders and yanked.

Dennis started to lift his hands in the air and found himself being dragged backward, out of the room. Within seconds, the sprinkler system was off, and he was able to focus on the man who'd foiled his plan.

Dennis felt the man's fury as if it had physical form. Something told him that this man was capable of breaking his neck without a moment of regret. All he had to do was resist and his misery would be over.

Just. One. Simple. Move.

Come on, Dennis. For once in your life, try to do something right.

The taunt was as real to him then as the man behind him.

One move. One act of rebellion and he would be standing before God.

But he didn't have the guts, and in that moment, Dennis Rawlins faced the worst of his fears. He was going to his maker with the blood of children on his hands and the eternal knowledge that, when push came to shove, he'd been too much of a coward to do the right thing.

Trey shoved the man face first against the wall and had him in handcuffs before security arrived. When he finally got a good look at the man's face, he was not surprised it was the man who'd carried the Baby Killer sign.

"Hold him," Trey ordered, and dashed back into Olivia's room.

Even though her bed and her clothes were wet, she was still asleep, oblivious to how close, once again, she'd come to dying.

Trey touched her arm, listening to the steady beeping of the machines measuring her heartbeat and blood pressure. They were as constant as they'd been before he'd run into the hall. When he laid the back of his hand against her cheek, he realized he was shaking.

Twice in one day they'd come so close to losing her. The thought made him sick. He touched her hair, lifting a stray wet lock away from her forehead, then took a deep breath, exhaling softly.

Her lips were slightly parted, the lower one somewhat swollen. There were scratches on the side of her cheek and a longer one on her forehead. She looked as if she had gone ten rounds with a wildcat and come out the loser.

And she'd never been more beautiful to him.

He pressed his lips to her cheek, then to her forehead, before he pulled slightly back. He was only inches from her face—from her lips. He could see her eyelashes fluttering, and the slight flare of her nostrils as she breathed in and out.

"Oh, Livvie . . . you're getting under my skin again, and you don't even know it," he said softly, then leaned down one more time, and this time, touched his mouth to her lips. It was little more than a brush of skin against skin. When he pulled back, there were tears in his eyes.

He took out his cell phone as he moved toward the door and, hospital regulations be damned, made a call to Chia Rodriguez. When she answered, he heard the sleep and anger in her voice.

"Whoever this is, it better be good," she said shortly.

"Chia, it's me, Trey. I've got your shooter."

Now he had her attention. She rolled over to the side of the bed, then sat up.

"What do you mean, you've got him?"

"I don't know his name, but he's lying on the floor out in the hall in my handcuffs. Hospital security is with him now, but since it's your case, I thought you'd like to take him in."

"What in hell happened? How did you—"

"He came to the hospital to finish the job. I caught him in Olivia Sealy's room with his hands around her neck. I'll fill you in when you get here."

9

Dennis Rawlins tried to pray on the way to the police station, but he felt empty. No matter how hard he listened, he couldn't hear God anymore. He wasn't sure what it meant, but back when he was little, if his mother got mad at him, she wouldn't talk, either, so he figured God was mad at him, too. Truth was, Dennis couldn't blame him. He'd been messing up his own life for years now; it seemed inevitable that God would finally have gotten disgusted.

When they booked Dennis into jail, he had nothing to say. Trying to explain why he'd tried to kill Olivia Sealy made his head hurt, and he sure wasn't going to tell them about the bombing of the abortion clinic. He knew he was obsessive, but he wasn't dumb.

While Dennis waited for a court-appointed lawyer to show up, in another part of the city, Foster Lawrence sat on the side of his bed, wondering what to do next.

Maybe he would go to Florida.

He'd always thought about living where it never got cold. Of course, he'd planned to have money to live in luxury when he got there, but that had taken a very disappointing turn. Just thinking about his million dollars going up in smoke made him crazy. Winding up with the police after him again was a nightmare. He couldn't go back to prison. He *wouldn't* go back to prison.

And while he was making those vows, he couldn't help but think of what had put him in prison to begin with. If he hadn't let emotional ties sway him into getting mixed up in the Sealy mess, there was no telling how different his life would have been. It was for damn sure he wouldn't have been in prison. He'd always been too smart for that.

But the day he'd gone to the old lake house and seen that little kid, he'd been stunned. Then, learning that she'd been snatched, had been a nightmare. He could still remember how she'd walked around the house, holding her blanket and crying for her mommy. He'd had himself a big fit, which had done no good.

But once he'd seen her, he'd been torn between whether to turn in one of his own or just say nothing. If he left without reporting to the authorities where the kid was, he could automatically be charged with aiding and abetting. To add confusion to the whole mess, he'd found out that no ransom call had been made, nor was it going to be. He'd cursed and raised all kinds of hell, unable to understand that kind of thinking.

Looking back, he wondered why in hell he'd stayed.

Even more, what devil had gotten inside his mind to make it okay to ask for the ransom for himself when he'd had nothing to do with the crime. All he could remember was that it had seemed like a good idea at the time. He had known nothing about any murders until news had hit the papers, but by then, he was in too deep.

Outside his hotel, it started to rain. He heard it hitting the window on the other side of the room and was reminded of the night he'd picked up the ransom. It had been raining then, too.

God.

If only he'd never made that ransom call. If only he'd just taken the kid and dumped her off at the mall, then left Texas without ever looking back. He'd had a good woman in Amarillo back then. He couldn't help but wonder how his life might have been different if he'd gone back to her and not let greed pull him under.

He stood up and walked to the window to look out on the streets below. The speeding cars splashed water up onto the sidewalks as they passed, washing everything clean. He wished he could be washed clean.

He laid his palm on the window, imagining he could feel the impact of the raindrops hitting the window on the other side, and wondered what ever happened to that girl in Amarillo. What was her name? Linda? No, Lydia. That was it. Lydia. Lydia Dalton. She'd been a little bitty bird of a thing, but she'd had a great laugh.

Lydia Dalton.

He turned away from the window, walked back to the bed and lay down. There would be time enough tomorrow to decide what to do next. Right now he just wanted to sleep and forget that the past twenty-five years had ever happened.

Marcus Sealy was asleep down the hall from the room where he'd put Anna.

Anna had unpacked her bags, said hello to Rose, had a meal with Marcus, then gone to her room. By the time she'd come out of her shower and was ready for bed, she had lost track of her world. For a time, she didn't know where she was or why she was there. When she began to remember, it came in bits and pieces. She knew she'd promised Marcus to look after Olivia, but she couldn't find her. She walked the halls of the mansion for hours, looking for the baby and listening for her cries.

Finally, too weary to look anymore, and lulled by the rain coming down outside, she fell asleep on a sofa in the library.

Olivia woke just before daylight. She heard rain hitting the windows. That was good. They'd been needing a rain. Then she opened her eyes, and the first thing she saw was Trey, asleep in a chair by her bed. She didn't know why it was him and not her grandfather who'd kept the vigil, but she was moved to tears by the sight.

For the longest time she just looked at him—at the long sprawl of his legs and the way the fabric of his jeans hugged the muscles of his thighs. She remembered how those long legs felt wrapped around her, and the weight of his body as they made slow, quiet love in the dark. She remembered all too well the tug of want in her belly, just watching him walk, and how a ghost of his smile would make her dizzy with joy.

But that was years ago. Now he was only inches away from her bed, and they'd never been farther apart. It seemed forever since they'd shared the banana split, and she wondered how long it had really been, how long she'd been asleep. If only she had gone with him instead of going home. If she'd stayed with Trey, she wouldn't have eaten lunch alone and most likely wouldn't have gone to Anna's. She wouldn't have been on the freeway in just that spot at the very moment somebody tried to kill her. Trey had wanted her to stay with him, but she'd edged away, just as she'd done all her life, and look what she had to show for it.

She gazed her fill of him then, wondering how the boy's body had changed since he'd become a man. Wondering if he still rolled up in a ball when he went to sleep. Wondering if he still ate peanut-butter-and-pickle sandwiches at midnight. Wondering how long he'd hated her after she'd knuckled under to Grampy's wishes, then knew it couldn't have been as long as she'd hated herself.

She sighed, and even that slight motion brought her pain. She bit her lower lip before glancing nervously at him again. When she did, she realized he was awake and had been watching her face.

Her heartbeat accelerated, and she heard the break in the monotonous beeping of the machine beside her bed. Within seconds, he was at her side.

"I'm here, baby," he said softly. "Do you hurt? Want me to get a nurse to give you something for the pain?"

When he cupped her face in the palm of his hand, she rested against it, unashamed of the tears that fell.

"You stayed," she said.

Trey saw the question in her eyes but wondered if she was ready for the answer.

"I needed to know you were going to be all right," he finally said.

"Part of the job?"

He hesitated again, then sighed.

"No, Livvie, this isn't part of the job."

"Is it too late?" she asked.

"For what, honey?"

"Us."

Trey's pulse upped the count as a cold sweat broke out on the back of his neck. He thought about how close they had come to being too late for everything. Even if he got another kick in the teeth from stepping into a world where he wasn't wanted, he couldn't bring himself to tell her no.

"You want there to be an us?" he asked.

She nodded.

"And your grandfather?"

"Will love you, too," Olivia said, and then sighed and closed her eyes. It took too much strength to stay awake. Besides, now that she knew Trey was here, she felt safe.

Trey thought about what she'd just said. Love me, too? Did that mean Olivia still had feelings for him, or was it just a figure of speech? Only time would tell. For now, just having her alive and breathing was enough.

But as he sat and watched Olivia falling back to sleep, he thought about the cold case they were working and wondered how, if at all, Dennis Rawlins played into that. Trey didn't think he was old enough to have been involved in a murder twenty-five years ago, but stranger things had happened.

It made no sense that the man had wanted Olivia dead, but he was beginning to suspect that good sense had nothing to do with Rawlins. If Trey wasn't mistaken, the man was missing a large dose of sanity. It wouldn't be the first time that some nutcase got involved in an ongoing crime without having had anything to do with it. If this was the case now, all Rawlins had done was put a muddy spoon into an already murky pot. It would be up to Chia and her partner, David Sheets, to sort out Rawlins's culpability. He still had the Baby Jane Doe case to deal with.

Marcus woke up with a start. One glance at the clock and he panicked. It was almost 9:00 a.m. He had called hourly when he'd first come home, then had fallen asleep and never called back. He sat up on the side of the bed and reached for the phone. Within moments, a nurse was assuring him that Olivia was stable. Breathing a sigh of relief, he asked if Detective Bonney was still there, and then relaxed even more when he learned it was so. It was all he needed to know to give him a breather before going to see Olivia. He had no idea how Anna had fared. He flew out of bed, made a quick trip into the bathroom and came out with his hair damp from a hasty combing. He pulled on a pair of sweats and a T-shirt, stepped into some tennis shoes sans the socks, and dashed across the hall to Anna's room.

She wasn't there, and the bed hadn't been slept in.

"Oh no," he muttered, and headed for the stairs.

Rose was in the kitchen when he got there.

"Anna's bed wasn't slept in. Have you seen her?"

Rose handed him a cup of coffee as she answered. "She's asleep in the library. I found her like that early this morning. She's all right, I imagine. Maybe she wasn't comfortable sleeping in an unfamiliar bed."

Marcus sighed with relief and then took a sip of his coffee, savoring the caffeine kick.

"Do you want breakfast?" she asked.

"No, coffee will do this morning. I want to get back to the hospital and check on Olivia, but I don't know what to do about Anna."

Rose waved him away. "Oh, go on with you. Don't worry about her. She'll be fine here with me."

"I don't know," Marcus said. "She's a little bit—"

"I know," Rose said, interrupting. "I saw. She gets a bit mixed up from time to time. Nothing wrong with that. I'll make sure she doesn't come to harm."

"Thank you so much," Marcus said. "I'll just go check on her before I dress for the hospital. I'll be gone most of the day, so don't fix any meals for me."

"Yes, sir," Rose said. "And you give Olivia my love,

now. Tell her I said everything is going to be fine."

Marcus eyed the tall, stalwart woman with relief and affection.

"Yes, I will," he said quickly. "And about Anna . . . if you need me, just call my cell phone."

Rose frowned. "When the day comes that I can't handle one ditzy old woman, then it will be time for me to turn in my resignation." Then she added, "Not that ditzy is bad . . . just a fact of life for some."

Marcus smiled, then took his coffee with him as he went.

He looked into the library long enough to see Anna sprawled out on the oversize sofa. Thoughtfully, Rose had covered her with a blanket and left her to sleep.

Marcus stared at Anna's face, trying to find the woman he'd known for so many years, but without success. The vibrant young thing with flashing blue eyes and a zest for life was missing and, he feared, lost. All that was left was a confused and aging shell.

He returned to his room and began to dress, and as he did, realized that in the upcoming days, he was going to have to face more than Olivia's recovery and the dissolution of Anna Walden's mind. All of this mess was bringing Terrence Sealy back into his life, which would inevitably open old wounds and bad memories—things Marcus could just as easily have done without.

Still brewing about Carolyn and Terrence's imminent arrival, he finished dressing and was just getting ready to leave the house when the phone rang.

It was Trey.

"Detective Bonney! I was just leaving to come to the hospital."

"I'm still here. I was calling to see when you were coming in."

"I should be there in about thirty minutes or so. Will you still be there?" Marcus said.

Trey could tell by the way Marcus was talking that he hadn't been watching the morning news and didn't know about the second attack on Olivia's life. He wondered why the department hadn't called Marcus, then guessed that Lieutenant Warren must have assumed Trey would call.

"Yes, I'll be here," Trey said, then added, "Sir . . . have you been contacted by the Dallas PD this morning?"

Marcus frowned. "No. Why? Has something—"

"No, no, don't worry," Trey said. "Everything is all right. Olivia is fine."

Marcus relaxed. "For a minute there I thought you were going to tell me bad news."

"On the contrary," Trey said. "We got the man who shot Livvie. He was arrested last night."

"Why, that's wonderful news!" Marcus cried. "Why didn't somebody call me?"

"Just a mix-up, I'm sure," Trey said. "They probably thought I would do it, and I assumed the two detectives on the case would call you after they'd booked the suspect."

"Who is he? Why did he do it? Did he tell you anything?"

Trey sighed. "His name is Dennis Rawlins. We don't know his motive and he hasn't said anything that makes much sense."

"At any rate, it's over," Marcus said.

"Yes, well, there's something I need to tell you. You'll hear it on the news, anyway, so I think you should hear the whole story from me."

Marcus's elation was tempered by Trey's tone. "What?"

"The man we arrested for shooting Livvie and causing her accident . . ."

"Yes?" Marcus said.

"He came here to the hospital last night to finish the job. Set a fire on the ward to distract attention and got into her room."

"Jesus, God almighty," Marcus muttered, and sank against the wall. "He didn't hurt her?"

"She never even knew he'd been there," Trey said.

"Are you sure?" Marcus asked.

"Yes."

Marcus started to ask another question when suddenly the answer dawned.

"It was you, wasn't it? You're the one who caught him."

"Yes, sir."

There was a long moment of unbroken silence, then Marcus spoke. The tremor in his voice gave away the emotions with which he was struggling.

"I owe you more than you will ever know," he said.

"You don't owe me anything," Trey said. "I was

doing my job." Then he added, "But just so you know, if I'd let anything happen to Livvie, I couldn't have lived with myself."

"I see," Marcus said.

"Sir, I sincerely hope you do see," Trey said. "Because a while ago I sort of gave my word to Livvie that we'd give our relationship another try, and I'm not the kind to break a promise."

"She regrets the lost years, doesn't she?" Marcus asked.

Trey sighed. "No more than I do, sir."

"It's all my fault," Marcus muttered. "I didn't know . . . I didn't realize that—"

"Look . . . we were kids," Trey said, then added, "But we're not anymore. I don't want to cause trouble between you and Livvie, but I won't walk away again."

"Olivia is a grown woman, fully capable of making up her own mind," Marcus said. "And trust me, the last thing I would ever do is knowingly cause her pain. You're obviously an upstanding man, and I owe Olivia's life to your diligence."

"As I said before, you don't owe me anything. I'll see you shortly, then," Trey said, and hung up.

As he was dropping the cell phone into his pocket, he heard someone calling his name. He turned around just as Chia was getting off the elevator.

"Hey, cowboy," Chia said. "Caught any more bad guys?"

He grinned but ignored her sarcasm as he began grilling her about Rawlins.

"Did he say why he'd targeted Olivia?"

Chia rolled her eyes.

"He's loony, but that's another story. Guess what we found when we ran him through NCIC?"

"What?"

"He's wanted for questioning in the bombing of an abortion clinic up in Boston about nine years ago."

"No kidding?"

"No kidding," Chia echoed. "Not only that, but seven kids and their teacher died in the blast."

"How did that all come about?"

"Seems the church bus they were on had engine trouble and caught fire. It was snowing, so when the teacher got the kids off the bus, she hurried them up the sidewalk to the big overhang at the entrance to the clinic, thinking she would be sheltering them until another bus was sent. Instead, they died in the blast."

"And they think Rawlins is responsible for that?"

"He was one of the main suspects," Chia said. "Then he disappeared. Why he targeted Olivia Sealy is a mystery, but mine is not to reason why, and yours is to solve the Baby Jane Doe case. If they link up in any way, we haven't found it yet."

"Thanks anyway," Trey said.

Chia shrugged. "Lieutenant Warren wants to see you."

"I'll call him. I'm not leaving here until Olivia's grandfather arrives."

"Hey, we caught the bad guy, or *you* caught the bad guy. So what's the fuss? She should be fine now."

"Yeah, but I'm not," Trey muttered. "And I won't be, not until I know she's all right."

Chia's eyebrows arched as she pursed her mouth and let out a soft *ooohh*.

"What's the deal here, cowboy? Don't tell me the mighty Bonney has fallen for the poor little rich girl? If you ask me, that was pretty fast work, even for you."

"There is no deal here, and nobody needs to tell you a damn thing," Trey snapped.

Chia held up her hands. "Sorry. I didn't mean to step on any toes."

"No, I'm the one who's sorry," Trey said. "I shouldn't have snapped. And just for the record, there's nothing fast about what I feel for Livvie. I've known her since high school."

The smart-ass answer Chia had been about to utter died on her lips. Her eyes widened, and her lips went slack.

"No shit?"

Trey shoved his hands through his hair.

"No shit."

"So . . . I'll talk to you later?" Chia said.

"Yeah . . . later," Trey said, and headed back to Olivia's room.

Someone was in the room with her. Anna knew it, even before she opened her eyes. Panic hit her like a fist to the belly. She sat up with a jerk.

"Who are you?" she cried.

Rose set a cup of coffee down on the table in front of

the sofa where Anna had been sleeping.

"You know who I am," Rose said firmly. "It's me. Rose. I'm the housekeeper for Olivia and Mr. Marcus, and you're Anna. You took care of Olivia when she was a baby."

Everything the woman was saying seemed familiar. Anna leaned forward, took the cup of coffee and then sniffed it, as if testing it for something vile that didn't belong.

It seemed fine.

She took a sip.

It tasted wonderful.

She took another, then looked at Rose anew. Suddenly she smiled.

"You make good meat loaf," Anna said.

Rose grinned.

"Why, thank you, Anna. Now come with me. I'm going to make you some breakfast. Then you can get dressed and help me in the kitchen."

Anna stood. A plan. She had a plan. Plans were good. They made her feel steady, as if she'd suddenly been balanced.

"I will have two eggs over easy," Anna said. "And bacon? Will there be bacon?"

Rose laughed. "In this house, there's always bacon."

Anna smiled. The laughter felt good against her ears. She liked being here. It wasn't nearly as lonesome as it was being at home.

She followed Rose into the kitchen, and with each step moved further and further away from the life she'd been living in Arlington and closer and closer to the world of her past.

10

It had been three days since Olivia had come out of surgery and turned Trey's world upside down. He'd been so worried—so sick at heart for what had happened to her—that he'd been blindsided when she'd asked him for a second chance. Now he went through his hours at work just waiting for the moment when he could get back to the hospital. Even if she slept through most of his visit, it was enough to just watch her breathe.

Although Dennis Rawlins had finally confessed to his crimes, his mental state had been compromised enough that a judge had ordered a complete psych evaluation. He'd been temporarily committed to a facility for the criminally insane, which, to Trey, meant he was going to get away with murder.

But one thing had come out of the Rawlins investigation that related to Trey's case. Dennis Rawlins had been fourteen years old and in a military academy when the Sealy kidnapping and murders occurred, which meant there was no way this attack was connected to the first crime.

While this was a process of elimination that had to be done, it also put Trey back at square one regarding suspects. They still had a BOLO out for Foster Lawrence, though it was only for questioning. But the "Be on the Lookout" was old, and Trey figured if Lawrence had been anywhere in the area when it went out, he was long gone now. Trey was down to waiting for the DNA results from the lab, and for Terrence and Carolyn Sealy to arrive from Milan. Unless something broke from one of those areas, they were at a dead end.

With all the leads coming up blank, he wanted a second look at the things that had been in the suitcase with the baby's remains. Maybe there was something there they'd missed—something that would give them a new direction—and that meant a trip to the lockup where evidence was logged and stored.

Trey's mind was on the task at hand as he approached the evidence desk. The skinny sergeant in charge eyed him curiously as he grabbed the sign-in sheet.

"Hey, Bonney, rescued any more damsels in distress?" the sergeant asked.

"What's the matter, Bodine? You jealous?" Trey countered.

"No, I ain't jealous," Bodine muttered. "I was just asking."

Trey grinned. He knew all about Russell's aversion to flirting with other women. Everyone on the force knew his wife, Peggy. They also knew about the knife.

Russell Bodine was six months from retirement and almost forty years married, and the only time he'd stepped out on his wife, he'd been found out before he ever made it home. He'd fallen into bed and woken up with the sharp edge of a butcher knife against his groin.

Without a word, Peggy had taken the knife and proceeded to shave every hair from around his penis while he pleaded and begged for her not to hurt him. He'd made promises to her, and God, and everyone he knew, that he would never stray again if she would just leave him with his manhood intact.

She had, but with a nightly reminder that never failed to work. The last thing he saw at night before he closed his eyes was the butcher knife that she'd had mounted and hung on the wall opposite their bed.

"What you needin' to see?" Russell asked as he opened the door and let Trey in.

"The stuff that came in with Baby Jane Doe from up at Lake Texoma."

Russell frowned as he led the way back through a maze of shelving and boxes.

"Someone was a real bastard, doin' that to that poor little baby," Russell said as he pulled a box from the shelves and carried it over to a table. "You gonna need this long?"

Trey shrugged. "I don't know if I'm going to need it at all. Unless we get a hit on the DNA from the crime lab, we've run out of leads. I thought this might turn up something we haven't considered."

"Good luck," Russell said, and then added, "I didn't mean nothin' by that remark 'bout bein' a hero and all."

"No offense taken," Trey said.

Confident that he'd done the right thing, Russell

ambled off, leaving Trey with the contents of the box.

He grabbed the lid, then braced himself as he took it off. Besides the suitcase itself, there were only four small plastic bags inside, each one labeled and dated. Four remnants of a brief young life that had been snuffed out all too soon.

He gave the suitcase the once-over but came to the same conclusion Jenner had come up with. It was like thousands of others that had been made in the seventies. It was old and peeling, with not one remarkable thing about it that would help him in finding the owner. He moved on to the bags.

He took out the first bag and opened the Ziplock top. Inside was a single sock about the length of his index finger—originally white, now a dirty color, as if it had been dipped in tea and left out to dry. There was a small dot of yellow near the edge of the cuff, and on closer examination, he decided it was what was left of a yellow embroidered duck. It told him nothing.

The second bag yielded a small pink nightgown. There were a series of dark stains near the shoulder, then down the back. Bloodstains, he guessed, and fingered the spot where the lab had taken a snippet of the same for testing. The label that would have been at the neck had been cut out, but he knew from experience that people often did that to prevent chafing, rather than from a need to conceal. He always cut off the tags on his new T-shirts as soon as he got them home. It was simply a matter of preference, and he decided the missing tag didn't mean anything.

Laying that garment and bag aside, he pulled out the third. It was the largest, yielding most of a baby's blanket. The fabric was a dirty, faded pink, with frayed remnants of a pale satin binding. There was no manufacturer's tag, no identifying marks whatsoever that would aid him in giving Baby Jane Doe a name.

He laid that aside, too, and picked up the last bag. The wooden cross inside was approximately twelve inches high and obviously handmade. He took it out of the bag and turned it around, hoping to find the name of an artist, but found nothing.

He turned it over, eyeing the three words that had been etched into the cross with a wood-burning tool.

Sleeping with angels

What the hell did that mean? Had someone actually made this after murdering a child, or had it been tossed in as an afterthought? It gave him the creeps to think that someone had been callous enough to stuff that baby's body into a suitcase and plaster it up inside a wall, yet had still included what amounted to an epitaph—and a religious one, at that.

Frustrated that the items hadn't given him anything new to go on, he bagged them back up, put the lid on the box and left it on the table for Russell to deal with.

Russell looked up as Trey came around the aisle empty-handed.

"Didn't do you no good?" he asked.

Trey shook his head.

"It's a shame," Russell said. "Hope you catch whoever did that."

"Yeah, I do, too," Trey said. "Thanks for your help. Tell Peggy I said hello."

Russell made a face. "Peggy's sort of pissed at me right now."

"Mad enough to take down that knife?" Trey asked.

Russell saw the gleam in Trey's eyes and frowned. He wished to hell and back that everyone on the force didn't know the story about the knife, but he couldn't complain. It was his own fault for getting drunk one night and telling it on himself. Now everyone knew, and no one seemed to want to let the story die.

"No, not that pissed, but enough that I reckon I'll be coughin' up some jewelry. Peggy's real fond of jewelry, you know."

"What did you do?" Trey asked.

"Well, hell, I accidentally mowed some flower she'd been babyin' along. Looked like a dang weed to me, so I mowed it. Any other time she would'a fussed at me for leaving the weeds."

Trey grinned.

"Sometimes it's hard staying on the good side of a woman," Russell muttered. "You're a single man. If you're smart, you'll stay that way."

Trey thought of Olivia and then shook his head.

"I'd rather take my chances with the woman and the flowers than live a life without them."

Russell thought about that a minute and then nodded.

"Yeah, I reckon you're right. Let me know if there's anything else I can help you with," he said.

"I'll do that," Trey said, then left.

• • •

Olivia was sitting on the side of the bed. Her jaw was clenched against the pain of movement, and a cold sweat had broken out on her forehead. Her left shoulder was in bandages from the surgery, and her arm was in a sling. The IV needle was taped to the top of her right hand, which left her with nothing to brace herself with if she stood, although that was highly unlikely. She had a pounding headache, caused by the concussion, and her lower lip was still a little bit swollen. The only thing she could eat without wincing was soft cold stuff, like Jell-O and ice cream, and that diet was getting old fast.

It was only a few feet from her bed to the bathroom, but it might as well have been a mile. Just as she was about to give up and ring for a nurse, the door opened. She looked up, unaware there were tears on her face.

It was Trey.

Within seconds, he was at her side.

"Livvie, sweetheart, what are you doing? Why didn't you ring for help?"

"I was trying to go to the bathroom," she mumbled, then started to cry in earnest.

"Oh, honey, don't cry," Trey said, and picked her up in his arms. "I'll help. Can you grab your IV or do you want me to get it?"

"I can do the IV," she said, and then hiccuped on a sob.

She pulled the pole along as Trey carried her to the bathroom. When he put her down inside, he held on to her shoulders until he was satisfied she wasn't going to fall.

"Can you manage from here?" he asked.

She wouldn't look at him, only nodded.

"It's okay," he said softly. "It's part of what comes from being friends."

She looked up at him then, tears welling in her eyes.

"Are we friends, Trey? Really friends?"

He leaned down and kissed the side of her face, near her lips.

"Yes, baby . . . real friends. I'm going to be right outside the door. Just call out when you're done and I'll help you back to bed."

He stepped outside, pulling the door closed as he went.

A couple of minutes later, he heard the toilet flush.

"Livvie?"

The door opened. She was swaying on her feet.

"Come here, darlin'," he said softly, and picked her up in his arms so gently that she hardly knew when her feet left the floor.

She pulled the IV pole as they went, and moments later he had her back in bed, the IV pole shoved back in place against the wall.

"Feel better?" he asked.

She nodded and closed her eyes.

He picked up a washcloth from her bedside table and washed her face, then her hands, careful not to jar the sling or the IV needle.

Olivia was still crying, but without making a sound.

The sight of the tears seeping out from under her eyelids undid him.

He dabbed at her eyes with a handful of tissues, then, on impulse, leaned over and kissed her square on the lips.

The contact was gentle—the tremble of Livvie's lips matching the tremor of his own. It was the first time in eleven years that he'd had the pleasure, but it was as if the break in time had never been. His ache for her was as familiar as the sound of his name on her lips. When he pulled back, Olivia opened her eyes.

"Oh, Trey," she whispered, and reached for him.

He took her hand, tenderly kissing her palm as he gazed down at her.

"What's happening?" Livvie asked.

"You mean here and now, or with the world in general?"

"Both," she said.

"With regards to the here and now, I'm falling in love all over again. As for the world in general, well . . . I guess you might say there have been better days."

"Are you really?" Olivia asked. "Falling in love with me again?"

His eyes darkened, but he couldn't lie.

"Yes."

She tried to smile, but the tears only came faster.

"That wasn't supposed to make you sad," Trey muttered as he grabbed a second handful of tissues and swiped them across her cheeks.

"I'm not sad, just humbled by your ability to forgive."

Trey sighed. "Aw, Livvie . . . we were kids. I loved you so damn much, but if we'd tried to make a go of it back then, it wouldn't have worked, and we both know it."

"Maybe." Then she shifted until she could see straight into his face. "Have you given much thought to the fact that we might never have met up again if it wasn't for the discovery of that poor little baby?"

"Yeah, I've thought about it," Trey said. "And you know what I think?"

She shook her head.

"I think things happen for a reason, and at the time they're supposed to happen. Last week I would never have dreamed of having you back in my life. Then, a few days ago, I found you and nearly lost you, all within twenty-four hours. When I got the call about your accident . . . well, let's just say that I don't ever want to feel like that again."

"Do you know what I was thinking when my car flew up in the air the first time?"

A muscle jumped in Trey's jaw as he cupped his hand against her cheek.

"I can only imagine," he said.

"I was thinking how stupid I'd been to find the love of my life not once, but twice, and walk away from him both times. I was wishing I hadn't left you. I was wishing I didn't have to die."

"You're not going to die. A lot of people made sure of that."

"Including you," she said. "I heard the nurses talking.

172

The man who shot at me . . ."

"What about him?" Trey said.

"He was here, wasn't he? He came that same night and tried to finish what he'd started."

Trey sighed. It was inevitable that she would learn of the incident sometime, but he would have preferred it to be later, rather than sooner.

"Yes, he came back," Trey said. "But he didn't hurt you. I made sure of that."

"I know," Olivia said. "You saved my life."

Trey shrugged.

"What about the man?" Olivia asked. "Is he locked up?"

"Rawlins? Yes, he's gone. Locked up where he won't ever hurt you or anybody else again."

"So . . . now what? What about that baby?"

"The case is going nowhere, and I've got this overwhelming sense of guilt, as if I'm somehow letting her down."

"What about the DNA tests? When will you know something about them?"

Trey shrugged. "Who knows? I asked for a rush, but that stuff just takes time. And there's still Terrence Sealy to test, too, you know."

Olivia nodded.

"What's with him and your grandfather?" Trey asked.

A frown line ran the length of Olivia's forehead.

"You know . . . until the other day, when you mentioned he would be coming back to the States, I don't think I really knew there were bad feelings between them. I can remember my grandfather talking about Aunt Carolyn and Uncle Terrence coming to the house for the holidays . . . Thanksgiving, Christmas . . . you know, the times when families usually get together. But I was too young to remember. I think they moved to Italy before the kidnapping." She thought for a moment.

"Aunt Carolyn is a lot younger than Uncle Terrence, you know."

"How much younger?" Trey asked.

"I'm not sure, but I'd guess at least twenty years. I think she's around the same age as my father."

A thought came and went in Trey's mind so fast that he almost didn't bother to focus; then he ran it back through his mind one more time.

"Hey, honey?"

"Yes?"

"Do you ever remember hearing your grandfather reminisce about your parents during the holidays . . . you know, stuff like how much he missed them, or funny stories about them?"

"No. No one talked about my parents in my presence. Ever."

"Why not?"

"I think it was because they were all afraid it would bring back horrible memories, but the truth of it is, I can't remember either of them. Not their faces. Not anything we did together."

Then her expression shifted, and she began to pick at the sheet with a nervous motion.

"Do you think that's strange?" she asked. "Wouldn't you think I would have at least one memory?"

Trey saw the fear in her eyes and regretted bringing up the subject. She needed to concentrate on getting well, not wondering if she'd grown up in a house where she didn't belong.

"No, I don't think that's strange at all. I don't know anybody who can remember things from when they were that young."

Olivia sighed.

"What?" Trey asked. "Talk to me."

"The only memories I have are of Anna and Grampy, and of Rose."

"And that makes you believe you lived somewhere else before? Are you trying to convince yourself that the wrong child was returned to the Sealys?"

Olivia looked away.

"Are you?" Trey persisted.

Olivia continued to pick at the sheet. Trey glanced down and saw her fingers shaking, and his heart went out to her.

"Livvie . . . darling . . . whatever happened, it was not your fault. You were . . . are . . . an innocent victim in this mess."

"I know, but—"

"But nothing. And there's one more thing you need to keep in mind."

She looked up then, and saw the love in Trey's eyes.

"Remember that no matter who you started out to be, you were always the same to me. I loved you when you were a girl, and I'm falling in love with you all over again. You will always be my Livvie, okay?"

Her chin quivered, but it was her only concession to emotion.

"Oh, Trey, I don't deserve you, but I'm so glad you're in my life again."

"Yeah, baby, so am I," Trey said softly, and this time, when he bent down to kiss her, she kissed him back.

The pull of her lips was sweet, the softness of her breath against his face even sweeter. He could remember the soft, uneven sound of her breathing as they'd made love, and the way she'd arched up to meet him at the moment of climax. It had been passion at its best—new and hot between hearts yet to be broken. He wanted to make love to her again. He wanted to know the woman as he'd known the girl.

11

Anna was settling in with Rose better than Marcus could have imagined, but every time he visited Olivia in the hospital, he had to reassure her that Anna was okay. She was upset by her old nanny's mental deterioration and, like him, felt a great amount of guilt for having neglected Anna. What he didn't talk to her about was the impending arrival of his cousin, Terrence.

Marcus remembered the family gossip about Terrence's father. He'd been the black sheep of the Sealy family, and Terrence had been well aware of that fact

176

while growing up. He'd had a constant chip on his shoulder and swaggered his way through his teenage years and into his early twenties in an effort to make up for that fact.

During that time Marcus and Terrence met a girl named Amelia Fisher at a party. They both fell in love with her, but she chose Marcus. Two years later, when Marcus married Amelia, Terrence was noticeably absent from the wedding.

It wasn't until Marcus and Amelia were on their honeymoon that Amelia broke down in hysterics. Through choking sobs, she admitted to Marcus that, in a drunken rage, Terrence had forced himself on her the night before their wedding, and that she had been too shocked, then too ashamed, to tell. Marcus was stunned, then furious enough to kill. Even while he was assuring Amelia that he didn't blame her and would love her forever, he was planning what he would do to Terrence when they returned.

With Marcus's patience and love, they managed to regain some happiness during their honeymoon, even though the taint of what Terrence had done was constant fuel to his rage. By the time they returned and set up their own household, Marcus could stand it no longer.

One night, after Amelia had fallen asleep, he left their house, got in his car and drove to Terrence's apartment. He let himself in with Terrence's extra key, the key he kept under a potted plant in the hallway, and quietly locked the door behind him as he entered.

Terrence was asleep in his bed when he was awakened by the sound of footsteps coming down the hall. He knew, even before he saw Marcus appear in the darkened doorway to his bedroom, who it would be. On one hand, he was as afraid as he'd ever been in his life, and on the other, almost relieved that this moment had come. When he'd sobered up and realized what he'd done, he'd been horrified, but it was too late to change what had happened.

Now justice was coming for him, and he welcomed it. He threw back the covers and sat up in bed just as Marcus came into the room.

"I'm sorry," he said. "I'm truly sorry."

Marcus doubled up his fist and hit him square in the mouth. The sound echoed in Terrence's head like the crack of a whip as blood spurted between his teeth. Before Terrence could get up, Marcus had him by the hair and was dragging him out of the bed.

"You bastard," Marcus muttered, his voice shaking with rage. "You unmentionable, disgusting excuse for a man. You're nothing but a dog . . . an animal. As for being sorry, you've been that since the day you were born."

The words stung more than the blow to his mouth, but Terrence couldn't bring himself to argue. It was true.

Then Marcus hit him again.

Terrence did his best to defend himself but was helpless against his cousin's rage. The fight went on for what seemed like hours. Furniture was overturned; lamps were broken; revenge ruled. Just when Terrence thought he'd drawn his last breath, it was over.

Marcus staggered backward, then dragged himself upright. Blood poured from a cut over his eyebrow, and his mouth was bloodied and swollen. He'd broken two fingers on one hand and knocked a knuckle out of place on the other. His hands were so swollen he could no longer make a fist, and the pain in his chest had been replaced by a horrible sense of loss. Because of Terrence, their family unity had been forever destroyed. To protect Amelia's reputation and pride, he would never tell what Terrence had done. But the damage had been done and would forever stand between them through the years.

When he'd gotten home, Amelia had been waiting for him at the door. She took one look at his bloodied face and hands and started to cry. Nothing was ever said of that night, but it seemed to Marcus that Amelia's behavior changed for the better afterward. Where she'd been solemn and even withdrawn, she began to laugh again. What Marcus had done gave her a sense of justice having been served.

Years later, it was Amelia who had fostered the end to their silent war. The day Terrence married Carolyn, Amelia told Marcus that their outward animosity had to end. She said she wouldn't have an innocent young woman like Carolyn suffering an unfair estrangement from the family into which she'd just married. Against every instinct Marcus had, he'd given in to Amelia's decision.

Through the ensuing years, Terrence and Carolyn

were often honored guests in Marcus's home and part of the event when Marcus's son married. Even after Amelia died, Marcus continued to include the couple in family gatherings because his beloved Amelia had wished it to be so.

Olivia's birth was a celebrated event and Terrance proudly took on the title of Uncle although he was only a cousin. Then they moved and Marcus was relieved. But it was with those memories that Marcus Sealy still lived. After all these years, he still hated the man. Despite his regard for Terrence's wife, when they'd moved to Italy, Marcus had hoped to never lay eyes on him again. But the discovery of the murdered baby had changed all that. He couldn't help but consider the possibility that Terrence might be the child's father. It would explain everything. Because of what had happened to Amelia, he believed Terrence capable of cheating on Carolyn, although he couldn't quite wrap his mind around Terrence being capable of murder—especially a child of his own. He'd been crazy about Olivia and doted on her to the point that he became her favorite relative—other than her Grampy, of course. But back then she'd just been a baby. Terrence and Carolyn had left before the kidnapping had occurred.

And tomorrow they would be back. It was almost more than Marcus could absorb. He carried the burden of his thoughts as he set out for his daily visit to the hospital.

Olivia was sitting up in a chair, watching the two

nurses changing the sheets on her bed and listening to their chatter without paying much attention to what they were saying. It wasn't until she heard one of them mention Trey Bonney's name that she sat up and took notice. She'd heard bits and pieces of the accounts of his heroism, but she was about to hear it from front to back.

"Excuse me, but what is that you were saying about Detective Bonney?"

The little redheaded nurse rolled her eyes in a mock swoon.

"Besides the fact that he's such a honey?" she said.

Olivia grinned. "Yes, besides that."

"We were just talking about how he caught that man who set the fire in the janitor's closet."

"The man who was after me?" Olivia asked.

"Yes. It was like something out of the movies. We were all out in the hall. Smoke was everywhere, and everyone was getting panicked, and then the sprinkler system came on. What a mess! We ran out of dry sheets, and the laundry room worked overtime for the first time in years. Anyway . . . Detective Bonney came flying out of your room and went straight to the source of the fire. We were just getting that under control when he saw the door to your room was shut. Well, let me tell you . . . he yelled at us to call security and charged back inside. Before we knew it, he was dragging this guy out of your room by the neck, and he shoved him to the floor and handcuffed him right before our eyes. Like I said . . . just like in the movies."

Olivia shivered. She had seen the man's face—seen the maniacal glitter in his eyes. To think that he'd been in her room, by her bed, moments away from finishing what he'd started, was overwhelming. Except for Trey, he would have succeeded.

She shuddered, then leaned back and closed her eyes. A few minutes later, the nurses were through.

"You want to get back in bed?" the redhead asked.

"I think I'll just sit here a while longer," Olivia said.

"Doctor says you'll go home tomorrow," the nurse added. "I know you'll be glad. You're doing great, you know."

"Yes, I do know," Olivia said. "I'm a very fortunate woman."

"Yes, you are. Honey, someone is for sure looking over you . . . besides that yummy detective, that is."

Olivia managed a smile, but inside she was shaking. The stress of the past two weeks was catching up to her fast. No sooner had the nurses left than she began to cry. For the first time in her life, she was beginning to understand how swiftly things could change. One day she and her grandfather had been living a privileged and luxurious lifestyle, and the next their past was spread all over the papers. Before she'd even come to terms with that, someone had tried to kill her—twice. She wanted to feel safe. But right now, she felt used up and bereft.

And that was how Marcus found her.

Marcus got off the elevator with a heavy heart. His

steps were dragging as he started down the hall to Olivia's room. He had to get past this feeling of impending doom, but he didn't know how. There was so much turmoil in their lives. Between the media, the police investigation and the arrival of unwelcome guests, he was more than a little overwhelmed. There was a part of him that wished he and Olivia could go back to that wonderful trip they'd had in Europe and never come home.

On top of everything, he was concerned about Anna. Her presence in their home should have seemed normal. After all, she'd spent nearly sixteen years with them before she'd retired with a generous annuity, a home and a car. Instead, her diminishing sanity added to the strain of dealing with Olivia's injuries and the constant meddling of the media.

Then there was the guilt he was still trying to sort through regarding Olivia's personal life. He didn't know who he was more disgusted with—himself for riding roughshod over every man she'd ever shown an interest in, or her for letting him do it. Only now was he coming to realize that Olivia had been living with a lifetime of guilt. Somehow she'd blamed herself for the murder of her own parents and for getting kidnapped. It didn't make sense, but guilt rarely, if ever, did.

And then there were Terrence and Carolyn.

Old ghosts.

New fears.

Could the Sealy family actually be connected to the murder of a child? And, if so, who was that little girl?

Who did she belong to?

As he neared the door to Olivia's room, he shook off his malaise. She needed positive feedback, not more problems, but when he walked in, it was obvious she was having a bad day of her own.

Olivia's shoulders were shaking from the strength of her sobs. She didn't hear the door open or see her grandfather enter. But she heard the concern in his voice as he hurried toward her.

"Olivia! Darling! What's wrong? Has something else happened?"

Olivia struggled to regain her composure, but she was too far gone to make it happen.

"Oh, Grampy . . . everything is such a mess."

Gently, Marcus pulled her out of the chair and into his arms.

"I know, darling, I know. But it will get better, you know. Eventually, everything always does."

"I don't know how to deal with all this. Every time someone I don't know comes into my room, I wonder what they think of me. Of the fact that someone wanted me dead. And then there's that poor little baby. Last night I dreamed it was me in the suitcase, and I was crying and crying and nobody came."

Marcus groaned. "Oh, sweetheart, you've had too much to deal with. That didn't happen, and you know it. I would give anything to have been the one that crazed man went after, instead of you. I wish with all my heart that I could prove to your satisfaction that you belong. But I can only tell you over and over what I believe. You are my grandchild. You are innocent of anything except being a victim. And tomorrow I am taking you out of this place and back home where you belong."

"I want to go now," Olivia said. "I don't want to spend another night in this place, afraid to close my eyes for fear another crazy person will take it into his head to finish what the first one started."

Marcus frowned. "I'll talk to the doctor. If he won't let you go home this evening, I'll put a guard on your room. It's as simple as that."

Olivia shuddered as she leaned against her grandfather's strength. She was still crying when Trey walked into the room.

Trey had been dreading his visit to Olivia ever since he'd gotten the report on the DNA. Instead of eliminating confusion, the results had added to it. When he'd called the Sealy estate to talk to Marcus, he'd been told that Marcus was already at the hospital. Despite his reluctance to confront them, he was thankful to have to explain this only once.

And so he'd driven to the hospital in haste, anxious to catch them together before Marcus could leave. He'd seen Olivia only last night, and she'd been doing so well that he wasn't prepared to find her an emotional wreck in her grandfather's arms.

"What's wrong? Has something happened?" Trey asked as he crossed the room in three strides. His hand was on Olivia's back even as he was looking at Marcus for answers.

Marcus shook his head.

"No, she's all right, at least in the physical sense," he said.

Trey's legs went weak with relief. He touched the back of Olivia's head, then her shoulder.

"Honey, we need to talk," he said.

Olivia shuddered, then turned around and looked at him.

His spirits sank. If she felt as distraught as she looked, what he had to say wasn't going to help.

"What is it?" she asked.

"The test results on the DNA samples came back."

Olivia stiffened, as if bracing herself for a physical blow.

"And?"

"You are definitely a Sealy," Trey said. "All the markers are there to prove it."

"Thank God," Olivia muttered, then swayed where she stood.

Marcus grabbed for her, but Trey caught her first and led her to the bed.

"Lie down, Livvie . . . you're white as a sheet."

It wasn't until her head hit the pillow that Olivia realized she was shaking. She broke out in a cold sweat, while the bed felt as if it was rolling.

"I'm okay," she mumbled, but closed her eyes anyway until everything stopped spinning.

"You're not okay," Marcus said. "You've been up too

long, and our discussion didn't help."

Trey eyed them curiously. Unless they offered, he didn't feel as if he had the right to ask.

"It's over, isn't it, Trey?" Olivia asked. "I really am Michael and Kay Sealy's child?"

He frowned. What he was going to say wasn't going to help. In fact, it only added to the mystery of this mess.

"I can't say that for sure, but you are definitely Marcus's granddaughter."

Both Marcus and Olivia frowned.

"What do you mean?" Marcus asked.

"Both Olivia's DNA and Baby Jane Doe's DNA show that they're related to you."

Now Marcus was the one in shock.

"Dear God," he said, and stumbled to the nearest chair.

"I don't understand," Olivia said.

"Michael," Marcus muttered.

Olivia frowned.

Trey sighed. He was glad he didn't have to explain the implications to Marcus.

The old man seemed to wilt where he sat, but Olivia still wasn't connecting.

"Will somebody please explain what the hell is going on?" she said.

Trey sat down on the side of the bed, then laid his hand on her arm, wishing he could soften the impact of what he was going to say.

"Michael and Kay Sealy had a daughter they named Olivia."

"Yes. Me," Olivia snapped.

"Not necessarily," Trey said, avoiding her eyes. "You and the victim shared a father, but not mothers. Without DNA from Kay Sealy to compare to both you and Baby Doe, we can't prove which was which." He glanced toward Marcus. "Does Kay have any surviving family members?"

"No, none that I know of."

"That complicates things a bit," Trey said.

Olivia started to shake as she clutched at Trey's hand.

"Even if we resembled each other, surely half siblings wouldn't have been identical. Grampy would have known if I wasn't the right one." She looked to Marcus for backup. "That's what you said, right, Grampy? You would have known if they returned the wrong baby."

"Absolutely," Marcus said, but he was so shaken, he was no longer sure. He wasn't sure about anything anymore.

Trey glanced at Olivia, then turned his attention to Marcus.

"I have some more questions I need to ask you," Trey said.

Marcus nodded. "Yes, I suppose you do."

"Were you aware that your son was having an affair?"

Marcus reeled from the question as if it had been a physical blow.

Olivia stared at her grandfather's face. His expression raised new doubt.

"Oh, God, Grampy, what if—"

"Stop it," Marcus said. "Just stop it right there. I said

I knew my own granddaughter, didn't I? I won't say it again." But even as he said it, the seeds of doubt had taken root.

Olivia covered her face, then rolled over onto her side.

"This is a nightmare," she whispered, and closed her eyes.

Trey would have given anything not to have been the bearer of this news, but he'd been handed the case, and he had to see it through. He eyed Marcus again, waiting for him to answer. When he didn't, Trey prompted him.

"Marcus?"

"I never knew. I swear," Marcus muttered. "Michael was always so loving toward Kay. The only other woman I ever saw him pay any attention to was Carolyn, Terrence's wife, and she was family."

"That doesn't eliminate her," Trey said. "Are you sure there weren't others? Maybe someone at work? Someone he came in contact with on a daily basis? Were you ever aware of another woman in your son's world who was pregnant at the same time that Kay was carrying her child?"

"God in heaven," Marcus said. "This can't be happening. I will not believe that my son had a child and let it be murdered."

"That's not the only possible scenario here," Trey said. "I would advise against drawing any kind of conclusions until we know more."

"What more is there to know?" Marcus muttered. "My son got two women pregnant, virtually at the same time. The dead baby and my kidnapped granddaughter were the same age, right?"

"The coroner thinks they couldn't have been more than a month apart in age when the kidnapping occurred."

"I'm still missing something obvious, aren't I?" Olivia asked.

Marcus couldn't look at her, and Trey couldn't look away.

"Back when the kidnapping occurred, the authorities never could reconcile Foster Lawrence as having been the only kidnapper. He was the one who picked up the ransom, but they were never able to link him to the murders. It was one of the reasons why he didn't get the death penalty. According to my lieutenant, they always thought there were at least two people involved, and that the other one did the killing. At the trial, Lawrence kept swearing he'd had nothing to do with murder, that he was the one who'd turned the baby loose. He told them where he'd parked at the mall and the door through which he'd carried her in. There was a store clerk who remembered seeing a man who looked like Lawrence carrying a child into the mall about the same time that Lawrence swore he was turning her loose. But if Lawrence had an accomplice, he never gave him up."

"Only now you think it could have been a woman . . . a woman scorned, couldn't it?" Marcus said.

"The possibility exists," Trey said.

"I don't know. I can't think," Marcus mumbled. "I need to go home. Maybe if I go through some old photo albums, someone will come to mind."

"What about Uncle Terrence and Aunt Carolyn?" Olivia asked. "If my father is . . . responsible for both children, then that lets Uncle Terrence off the hook."

"Yes, I suppose it does," Trey said. "But now that we're looking for another woman, what about Carolyn? You said she and Michael were friendly?"

Marcus's face turned a dark, mottled red.

"She can't possibly be a suspect! I never intended to degrade her reputation. I only meant that she and Michael got along. I didn't add, but I will now, that she and Kay were also best friends, and there is no way that Carolyn Sealy got pregnant from my son, gave birth and then hid a two-year-old child from our entire family before . . . before . . . killing it and plastering it up in some wall."

Trey's chin jutted. He was just as determined to solve the case as Marcus was to make this all go away.

"I was not insinuating that Carolyn Sealy was the mother," Trey said. "But if she and your son were friendly, there is a possibility that she knew something about Michael's other life that you and his wife did not. I'll have to interview her."

Marcus's posture sagged.

Trey regretted his anger.

"Look, Marcus . . . I'm not trying to be difficult about this. I know how everything that's happened has affected you and Olivia, but let's not forget what started this whole damn mess. A child is dead. And all I've got to go on are a bag of bones in the coroner's office, and a suitcase, one sock, a bloodstained nightgown, a wooden cross and most of a dirty pink blanket. I told you once before, and I'll say it again. I will find out who killed her, and I won't quit until it's done."

Marcus nodded once.

"I'm sorry. This is your investigation, and I never intended to try and influence you. I was just looking out for my family."

"I understand that," Trey said. "But after what I've just told you, you also have to understand that you can't keep your family out of this anymore. Your son was involved with the mother of the murdered child. When we find out who she was, then I think we'll be able to find out who killed Michael and Kay Sealy and kidnapped Olivia."

"But who killed the baby in the suitcase?" Marcus asked.

Trey wouldn't look at Olivia as he answered.

"I think it all depends on which baby it was that died."

Olivia turned her back to both men and curled into the fetal position. She felt sick and afraid—as afraid as she'd ever been.

Marcus tried to talk to her, but was so rattled by the revelations that he made a feeble excuse and quickly left with a promise to call soon.

12

Trey waited until Marcus was gone, then moved to Olivia's bed. She hadn't moved or spoken since she'd turned her back on both of them, and he worried that she blamed him for the news he'd brought.

He scooted onto the side of her bed, then put his hand on her shoulder. When he felt her flinch, his heart sank.

"Livvie?"

"Go away, Trey. I don't want to talk about this anymore," she said.

He heard tears in her voice. She was crying again. He couldn't blame her.

"I'm so sorry," he said softly.

She braced herself as she turned, trying not to disturb the sling on her arm, and rolled over onto her back.

"You have nothing to apologize for, and as you reminded us, your main purpose here is finding a murderer."

"That's my job," he said shortly. "Loving you is a complete and separate thing, and I would like to remind you that I don't intend to be bullied into giving you up again, no matter how pissed off you or your family get at me."

For a long silent moment he and Olivia just stared at each other.

"Are you okay with that?" he finally asked.

She swallowed once, then nodded.

His voice was a little softer, but there was determination in his hands as he cupped her face, then leaned down.

"All right, then," he said softly, and kissed her, only this time the kiss was filled with passion, rather than his previous restraint. He felt the tremble in her lips, heard the catch in her breath, and knew she was feeling it, too.

When he finally pulled away, Olivia was shaking.

"I remember what it was like making love to you," she said.

The hair stood up on the back of Trey's neck.

"Oh, baby, I remember what it was like making love to you, too, and when you get well, we'll make new memories, okay?"

"More than okay," she said softly.

Trey touched her lips one last time, but with the tip of his finger, then slid his thumb the length of her mouth before tilting her chin just a bit.

"Look at me," he urged.

She looked her fill and then some.

"No matter what happens with this case, it doesn't change anything that's between us, right?"

This time she didn't hesitate.

"Right."

He grinned. "So you go home tomorrow, right?"

"Yes, and none too soon."

His grin faded. "Something wrong?"

"I don't like being the object of so much curiosity."

His voice deepened, as did the frown between his eyebrows.

"Are you being bothered here?"

"Not really, but someone is always staring."

"You're a damn beautiful woman. I don't blame them. Now, quit reading stuff into what's probably just natural curiosity."

She sighed. "Yes, you're probably right."

"I can put a guard on your door," he said.

"Grampy said the same thing, but there's no need. I'm just being silly. Besides, by this time tomorrow I'll be gone."

"I'm going to be keeping the road hot between the station and your house."

"You'd better," she said.

He pointed to her sling.

"Speaking of better, when does this come off?"

"Soon. The doctor is going to start me on some kind of therapy to help loosen the muscles. We have a complete gym in the basement at home, so all I'll need is some instruction and then I can do it myself every day."

He nodded and would have said more, but his pager went off. He glanced down at the number, then frowned.

"I'm going to have to go, honey. I'll check back with you this evening, okay?"

"Okay."

A moment later he was gone, leaving Olivia with the memory of his kiss tingling on her mouth and the anticipation of more to come.

Foster Lawrence had settled on a plan. He was getting

out of Dallas now, even if he had to hitchhike to make it happen. He had less than three hundred dollars to his name, with no prospects of adding to that unless he went to work. But he couldn't do that here unless he bought himself a new identity, and that would cost more than three hundred dollars.

When the police arrested the man responsible for the attempted murder of Olivia Sealy, he'd breathed a huge sigh of relief. One less monkey on his back. But there was still that matter of a dead baby and a suitcase, and while he hadn't witnessed anything, he knew the name of the person who was responsible. Trouble was, even if he decided to give that up, he had no earthly idea where to tell the cops to start looking, and they were bound to press for that information before letting him off the hook.

He'd divided his money into three separate portions and hidden them in three different places. One third was in his bag, another in his wallet and the last in his sock. He had a switchblade in his pocket, and a freshly shaved face and head to keep him from being recognized. He gave his hotel room a last lingering look to make sure he'd left nothing of himself behind, then went out the door, closing it behind him.

He'd cleared the fourth-floor landing and was just starting down to the third when he suddenly smelled smoke. He thought nothing of it. Some down-and-out resident was cooking on a hot plate in the room. It wasn't allowed, but it wouldn't have been the first time the rule had been broken.

He readjusted the strap on his duffel bag and moved a few feet farther down the stairs. He was almost to the second-floor landing when the smoke came up to meet him, spiraling up the stairwell, as if drawn up a chimney.

"Son of a bitch," Foster muttered as his heart skipped a beat.

He took another couple of steps down, and as he did, the steps seemed to disappear beneath his feet. Where treads had been, there was now nothing but smoke. He looked down and realized he couldn't see past his knees.

"Oh God, oh no. No. No." His voice kept rising until he was shouting the last two words. Then he started to scream. "Fire! Fire! Somebody help! Fire!"

He was frozen to the spot, watching the smoke as it continued to rise, and then suddenly realizing he was beginning to feel heat.

He turned abruptly and began running back up the way he'd come, convinced there had to be more than one set of stairs to each floor, certain that if he could just find them, he could get out another way.

He reached the fourth floor, and then kept going up, up, until he reached the door that led to the roof. He could hear footsteps behind him—the sounds of people crying, someone screaming—and always there was the continuing accumulation of heat and smoke.

He burst through the door and out onto the roof, and for a few seconds could almost believe he'd outrun the fire. Then reality surfaced as a swarm of people came out behind him and began running to the edge of the building. He followed and, like the others, found himself leaning over the edge and screaming down below to the people who were beginning to gather.

"Help! Help!" they screamed, as if the mere uttering of the word would automatically keep them from harm.

Foster could hear the fire trucks coming now, racing through the streets below with their sirens signaling their imminent arrival. Fire had jumped from the second-floor windows to the third, and there was smoke beginning to come out of the fourth-floor windows, as well.

Foster panicked. Was this going to be his end? Was he going to go up in smoke like the money he'd fraudulently obtained so long ago? It seemed impossible, and yet, in a cruel and ironic twist, almost justified.

He began to circle the rooftop, running as fast as he could, looking for a break in the smoke, but it seemed now that it was coming up from all four sides. His panic was echoed by the others on the roof. Two of them found a small stack of wooden planks and began frantically dragging them to the edge of the building, intent on using them as a bridge to the next building over.

But when they extended the planks as far as they would go, they discovered the boards were about three feet too short. A wail went up from the group en masse as if one brief window of escape had suddenly closed before them.

"The fire trucks! They're here!" someone yelled, and pointed as the trucks turned a corner up the street.

"We're saved! We're saved!" another cried, and began to weep.

But Foster wasn't as elated. He didn't see how any of them could be saved when it was obvious that the firemen couldn't see them on the roof any better than they could see the firemen below. The way he looked at it, they were about to be royally screwed—or fried, as the case might be.

When he was just at the point of making peace with his sins and asking forgiveness from God, he heard shouts from the building directly north. He turned. The building was at least six floors higher than the one they were on, but at the edge, he saw a group of firemen strapping on rescue gear. Immediately, he understood what they were about to try.

"There!" he yelled, pointing up, and watched in open-mouthed amazement as a helicopter suddenly appeared, then unfurled a rope ladder from one of the open doors.

Within seconds, the powerful downdraft from the rotors threatened to sweep them off the roof. Foster ran with the others to a central portion of the roof. As they watched, a fireman jumped onto the ladder, locked one arm through the rungs, and then rode it down to the top of the burning building.

The fireman leaned down and grabbed a victim, then pulled her onto the ladder, positioning himself behind her so that she was pinned between the ladder and his body. The ladder was swinging wildly, partly from the downdraft of the chopper's blades, and partly from the wind being churned by the growing wall of heat below.

The chopper rose slowly to keep from slamming the people against the wall of the next building. In moments the woman was dropped into the waiting arms of the firemen on the other roof.

One after another, they were removed that way until there were only two men left—Foster and an old man he knew only as Ralph. The roof of the building was so hot now that he could feel the heat through the soles of his shoes. He saw the chopper coming, calculated that there might be time for one more run before the roof caved in, and knew if they had to choose, they wouldn't choose him. Desperate to save himself, he grabbed hold of Ralph's arm and started to run toward the dangling ladder and the fireman hanging on to the rungs.

Only seconds after they'd moved from where they had been standing, the center of the roof began to give way, sinking slowly inward as the structure was devoured by the fire.

"Hurry!" he screamed, and motioned for the fireman to climb up out of the way.

The fireman was waving his arm and pointing to the far corner of the roof, where the outer wall still held. At that moment, Ralph stumbled. It was instinct, not a sense of bravery, that made Foster grab him under the arms and lift him off his feet. In one last desperate sprint toward safety, they reached the corner just as the ladder swung across his line of vision. With a desperation born of fear, he grabbed the ladder just above the last rung and screamed in the old man's ear.

"Put your arms around my neck and don't let go."

"We'll fall," the old man wailed.

"Do you want to die?" Foster shouted.

"No!" Ralph cried.

"Then hold the hell on. I won't let go if you don't," he promised.

At that point, the rest of the roof began to fall inward. He could feel the outer wall as it began to sway.

"Now!" he screamed.

The old man's arms went around his neck. He grabbed the ladder with both hands and locked his legs around the old man's waist just as the ladder swung out into space.

He looked up once and found himself staring straight into the soot-streaked face of the fireman, then looked away.

The chopper went up. The burden of the old man's body was more than he'd expected. Almost instantly, his shoulder muscles began to burn from the pull of the weight. Ignoring everything but the feel of the rope against his palms, he closed his eyes, focusing all of his energy into his grip.

It seemed as if they were suspended forever, when in fact it was only seconds. Just when he thought he would have to let go, he heard the sounds of people shouting and then felt hands grabbing his ankles, pulling him down, down, to the safety of the other roof.

"Let go, man! Let go!" someone shouted as fingers grabbed at his hands, trying to make him turn loose of the ladder.

So he did—and immediately collapsed.

In the few moments it took him to realize they were safe, he opened his eyes and looked up. There were faces looking down at him, then hands pulling at his clothes and yanking him upright.

"Can you walk?" someone asked.

Foster nodded.

"Follow me," one of the firemen ordered.

Foster did as he was told. It wasn't until they reached the street below that he accepted they'd been saved. He stood for a moment, his legs trembling, his heart hammering against his chest, and then dropped to his knees.

"Good job," someone said, and clapped him on the back as they moved past.

"Way to go, mister," another said, and thumped him on the shoulder as he, too, passed.

While he was still trying to catch his breath, two men scooped him up by the arms and all but dragged him to a curb.

"Hey . . . I'm all right," he mumbled. "Let me go. Let me go."

They patted him on the back, shoved a bottle of water into his hands and draped a heavy blanket across his back before running back to the other survivors.

Rose was in the kitchen, preparing vegetables for the evening meal. The portable television she kept tuned to her favorite soaps was on a nearby shelf. She listened as she worked, and every now and then had to pause to watch a particular scene.

"That crazy woman," she muttered as she stopped to

point at the screen. "She breaks up every romance on this show. You'd think they'd have at least one man who could resist her charms."

Anna nodded in agreement, although she was completely lost as to what Rose was saying. Her gaze was caught on a pair of daisy fabric pot holders hanging on a hook beside the stove.

"I like daisies," Anna said.

Rose was getting used to the way Anna's mind wandered and nodded without looking to see what had prompted the remark.

"Yes, I do, too," she said. "And zinnias. I like zinnias a lot. I know they're not as delicate and their colors are less subtle, but they're sturdy. I like sturdy things. They survive when other things don't."

Anna moved toward the pot holders as Rose turned away from the stove to focus on a particularly intense part of her story.

"Look at that hussy!" Rose said, pointing to the television screen. "Someone needs to teach her a lesson."

Just as the actors were about to reveal some plot secret, the broadcast was interrupted by a news flash.

"Oh, for goodness' sakes," Rose muttered. "They were just about to—" Then she gasped as the station began broadcasting footage they'd shot at a fire in an old downtown hotel. "Oh my! Anna! Would you look at that fire!"

Rose's gaze was fixed on a helicopter and the fireman hanging on to the ladder hanging from it. She was watching, transfixed as, one by one, the helicopter moved people from the roof of the burning building to a place of safety, until all but the last two men had been rescued.

Then, to her horror, she watched as the helicopter started back and the roof of the burning building began to collapse. She squealed in horror, then covered her mouth, frozen to the spot by the drama unfolding before her.

"Oh lordy, lordy, the fire, the fire," Rose mumbled.

Anna laid one of the daisy pot holders onto a burner, then took down the other one and piled it on top. A flame shot upward, past the cooking pots and up into the vent hood. Without missing a beat, Anna punched the switch on the hood. The motor started, instantly sucking fire up into the vents and the ceiling.

"Fire," Anna said without moving.

Rose nodded. "Yes, it's a big fire, but thank the Lord they've rescued all those poor people."

"Fire," Anna said again.

Rose turned. Her eyes widened, and she let out a scream.

"Oh Lord! Oh Lord! Fire! Fire! Oh, Anna, what have you done?"

She turned off the stove and the exhaust fan, then grabbed the cell phone and Anna's hand as she ran, dialing 911.

Marcus was signing the last of some papers for his secretary when his cell phone rang. He frowned, glanced at the number, then picked up.

"Hello?"

Rose was screaming and crying, and he could hear sirens in the background. He jumped to his feet and raced to the window, as if by moving six feet to the right he could be closer to whatever was happening at home.

"Oh, Mr. Marcus . . . the house, the house . . . Anna set it on fire. I turned my back for just a minute and—"

Marcus stifled a groan. "Are you both all right?" he asked urgently.

"Yes, yes, we're all right. The firemen have it under control, but the kitchen is ruined, and the fire went up to the room over it, too. I'm so sorry. I'm so sorry."

"Rose! It's all right. Things can be fixed. I just needed to know you're both alive."

Rose was sobbing.

His heart sank. What the hell else was going to happen to their family? Then he stifled the moment of self-pity and got to the point.

"Don't cry, dear. It's not your fault, it's mine. I shouldn't have left an unstable woman in the house for you to deal with. We knew Anna had problems. I put off getting her help, and now this is a result."

"What do I do?" Rose asked.

"I'm on my way. Just stay with Anna for the time being. When I get home, I will take care of it all."

"Yes, sir, Mr. Marcus, and I'm so, so, sorry."

Marcus dropped his cell phone in his pocket and grabbed his sports coat just as his secretary came back into the room.

"Devon, I'm going home. There's been a fire at the house."

"Oh no! Is there anything I can do to help?" she said.

He thought of Olivia. She was due to come home tomorrow, and Terrence and Carolyn were arriving today. He paused by the door, then nodded.

"Yes. Call Detective Trey Bonney at the Dallas PD, in homicide. Tell him to call me as soon as possible. I don't want Olivia to hear about this from the news and suffer any more distress. She's had more than enough to bear."

"Yes, sir. Right away, sir," Devon said. "Anything else?"

"Yes, actually, there is." He pointed to his desk. "See those brochures?"

She nodded, picking them up, then followed Marcus out of his office to the elevators.

"Find out how many of those assisted-care living centers have vacancies. I'll call you back later to see what you've found out."

"I'm so sorry about your home," she said.

"It can be fixed. Losing people can't. I'm just grateful that Rose and Anna are all right."

"Is there anything else?" Devon asked.

Marcus thought of Terrence and Carolyn, due to arrive at DFW airport later that evening. They were supposed to take a cab to his house, but that wasn't going to work out now. Thankfully, Rose had a sister who lived close. He knew she would want to go there.

"Yes, one more thing," he said. "Call the hotel at the

Mansion on Turtle Creek. Make a reservation for me, as well as one for Terrence and Carolyn Sealy, arriving this evening, with an open departure date. Then send a limo to the airport to pick them up. Give them a detailed explanation with the number to my cell phone, and tell them I'll join them for dinner at the hotel tonight . . . say, around eight o'clock. If there's anything else, I'll let you know," he said.

The elevator arrived. He rode it down as Devon returned to the office.

Trey got the phone call from Marcus's office just as he was arriving at the scene of the hotel fire. Four bodies had been brought out by the firemen before the building collapsed, and more than a dozen people, some burned, had been rescued from the roof. The arson investigator was already on the scene, making sure that it stayed as intact as possible, while emergency personnel were working frantically on the burn victims, trying to stabilize them for transport.

He pulled up to the perimeter, parked, then quickly dialed Marcus's number as he was getting out of the car.

"Marcus, it's me, Trey. What's up?"

"We've had a problem at the house. I know this is an imposition, but I don't want Olivia hearing this second-hand and getting all upset."

Trey stopped walking. Marcus's voice was shaking, and there was an exhaustion there that Trey wasn't used to hearing.

"What happened?" he asked.

"Anna set fire to the kitchen. It spread to a couple of rooms upstairs, as well, before they got it out. No one is hurt, but for the moment, the place is unlivable. I can't have Olivia coming home from the hospital to this mess, and Rose is a basket case."

"Don't worry about Olivia," Trey said. "I'll take her home with me. Are you all right?"

Marcus sighed. "I will be. Just knowing that Olivia will be in good hands is relief enough. I've got Anna to place in assisted-living quarters, and the arrival of a cousin I can't stand. Other than that, everything is fine. Oh! I'll be staying at the Mansion on Turtle Creek."

"Got it," Trey said. "And please don't worry about anything on this end. I'll make sure Olivia understands what happened without frightening her."

"Thank you," Marcus said. "Thank you more than you can know."

"On the contrary," Trey said. "I'm the one who should be thanking you for trusting me enough to do this. I know how much Olivia means to you. Please know that I will make sure she's well cared for. Do you have a pen? I'll give you my address and home phone number."

Marcus patted his pocket, then took out a pen and paper.

"Yes, I'm ready," he said.

Trey rattled off the information, then quickly disconnected. He had to get through with this as quickly as possible, then head to the hospital—and Olivia.

13

Foster had never been on the right side of the law before, and being hailed as a hero felt good. He considered the consequences of staying around and taking the acclaim the media wanted to give him, but if he didn't make himself scarce and soon, it wasn't going to last.

"Hey, mister! This way! This way!" a reporter shouted.

Foster looked up to find a camera aimed straight at his face. Startled, he wanted to look away, but he was frozen in the spotlight.

The cameraman moved closer, as did the reporter with the mike.

"Can you tell us what it was like up on that roof?" the reporter asked. "Did you think you were going to die?"

"Uh . . ."

It was as far as Foster got before another reporter appeared on the scene with a second mike.

"What's your name? Do you know how the fire started? Was the man you saved a friend?"

Foster covered his face with his arm and pretended to be overcome.

"Get back!" an EMT shouted as he grabbed at Foster and began forcing him onto a gurney.

Trey came up just as they were strapping Foster down and flashed his badge at the EMT.

"Where are you taking him?" he asked.

"Dallas Memorial," the EMT said as they pushed the gurney into the back of a waiting ambulance.

Trey nodded, slammed the door shut and then gave it a thump to indicate they were clear.

The ambulance pulled away from the scene, then sped off into traffic. Trey saw Chia about thirty feet away and headed toward her at a jog.

"What have you got?" Trey asked.

Chia looked up, then brushed at a lock of hair dangling between her eyes, which spread a streak of soot all the way across her face.

"We've got at least four dead and a suspicion of arson. Other than that, no one knows anything," she muttered.

"Warren said you and Dave were primaries, so what do you want me to do?"

She scanned her notes, then looked up. "Follow the ambulance to Dallas Memorial and talk to the hero of the hour. He might know something we can use."

"Will do," Trey said. "Anything else?"

"They've already transported some of the worst-off burn victims there," Chia said. "See if they know anything. Dave and I have this covered. We'll trade info later."

Trey nodded, then handed her his handkerchief.

"What's that for?" she asked.

He pointed to her face.

She rolled her eyes, dipped the handkerchief in a standing puddle of water and began scrubbing at her face as she walked away.

Trey grinned, then headed back to his car on the run. With media interest in the Sealy family at an all-time high, it followed that the fire at their home would merit coverage. He needed to get to Olivia before the gossip did.

Olivia had fallen asleep in the tangle of her sheets. Her arm had slipped out of the sling and was lying awkwardly across her chest. At her insistence, they'd finally taken the IV out, but there was a large bruise on the back of her hand where the needle had been. Her face was a mixture of healing scrapes and bruises, her hair a jumble of curls escaping from the twist on the top. Her lips had parted slightly, leaving her with a hint of a smile. In sleep, she'd been able to go where tragedy was just a part of her past, where there was nothing before her but a bright and hopeful future—back to where the love of her life had taught her how to be a woman.

Dallas, Texas—Eleven years earlier

Tonight was the homecoming game. Olivia had less than an hour to get changed and back to the stadium before kickoff, and she was determined not to be late. Her hair was in curlers, and she was still barefoot, but she had on her new sweater and slacks. She loved the sensuous feel of the soft wale corduroy pants and the chunky-knit, cowl-neck sweater against her skin. She'd chosen the style for herself but the color for Trey. Her

Trey. He loved blue, and she loved Trey, so it was an easy choice all around. She was taking the last of the rollers out of her hair as a knock sounded on her door.

"Come in!" she called, slinging curlers onto the bed as she made a frantic dash to the closet for her shoes.

"Olivia . . . I—"

"Oh, Grampy! I'm glad you're home. I thought I wasn't going to get to see you this evening before I left."

"That's what I wanted to—"

Olivia grabbed her shoes and ran to the side of the bed to put them on.

"It's homecoming tonight! Did I tell you?" she asked as she yanked the last of the curlers out of her hair and slipped her feet into the shoes. "Tammy Wyandotte is picking me up in less than fifteen minutes."

Marcus sighed. He'd been about to suggest that Olivia stay home tonight. He was concerned about her attachment to a certain boy but didn't know how to broach the subject. This was one of those times when a girl needed her mother, but he was all she was going to get. He knew she was keeping company with a boy from a less than desirable family, and he worried about the consequences. Still, the excitement in her voice was so genuine and her joy infectious. Instead of saying what he'd come in to say, he gave her a hug, told her to be home before midnight and kissed her goodbye.

"You have enough money with you?" he asked.

"Yes, Grampy, I'm fine. Keep your fingers crossed for our team, okay?"

He couldn't bear to take that joy from her face, so he sighed, then smiled.

"Absolutely," he said.

She threw her arms around his neck and kissed him soundly on the cheek.

"Oh, Grampy, you're the best."

The doorbell rang.

"That will be Tammy!" she said, grabbed her purse and dashed from her room.

Marcus followed her to the head of the stairs, then watched as she ran out the door.

By the time she and Tammy got to the football field, the captains of each team were on the field with the referees, who were in the midst of the coin toss.

Tammy squealed as they sat down.

"We won the toss! We're kicking off first," she said, and waved hysterically at her boyfriend, who was the second-string quarterback.

Olivia nodded, but she was more focused on the tall, long-legged running back standing near the bench. His thick black hair was just long enough to brush the padding around his neck, and there was a defiant jut to his chin that was unmistakable.

Trey Bonney.

Her heart stuttered just at the thought of his name. Two weeks ago, their relationship had taken a long leap from boyfriend and girlfriend to lovers. For Olivia, it had been the most frightening, and yet the most uplifting, moment of her life. She'd gone from being a girl to a woman in Trey Bonney's arms. She'd spent every waking moment since dreaming of a repeat performance and how they would spend the rest of their lives together.

Trey was graduating in the spring, and she had one more year of high school to go. They'd already talked about attending college together and sharing an apartment. They were so into each other that it never occurred to them that the rest of the world might object.

She held her breath, watching—willing Trey to turn around and see her. And then he did. She saw that moment of surprise roll over his face, then that slow, sexy smile. He winked, then pulled his helmet on his head and ran out onto the field.

For Olivia, the game passed in a fog. The fact that one of her friends was crowned homecoming queen was secondary to knowing she would be with Trey after the game was over. The moment the last seconds ticked off the clock and the whistle blew, she was on her feet and running toward the lockers. Trey would look for her to be waiting on the benches outside. That would leave them almost two hours to be together before her curfew.

She got to the benches and scooted into the shadows beyond the night-lights, waiting anxiously for Trey to come out. Nervous, she kept glancing often at her watch, trying not to think of the precious minutes being wasted.

Suddenly she saw him, silhouetted in the doorway with the light behind him as he stared out into the darkness.

She stood.

Alerted by the motion, he moved toward her at a lope, then caught her up in his arms and kissed her hungrily.

Olivia moaned and then sighed.

"You were wonderful tonight," she said softly.

Trey grinned, then leaned down and kissed the side of her neck below her ear.

"Thank you, Livvie, although the night's not over."

She blushed at the hint of things to come, but her heart was willing.

"I love you, Trey."

The smile died on his face as he took her in his arms and hugged her close. His voice was soft against her ear. "I love you, too, baby . . . more than you will ever know." Then he took her by the hand. "I've got Mom's car."

Livvie blushed again, but it was dark, and he didn't see.

"I have to be home by midnight."

Trey glanced at his watch.

"We've got an hour and thirty minutes," he said.

Within fifteen minutes, they'd made it to a secluded park near a small, man-made lake.

Trey parked the car, turned the radio down low, then took her in his arms. The nervousness they'd experienced their first time was gone. Familiarity choreographed their actions, and young lust led the way. Within a couple of minutes, Olivia was in the back seat of the car, minus the new blue corduroy pants.

She ran her hands up under Trey's sweater, caressing the hard muscles beneath his hot, smooth skin.

"Oh, Trey . . ."

"Shh," he whispered as he grabbed a condom and fitted himself.

He moved over her, then into her, in one smooth, fluid motion. Without foreplay, without hesitation, they began the act of love in innocence and haste.

Olivia gasped as he filled her, and when he started to move, she locked her arms around his neck and her legs around his waist. The heat of bare skin against bare skin quickly warmed the cooling interior of the car. The music shifted from a slow, sexy love song to the hard-rock rhythm of The Rolling Stones. Their bodies moved with it in perfect harmony, following the drumbeat all the way to a climax that rocked their world.

The present

Trey stopped in the E.R. long enough to ascertain that the man he'd come to talk to was still being examined. The injured who'd been brought in had already been transferred to the burn unit, which meant they probably wouldn't be available to interview tonight. With a promise from one of the nurses to give him a buzz when the hero of the hour could speak freely, Trey headed for the elevator to Livvie's room.

Just as he walked into her room, she moaned.

He moved quickly to her side and leaned over.

"Livvie . . . darling . . . are you in pain?"

Olivia moaned again, then sighed. She could still hear Trey's voice and was reluctant to give up the dream.

"Livvie?"

She flinched, then opened her eyes.

"Trey? You're here."

He frowned. "Where else would I be, honey?"

She ran a hand over her face. "I think I was dreaming."

He smiled. "About me, I hope."

"Actually, yes."

His smile widened.

"Really? What was I doing?"

"Making love to me in the back seat of your mother's car."

The smile shifted sideways as a wave of want washed through him.

"Jesus, Livvie," he said softly. "You sure know how to bring a man to his knees."

"It was a good dream," she said.

"Thank you . . . I think."

She smiled back at him, then put her good arm around his neck and pulled him closer.

"I think I could get used to waking up like this."

He leaned closer, then closer still, until their lips were nearly touching. Trey brushed the surface of her lips with his mouth, gently, then settling firmly on the center. He felt her hand at the back of his neck, pulling him closer. It would be so easy to lose himself in the moment, but that wasn't why he'd come. It was with reluctance that he was the first to pull away.

"Honey . . . we need to talk," he said.

Olivia heard concern in his voice and frowned. She

didn't think she could bear any more trouble.

"Please don't tell me something else is wrong."

"Your grandfather called me and asked me to come by. He didn't want you to hear the latest from your home front on the evening news."

Olivia's thoughts went instantly to Anna.

"Is everyone all right?" she asked. "Is it Anna? Has something happened to Anna?"

"Everyone is safe and sound, although your first instincts were right on. Somehow, Anna set fire to the kitchen. It burned through to a room upstairs, but the fire is out, and your grandfather wanted me to assure you it's nothing that can't be repaired."

"Oh my God," Olivia muttered. "Poor Grampy. On top of everything else, now this." Then it hit her that no one had mentioned Rose. "Is Rose all right, too?"

"Yes. Everyone is okay."

"Thank goodness, but this is all my fault. I shouldn't have insisted on having her come home with us. I could tell she was losing her grip on reality. I just didn't realize it could be dangerous. What is Grampy going to do? Where will we go?"

"It's going to be okay," Trey said. "At least, from where I'm standing, although if it makes you uncomfortable, I won't be insulted."

"What would make me uncomfortable?"

"I told your grandfather that I would take you home with me tomorrow when you're released. I have a next-door neighbor who would be more than happy to stay with you during the day until I come in from work. Her name's Ella Sumter, and she's eighty-one, but she's a hoot. Does tai chi on her front lawn every morning and doesn't look a day over sixty."

"All right," Olivia said.

Trey stifled the urge to do a little victory dance.

"You will?" he asked.

Feeling suddenly proper, Olivia nodded.

"Yes, of course, and I thank you for the offer."

He grinned. "Oh, trust me . . . you're very welcome."

"Where's Grampy going to stay?" she asked.

"The Mansion on Turtle Creek, as will your uncle Terrence and aunt Carolyn. As for the rest of it, he said for you not to worry, just get better. He'll stay in touch."

She sighed. "This has certainly become something of a mess, hasn't it?"

Before he could answer, his pager went off. He glanced down at it, then straightened.

"Honey, I'm sorry, but I've got to go down to the E.R. and interview a man. I won't be long, okay?"

She waved him away.

"Of course. Go do what it is you detectives do. I've got a dream to get back to."

Trey grinned.

"Save a place for me in that dream."

"I don't have to," she said softly. "You *are* the dream."

Trey was still thinking of Livvie as he got off the elevator, but his thoughts shifted quickly when he saw the man he'd come to talk to hurrying out the exit.

"Hey!" he yelled, and started toward him at a lope.

Foster turned. It was the cop who'd followed the ambulance to the hospital. He'd heard him talking to the nurses. The guy wanted to talk to him about the fire. With his luck, they would accuse him of starting it. He glanced out the door. Freedom was only a few feet away. But the cop was almost here.

Foster took a couple of steps toward the door, then froze as a police car pulled up to the entrance. His shoulders slumped; then he turned around.

It was over.

"Hey, man . . . where were you going?" Trey asked.

Foster shrugged. "Out. Don't like hospitals much."

Trey smiled, then clapped him on the back.

"Don't much blame you, but I need your help. My name's Detective Bonney."

When the man didn't answer, Trey let it slide for the time being.

"Are you feeling all right? That was quite a rescue you pulled off."

Foster saw the determination on the detective's face. Even if he ran now, even if he got away, it would only be a matter of time before they tracked him down. Truth was, he was tired of running. Tired of hiding. He'd fucked himself once by getting mixed up in something bad. He wasn't going to do it again.

"Yeah, I'm all right," Foster said, then held up his hands. "Just a few rope burns—and I need a new pair of shoes."

Trey looked down. The soles of the man's shoes were almost gone—melted by the heat of the roof on which he'd been standing.

"Let's find a place to talk," Trey said. "I want to get your take on the fire."

Foster lifted his chin. It was time for the unveiling.

"Let's just skip all the bullshit and get down to the truth. What you really want to know is, did I have anything to do with setting it."

Trey's eyes narrowed thoughtfully.

"Well . . . did you?" Trey asked.

Foster shook his head. "No, sir, I did not. If I had, I can guarantee I wouldn't have been so damn stupid as to get myself caught in the blaze."

Trey stared at him a moment; then he nodded in agreement. "Makes sense to me," he said. "So . . . now can we talk?"

"Yeah, why the hell not," Foster muttered. "I got plenty to say about a whole lot of things."

"Do we need to go down to headquarters?"

Foster shrugged. "I was leaning more toward Florida, but right now, I don't have anyplace else to go."

"My car is just outside," Trey said.

Foster fell into step beside Trey. Trey eyed the man cautiously, sensing he had yet to hear the whole story.

When they got to the car, Foster pointed to the back seat. "I reckon you'll be wanting me to sit back there," he said.

"Why's that?" Trey asked.

"Well, I understand the Dallas Police Department has

been wanting to talk to me for some time now."

Trey resisted the urge to feel for his gun and took comfort from the weight of it in the shoulder holster under his jacket.

"Why's that?" Trey asked.

Foster shrugged. "Beats me. I was sitting in my hotel room, minding my own business, when I heard my name on TV."

Suddenly Trey knew—even before the man made the admission—but he still had to ask.

"And what name would that be?" Trey asked.

"Foster Lawrence, late of Lompoc Federal Prison and most recently the Henry-Dean Hotel."

"Son of a bitch," Trey muttered.

Foster grinned. "Yeah, I heard that name a few times before, too." Then he held out his wrists.

Trey handcuffed him, then opened the back door.

"This is just a precaution," he said. "I'll take them off as soon as we get to the precinct."

The smile slid off Foster's face. "I heard that before, too," he said. "And just for the record, I don't know a damn thing about any dead babies, just like I didn't know a damn thing about those murders twenty-five years ago. But seein' as how nobody believed me back then, you can understand my reluctance to go through this shit again."

Without a cage between him and the back seat, and driving alone, Trey was reluctant to transport Lawrence. He took him by the elbow and escorted him to a police car parked nearby. One of the cops was standing by the unit, while the other was talking to an EMT driver.

When the uniformed officer saw the handcuffs, he began to pay attention.

"This is Foster Lawrence," Trey said. "He's just offered to come to headquarters and answer some questions. I wonder if you'd do me a favor and drive him for me. I'll pick him up down in booking."

Foster's heart dropped.

"Am I being arrested?" he asked.

"No," Trey said, then added, "Not unless you need to be."

"I need a lot of things, but that ain't one of 'em," Foster said, and scooted into the back seat of the police cruiser when Trey opened the door. "See you there," he told Trey, then leaned back against the seat and closed his eyes.

Trey eyed the melted shoes, the bandages on the man's hands, and the red, angry flush on his heat-scorched cheeks. It was ironic that this man had gone from hero to suspect within the space of five minutes. It was all about luck, and Lawrence's seemed to have run out.

14

Trey called Olivia from the car on his way back to headquarters. She answered on the second ring.

"Olivia, honey . . . it's me."

Olivia smiled to herself. "Hi, me."

Trey grinned. He couldn't remember the last time he'd felt this good about life.

"Just wanted you to know that something's come up. I'm on my way back to the precinct. I guess this was a night for fires. There was a bad one downtown at an old hotel, and I've got to talk to some of the survivors."

"Oh no. How awful."

"Yeah. Anyway, I won't be back tonight. Get a good night's sleep, and I'll see you in the morning, okay?"

"Okay. Be careful," Olivia said.

Trey chuckled. "Always, honey. Just think of it like this. I'm only going to the office. Sleep tight and dream some more good dreams of me. I'll pick you up in the morning."

Olivia smiled as she hung up the phone, then turned over and closed her eyes. The sooner morning came, the sooner she would be out of this place, but her phone rang again before she'd fallen asleep.

"Hello," Olivia said.

"Darling, it's me," Marcus said.

"Grampy! I'm so glad to hear your voice. Trey told me what happened. Are Rose and Anna all right?"

"They're fine, just a bit rattled. I've got Anna in an assisted-living home for the time being, although she argued all the way there, and Rose went to stay with her sister. Carpenters will be at the house in a few days. It's the best I could do."

"Oh, Grampy, I'm so sorry this is happening and I'm not there to help."

"You're right where you need to be, and besides, there's absolutely nothing you could do. Have you talked to Trey?"

"Yes. He's going to pick me up in the morning. Said he has a neighbor who can stay with me during the day when he's at work, although I don't need a baby-sitter."

"Let him take care of you, darling. I don't want to bring you home from the hospital to a hotel room, or I'd be the one coming for you."

"I know," Olivia said. "I'm not feeling abandoned. In fact, I'm feeling guilty."

"Whatever for?" Marcus said.

"For Anna."

"That's absurd. She needs help. We're all she has. Family doesn't abandon family, no matter what the price," Marcus said.

"Speaking of family . . . have Uncle Terrence and Aunt Carolyn arrived yet?"

"Yes. I'm meeting them at the hotel restaurant in an hour."

"Give them my love," Olivia said.

"I will," Marcus said. "Rest well, darling. I'll be in touch."

"Grampy."

"Yes?"

"Do you think it's true . . . about Daddy, I mean?"

Marcus slumped where he sat.

"I don't want to, but honestly, I don't see any other explanation."

"I'm sorry," Olivia said.

Marcus frowned. "Why? God knows none of this is your fault."

"I'm just sorry that this is happening. I don't have any memories of my parents, but you do. I know you're sad. I know you have to be hurting. I'm sorry that you have to go through this, that's all."

Marcus blinked away tears. "Thank you, darling. I don't know what I'd do without you." Then he thought of how possessive that sounded and quickly added, "Although, you know . . . I may have been short-changing myself all these years by being so selfish with you and your time. If I hadn't been so short-sighted, I might have had some great-grandchildren to spoil, too."

Olivia knew he was trying, in the only way he knew how, to apologize for pressuring her to stay with him all these years. Looking back, she had to admit that it was just as much her fault as his. She'd let him direct her life because it had been easier to give in than to fight. It was a shame that she'd had to come close to dying before she developed the gumption to go for what she wanted. She thought of Trey, picturing his face and the love in his eyes, and shivered.

"Oh, Grampy . . . where there's love, it's never too late."

Marcus thought of how many years he'd been without Amelia and suddenly felt old.

"You know something, darling? You're right. Sleep well. I'll be in touch."

"You, too, Grampy," Olivia said. She waited until she

226

heard the click of Marcus's disconnect, then hung up the phone.

She lay there a moment, thinking of all the possibilities the future held, then went to sleep, dreaming of Trey and babies with dark brown eyes and sweet smiles.

Foster was sitting in a chair beside Trey's desk, still handcuffed, when Trey got there. Chia Rodriguez was staring at him, trying to picture him stuffing a dead baby in a suitcase, while her partner, David Sheets, was leaning against a nearby desk with his arms crossed against his chest. They both looked up when Trey walked into the room.

"How do you do it?" Sheets asked as Trey walked past him and unlocked the handcuffs from Lawrence's wrists.

"Do what?" Trey asked, dropping the handcuffs into a drawer.

"Come out smellin' like a rose? Me and Chia Pet here bust our rumps, while you just dally here and there, catching bad guys between coffee breaks and making us look like slackers."

Chia frowned at her partner.

"Oh, shut up, Sheets. You cry like a girl." Then she snorted beneath her breath. "I just insulted my own gender."

"Thanks for keeping an eye on him," Trey said.

"No sweat," Chia said. "You want some company?"

"Stick around," Trey said. "He might have some

information for you about the fire."

Foster glanced at the female cop.

"The fire? At the hotel? Why didn't you say something sooner? Hell, lady, I thought you were just admiring the shine on my head."

Chia ignored his sarcasm.

"Tell me what you saw," she asked.

"I was leaving Dallas for good," Foster said. "If I'd left fifteen, maybe thirty, minutes earlier, I would have been long gone before all that happened."

"Did you see anything? Anyone suspicious?" Chia said.

"No. I was going down the stairs and ran into smoke between the third and second floors. It was knee high and climbing, so I backtracked. It wasn't long before I could feel the heat, too. I started yelling 'fire' and kept running up. About the fourth floor, I heard other people coming up behind me. We got to the roof. You know the rest."

"While you were on the roof, did you hear anyone mention anything?"

"Lady, there was just a lot of screaming and crying."

"Yeah, all right," Chia said. "But, if you think of anything—"

"I'll be sure and give you a call," Foster said, and then glanced at Trey. "Depending on how many calls I'm going to be allowed, of course."

"I keep telling you that you're not under arrest," Trey said.

"So talk to me," Foster said. "They said I'm wanted

for questioning. Question me. I have a life I'd like to get on with."

Trey sat down on the edge of his desk, then propped one shoe on the side of his chair as he stared down at the man.

"When you got out of Lompoc, why did you come back to Dallas?"

"To get the ransom I'd stashed," Foster said.

It was the last thing Trey had expected him to say.

"So did you get it?"

"Yeah, sure, and I was living the high life in the Henry-Dean Hotel when it caught fire." Then he laughed. "Actually, I think I'm jinxed by fire."

"What do you mean?"

"The ransom . . . I hid it in the basement of a restaurant called Lazy Days. So I come back to Dallas to retrieve it and find out that the damn place burned down years ago." Foster laughed and slapped his hand on his knee. "Isn't that a hoot? It's gone. What's worse, they went and built a federal savings and loan on the spot. Got guards out the wazoo, and I'm in no frame of mind to go back to lockup. I get myself a room to figure out what to do next and the hotel catches on fire. So I'm saying to myself that it's time to get out of Dallas. Then you came along, and, well, here I am."

The whole scenario was so outrageous that Trey had to believe it, but there were far bigger problems to consider than a pile of burnt-up money.

"Since you know you were wanted for questioning,

then I'm guessing you also know why," Trey said.

Foster's expression closed. "Somebody found a dead baby."

"Yes, somebody did find a dead baby, or what's left of her."

"I didn't have a damn thing to do with killing. I don't hold with it."

"But you stole a child from her parents and demanded money before you'd give her back."

Foster thought about what he knew and figured the more he told, the deeper the shit in which he'd be standing.

"I said it then, and they still put me in prison, so telling it all over again doesn't seem wise. However, I didn't have a damn thing to do with murder or kidnapping. I just walked in after the fact and did something stupid. I saw a way to make a bunch of fast money. And if it hadn't been for me, that kid would never have been returned."

Trey stood abruptly and circled his desk. He pulled out a file, shuffled through some pages, then tossed the file back on his desk before turning to Foster.

"You never said that before," Trey said.

Foster looked nervous.

"Said what?"

"That if it hadn't been for you, Olivia Sealy would never have been returned to her family."

"Yes, I did. I took her back to the mall, remember?"

"But you never said that it was against someone else's wishes," Trey said.

Foster shifted nervously in his seat, then looked down at the floor.

"Who was it?" Trey asked. "Who was the other person involved in the kidnapping?"

"I've done served my time," Foster muttered. "You can't put me back in jail for this, so why don't you leave me the hell alone?"

"I'm not trying to pin the kidnapping on you," Trey said. "I'm talking murder. Somebody killed a baby, stuck it in a suitcase and hid it behind a wall."

"It wasn't me," Foster said.

"You had your hands on one of them. Why should I believe you didn't kill the other one?"

Foster frowned. "I'm not getting this. What does one have to do with the other?"

"Both babies were the same age. Both babies were born with two left thumbs, an anomaly that runs in the Sealy family, and both babies had the same father."

Foster's eyes widened, and his mouth went slack. He shook his head. "I only saw one kid . . . the one I took to the mall. I don't know anything about a second one." Sweat beads formed across his bald forehead and his upper lip. "You have to believe me. I didn't know."

Trey glanced up at Chia and Sheets, who seemed as riveted by the new revelations as Foster Lawrence. Trey didn't know whether to believe him or not, and from the look on Chia's face, she didn't, either. Trey looked back at Lawrence, then started in on him again.

"So talk to me, Lawrence. Exactly how *did* you get

mixed up in the kidnapping?"

Foster thought about it long and hard. He'd served twenty-five years with his mouth shut, and all it had done was get him in trouble all over again. He wouldn't go back to prison.

"I want a lawyer," Foster said. "I don't trust any of you, so if you want any more information from me, I want it in writing that whatever I tell you, it will be my 'get out of jail free' card."

Trey stifled a curse. He'd been so close to finding out what he needed to know, and now Lawrence was going to lawyer up.

"You want a lawyer, you'll wait for him in jail," Trey said, and put the handcuffs back on Foster's wrists.

Foster's face paled, but he wouldn't budge.

"Damn you," he muttered as Trey led him away.

"No, damn you," Trey countered. "Somebody killed a baby and stuffed it in a suitcase, and I think you know who did it. You're protecting a baby killer, which means you could haul the entire first string of the Dallas Cowboys off a burning building and it still wouldn't make you a hero to me."

"I didn't set out to be no hero," Foster muttered. "I was just trying to save my own hide."

"Figures," Trey said, and kept moving.

Trey got down to booking and dealt with the paperwork, ignoring the constant muttering coming from Lawrence, then handed him over. Foster was still talking about his rights and demanding a lawyer when Trey left.

Marcus had taken some painkillers for a headache, then showered and shaved without particular care for how he looked. He just wanted the night to be over. Sitting across a dinner table from Terrence was going to be nothing short of misery, having to keep up a civil conversation was almost impossible. If not for Carolyn, he wouldn't bother.

He'd made a reservation at the hotel restaurant and was in the lobby, waiting for them, when they arrived.

Carolyn saw Marcus first, threw up her hands in a gesture of delight and came toward him. She gave him a big hug, then kissed him on both cheeks before turning to her husband.

"Terrence! Would you look at Marcus? I swear he hasn't aged a day since we left."

Terrence Sealy nodded and smiled, but, like Marcus, obviously felt uncomfortable.

"I'm afraid I can't say the same," Terrence said, and patted his thinning hair and thickening waist. "Too much good pasta and wine."

Carolyn smiled adoringly. "Oh, Terry, you always look wonderful to me."

Terrence's smile shifted, as did the tone of his voice.

"And don't think I don't appreciate it," he said softly.

"Our table is ready," Marcus said abruptly, which put a quick end to their billing and cooing.

They sat, ordered appetizers and wine, then, as they waited, addressed the subject of why they'd come.

"Am I to understand that they no longer need DNA from me?" Terrence asked.

Marcus hardly knew what to say. "I couldn't say for certain, but it's doubtful. It's too bad you were already en route, or you wouldn't have had to come after all."

"Oh, we didn't really *have* to come. We could have done all the testing from there, but we felt horrible about what was happening and wanted to come give our support," Carolyn said.

"Thank you," Marcus said. "I'm just sorry that Olivia isn't able to be here with us."

Carolyn fiddled nervously with the silverware as they waited.

"I still can't get over what happened to her. It's just awful. Some crazed man attacked her without provocation? Is that right?"

"Basically," Marcus said. "He was delusional and guilt-ridden over some previous crime, and he thought that killing Olivia would be reparation enough that God would forgive him for his first mistake."

Terrence's expression darkened. Neither man would have admitted or wanted to acknowledge it, but their resemblance to each other had grown as they aged. Carolyn, however, jumped right on it.

"Look at him," she said, pointing to her husband. "You two could pass for brothers."

A muscle jumped in Marcus's jaw, and Terrence quickly looked away.

Then Carolyn laid her hand on Marcus's arm and lowered her voice.

"This must be so difficult for you. Finding out that Michael . . . well, you know."

"They're going to question you," Marcus said.

She looked taken aback.

"Me? But why?"

"Because I made the mistake of mentioning that you and Michael had always been close friends. The detective, Trey Bonney, is hoping you'll be able to come up with something to help them find out who the mother of the other baby might be."

Carolyn's face flushed pink, then a ghostly shade of pale.

"I'm sorry, Carolyn, but I wanted to warn you."

Terrence's eyebrows knitted angrily.

"Look here, Marcus. Just because—"

"Hush, dear," Carolyn said sharply. "This is a horrible thing, and I'm happy to do my part, although, to be honest, I don't think I'll be much help."

"Thank you," Marcus said. "Oh good, here come our drinks."

"And the appetizers look marvelous," Carolyn said.

She picked up a small triangle of toast with a sliver of roast beef and a dollop of horseradish sauce, and popped it into her mouth.

"That is so good," she said, then picked up another and aimed it at Terrence's mouth. "Open wide."

He obliged, then made all the proper noises about the blending of tastes while Marcus wished him to hell and gone.

And so the evening passed.

• • •

Anna was crying. She didn't know where she was or how she'd gotten there. She kept opening doors and staring at the clothes hanging in the closet, and peering in drawers at her underwear folded there. She was pretty sure they were hers. She thought she remembered them in her laundry, but she couldn't find her washer or her dryer, and when she wanted to go outside, they wouldn't let her past this floor.

She felt as if she was in prison, but she couldn't figure out why. She hadn't done anything wrong. She was a good person. Everybody said so. And she kept looking for her little Olivia. She'd promised Mr. Marcus she would come home with him and look after her again, but they were nowhere to be found. She'd asked a woman for the telephone, but the woman had told her to go back to her room; then she'd taken Anna by the arm and walked her there herself.

Now Anna was sitting in the dark on the edge of her bed, watching the pictures changing on the television screen without acknowledging what she saw. It wasn't until the evening news came on and she saw the footage of a fire in a downtown hotel that she began to moan.

The fire was big. People were standing on a roof waving and crying while a helicopter took them one by one to safety.

There had been a fire at her house. No. Not her house. Someone else's house. The fire trucks had come there, too. She closed her eyes, trying to remember.

Rose was in the kitchen. They were cooking. The television was on. Rose saw the fire, too. It was big and burning up the building.

Daisies. There were daisies on the wall. *I took them off the wall and laid them down. Daisies aren't supposed to be on the wall. They're supposed to be in water. But there wasn't water. Only fire.*

Anna slid off the end of the bed and crawled into a corner of the room, then turned her face to the wall. A few minutes later, someone came into her room and called out a name, but she didn't recognize it. The footsteps came closer. Someone touched her shoulder.

"Anna . . . would you like me to help you into bed?"

"Who's Anna?"

"You are, dear. Now let's get up off the floor and into bed."

Anna grabbed at her arm, then pulled herself up.

"Somebody, please, I'm lost. I don't know the way home. Someone needs to come and get me now. I want to go home."

"I know, dear. But you don't feel very well, and I think you need to feel better first, don't you?"

Anna let herself be led to the bed; then the woman took off Anna's shoes and sweater, pulled back the covers and helped her lie down.

"There now, doesn't that feel better?" the woman asked.

Anna's arms felt empty. "I can't find my Olivia. I take care of her, you know. She likes to be rocked to sleep, and I can't find her."

237

"I'll help you look tomorrow, okay? Here, open your mouth."

Anna did as she was told and felt something being dropped on her tongue.

"Take a sip of water, dear. This will help you sleep."

"I'm tired, aren't I?" Anna said.

The woman stroked Anna's face, then her hair.

"Yes, dear, I believe you are."

Anna sighed. It was good for someone to tell her things. She'd forgotten so many things on her own that it was good to know what she was supposed to do.

15

Terrence Sealy stared at himself in the mirror, looking for signs of the man he used to be. He didn't know whether he was kidding himself or not, maybe letting himself believe that man no longer existed because he couldn't bear to be alive in this man's skin.

He touched his face. His jowls were sagging. He vaguely remembered his father's face looking a bit like this, although the eyes were different. He remembered his father's expression as more dissolute. He'd been such a bastard, his father, but as much as he'd hated him and as hard as he'd tried to be different, he'd turned out just like him. There wasn't a day of his life when he didn't relive what he'd done to Amelia or remember the hate and rage on Marcus's face when he'd come into his room. There were days when he could deal with it, and

238

then there were other times, like tonight, when he wished he'd never lived through the beating.

He heard a sound behind him. He didn't have to look to know it was Carolyn. When she came up behind him, he saw the tears in her eyes. He hated it when she cried.

"Don't," he said, and opened his arms.

"You're a good man, Terrence Sealy."

Terrence sighed as he pulled her close.

"You're the only one who thinks so."

"You didn't mean to. You were hurt. You were drunk."

He started to shake. "I fucking raped my cousin's fiancée the night before her wedding. If it had happened to you, would it have been okay?"

Carolyn's face crumpled. "I love you, Terry. I always have. I always will."

"I know . . . and I thank God every day of my life for you, but it doesn't change what I think about myself."

"We shouldn't have come back here," she said. "It's all my fault. I wanted to come home so bad that I didn't think of what it might do to you."

"No . . . no . . . don't talk like that. We had no choice, and you know it. We couldn't leave Marcus to deal with this horror alone." Then he looked at Carolyn closer. "Did you?"

"Did I what?" she asked.

"Know anything . . . about Michael having an affair, I mean?"

Carolyn frowned. "No . . . at least . . . I don't think so."

"What do you mean?"

Carolyn leaned against him, taking comfort from the strength of his embrace.

"Once or twice I caught Kay crying. I didn't think anything of it at the time. You know . . . couples fuss. Couples make up. But maybe she knew something."

"What are you going to tell the police?"

She shrugged. "What can I tell them but the truth?"

Rose sat in her sister's living room, trying to ignore the loud, obnoxious voice of her brother-in-law's demands. To this day, she couldn't understand how her sister could have married him. As children they'd been the darlings of the family; as young adults, they'd had many opportunities to succeed; and yet here they were, a cook for a rich man and a doormat for a drunk.

Rose rarely let herself dwell on the past. She'd had everything going for her. A man who loved her—or so she thought—and promises of a happy-ever-after life. It just hadn't happened.

She folded her hands neatly in her lap and pasted a quiet smile on her face as her brother-in-law fell asleep, passed out in a chair on the other side of the room. She was upset about what had happened with Anna. She'd assured Mr. Marcus that she could handle the woman; then, the moment she'd turned her back, Anna had set fire to the house. She wanted to cry. If they fired her, she would be devastated. Then she told herself that they weren't like that. They wouldn't blame her for something a crazy woman did.

Rose pushed off in the rocker and set it to moving. It squeaked softly with every motion. One of the rockers needed to be reglued. If it belonged to her, she would already have seen to the problem. She didn't know why her sister was so slovenly. Then she glanced at her brother-in-law and sighed. If she had to live with someone like him, she might let things slide, too.

"Rose . . . supper is ready. Come and eat!"

Rose winced. Her sister didn't have to shout. She was only in the other room. Still, beggars couldn't be choosers, so she got up and moved into the kitchen and tried not to think of the woman who'd set fire to her world.

Trey had been up for hours, going over everything he had on the case of Baby Jane Doe, which was little to nothing. He'd researched the brand of suitcase the bones had been in, looked for artists who specialized in woodwork and wood-burning art with a bent toward religion, and read all there was to be had on Foster Lawrence.

According to the background check, Lawrence was the youngest of five children, born to a single mother who seemed to make a living out of having babies, the total of her monthly welfare check going up with each birth.

The oldest child was a boy named James, who had died in a gang war when he was sixteen. The second child, a girl named Cheryl, had overdosed at the age of twenty-two and was in a coma in some state-run institution back in Cleveland. The next two children had been twin girls, Laree and Sheree. There was no information on them past the age of eighteen. Then there was Foster, the youngest, who, except for a couple of scrapes with the law in his teens, had no record whatsoever. Until the Sealy kidnapping.

And to Trey, that was what didn't add up. Kidnapping was a federal offense. Perps who got involved in high crimes like that usually had priors. It wasn't normal for some ordinary person to make that kind of leap—unless there were extenuating circumstances. Sometimes during a divorce one parent would kidnap a child from a custodial parent, but it wasn't common for someone to get involved as deeply as Foster Lawrence had done without a reason other than money. He needed to get Foster to open up.

He had gone to sleep dreaming of the case, trying to think what it would take to make a fairly decent man get mixed up in something as vile as murder and kidnapping. Lawrence hadn't been known to run with any particular crowd. There wasn't anyone—except his siblings—to whom Foster Lawrence had been attached.

It was with that thought in mind that Trey awoke. He knew what had happened to two of Lawrence's siblings. Just for the hell of it, he decided to find out where the twin sisters were. If Foster had stayed in contact with them, they might know who he'd been hanging out with. It could be the lead he needed to find the killer of Baby Jane Doe. Just as he was closing the last file, his alarm went off.

"Well, damn," Trey muttered when he realized it was time to start a new day. Then he remembered what was happening this morning. Livvie. He was bringing Livvie home today.

Exhaustion was forgotten as he headed for the shower.

Olivia was dressed and waiting when she heard Trey's footsteps outside her door. She stood up in anticipation, not just because she was finally getting out of the hospital, but because Trey was coming to take her home with him. She'd spent most of her high-school years wanting this to happen, but it never had. Back in high school, he'd been part of a family, however imperfect, and she'd been so envious. His father had a reputation for being a hard drinker, but Trey loved him. His mother waited tables in a restaurant and paid their electric bill from her tips, and he adored her. He had two older brothers, one who was career military, and the other a fireman in Houston, who bragged about their little brother, the football star, to all their friends. The Bonney family could have paid off the mortgage on their house with what Marcus spent in one year for Olivia's clothes. They hadn't wanted her in Trey's life any more than Marcus had wanted Trey in hers. Yet here they were, eleven years later, back in each other's lives. For Olivia, it was a dream come true.

She patted nervously at her hair, wishing she could have styled it, but heartily glad just to have it clean. She'd been given permission to shower this morning and had been almost giddy at the news. It wasn't until she'd had to endure several days of enduring bed baths that she'd realized the true freedom of being able to bathe on her own.

Her gaze focused on the door, waiting for it to move. When it began to swing inward, she caught herself holding her breath. Then she saw Trey silhouetted in the doorway. Tears suddenly blurred her vision, but she blinked them away.

"Hey, you're up and dressed," Trey said as he carefully took her in his arms. Ever careful of her injuries, he hugged her gently, then bent down and kissed her square on the lips.

Olivia groaned softly.

Trey sighed.

"Hold that thought," he said, and cupped the back of her head as she rested her forehead against his chest.

"Holding on for dear life," she said.

"Are you ready to go?" he asked.

"I just have to sign some papers at the nurses' station on the way out."

"Is that your wheelchair?" he asked, pointing to the one against the wall.

"Yes, they won't let me walk out."

"That's okay," Trey said. "I'm all about following the rules." He took her by the arm and led her to the wheelchair. "Your carriage awaits, my love."

Olivia shivered as she sat. "Am I, Trey?"

Trey grinned as he knelt to flip down the footrests.

"Are you what, Livvie?"

"Your love?"

The grin disappeared. "Yes, ma'am, you sure are."

"You don't think this is all happening too fast?"

"Do you?"

Olivia shook her head, then cupped Trey's cheek with her hand.

"No way, but what did happen too fast was the almost-end of my life. That's what was startling. After I woke up and realized I was still breathing, I made myself a promise that I would never live another day with regrets. So, for better or for worse, I'm baring my heart to you, Trey. I've always regretted the way our first relationship ended. When I asked you for a second chance, I was serious. I admit we have a lot of catching up to do, but I'm so ready for this to begin."

Trey turned her hands palms up, kissing first one, then the other.

"So am I, Livvie, so am I," he said.

Then he stood, slung the strap of her overnight bag over his shoulder and grabbed the handles of the wheelchair.

"Let's blow this joint," he said.

"Yes, please," Olivia said as he wheeled her away.

Within the hour, Trey was pulling into his driveway. He liked his house. It was comfortable in every way that mattered to him, but there was a moment of hesitation as he wondered how Olivia would view it.

The single-story three-bedroom redbrick house was about twenty years old. Trey had owned it for almost ten. Over the years he'd added a veranda in front and a small pool in the back. Crepe myrtle bushes encircled the yard in lieu of a fence. Olivia could smell the thick, sweet scent of their blooms as Trey opened the door.

"This is beautiful," Olivia said. "Did you do the landscaping?"

Trey shrugged. "Yeah, if you want to call it that. There's more in the backyard around the pool."

"You have a pool, too?"

He grinned. "Yeah, Livvie, I have a pool, too."

"Great. The doctor said water therapy would be helpful for my shoulder." Then she looked at him and grinned. "And seeing you in a swimsuit wouldn't be so bad, either."

Trey leaned across the seat until his mouth was just a few inches from her lips.

"I don't wear a swimsuit when I swim," he said.

Olivia's eyes widened.

"What about your neighbors?"

"There's a privacy fence in the backyard."

"Oh."

"Come on, Livvie, it's time to get you inside and in bed."

"My kind of man," Olivia muttered. "No sense wasting time on foreplay."

Trey frowned. "In bed as in resting."

"I know. I was just testing you."

Trey chalked her sarcasm up to nerves.

"Come on, Livvie, relax. We're going to get you inside, get your feet up and your shoes off. Ella will be over any time I give her the call, so after I leave, you won't be alone, okay?"

Olivia was feeling a little vulnerable and didn't know what she thought about being forced to spend the day with a stranger. But then she realized she'd been doing that very thing for the last week in the hospital. At least here she had the freedom of the house.

"Yes, okay," she said. "I am feeling a little tired."

Trey frowned. "Sorry, honey, why didn't you say so? I don't know what I was thinking."

He got her out, but instead of helping her inside, he picked her up and carried her to the door. He set her down only long enough to unlock the door, then picked her up again and carried her inside.

Olivia had fleeting glimpses of large, airy rooms, a big-screen television, overstuffed furniture, hardwood floors and a desk piled high with folders, papers and a computer.

"This will be your room," Trey said as he set her down on the side of a queen-size sleigh bed, then pulled back the covers. "My room is right across the hall, so all you'll need to do is call out and I'll come running."

"Okay."

He cupped the side of her face.

"Relax, Livvie . . . we've got the rest of our lives to get through this awkward stage. All I want from you now is for you to get well."

"I know. I want that, too."

"Do you want your nightgown?"

"What I would really like is my old T-shirt, but it's at

my house, so I guess the nightgown will have to do."

"What's so special about that T-shirt?" Trey asked.

"It's big and old and soft."

"Just a minute," Trey said, and hurried out of the room. He came back with what looked like a large white rag. "Try this," he said, and spread it out on the bed. There was a big DPD, Dallas Police Department, logo on the front.

Olivia started to grin. "How long have you had that?"

"Since the police academy . . . which would be at least ten years."

"You sure you don't mind me wearing it?" Olivia said.

"Honey, both I and the Dallas police force will be honored to know you've been inside it." Then he eyed her shoulder. "Need any help getting undressed?"

"No, I think I can handle it."

"I'm going to get your bag out of the car. You get comfortable and then crawl into bed."

He winked as he left, and Olivia had an urge to pinch herself. A month ago she'd been dallying across Europe with Grampy, resigned to the single life. So much had changed in such a short time. Their family was now under scrutiny by the media and the police and somehow mixed up in the death of a toddler. She'd been shot, lived through a wreck that should have killed her, and in the midst of all that sorrow and shock, she'd been reunited with her first love. It was difficult to believe, but here she was, in Trey Bonney's house.

Carefully, she took off her clothes and slipped into

Trey's old T-shirt. It was soft and threadbare in places, and it clung to the thrust of her breasts with the familiarity of an old friend.

Olivia savored the comfort of the soft fabric against the healing wound on her shoulder as she got into bed. The pillow cradled her head as the mattress gave way to her weight. She pulled the sheet and coverlet up to her waist, then wiggled slightly until she found a comfortable spot. The cool sheets and the crisp pillowcase smelled faintly of flowers, reminding Olivia of the beautiful border of dark purple crepe myrtle blooming outside.

A few moments later Trey was back, carrying her bag and a glass of water. He dug the pain pills out of her bag, poured the required dose into his hand, then handed them to her.

"Here, honey. You'll rest better."

She put them in her mouth, then sipped from the glass Trey held for her. By the time she'd lain back down on the pillow, she was exhausted.

"Thank you so much," she said softly.

Trey laid his hand briefly on the top of her head.

"You're welcome, baby. I'm going to call Ella to come over. You two can introduce yourselves later. Just rest, knowing that if you need help, someone will be here."

Olivia looked up at Trey as he hovered over the bed.

"I'll be fine. Go catch bad guys. I'll be here when you get back."

Emotion caught Trey unaware as he watched her

close her eyes. He stood there for a moment, trying to absorb the fact that Olivia was really in bed in his house. He wanted to believe that something good was going to come of this. He wanted to believe with all his heart that this was the beginning of the rest of their lives together. He wanted to—and a part of him already did—but he'd been burned before. Only time would tell if the memory of the love they'd once shared would be strong enough to sustain them through a renewal of more than passion.

"Love you, baby," he said softly.

Olivia's eyes were already closed, but she managed a sweet sigh, then an "I love you, too."

Trey waited until her breathing was slow and even, then he left to call Ella.

She answered on the first ring.

"I'm on my way," she said.

Trey grinned. "And how did you know it was me?"

"Caller ID," she said smartly, and hung up in his ear.

He replaced the receiver and headed for the door. She was on the doorstep by the time he opened it, wearing pink warm-up pants and a matching pink T-shirt.

"I really appreciate this," Trey said, trying not to stare at the large silver hoops dangling from her earlobes.

"Hey, I'm happy to do my part to get you married off," Ella said, and fluffed at her white, spiky hair.

"How do you like my new do?" she asked.

Trey grinned. "Pretty sharp. You look like you're dressed for the kill. Who's the lucky man?"

Ella smirked. "Hershel Mynor. He owns a chain of

funeral parlors. Pretty convenient, huh? Maybe I'll get myself buried for free."

"Lord, Ella. What a thing to plan for," Trey muttered.

"Well, it's what people my age do, you know. We can't leave everything for our kids to deal with. Besides, my daughter-in-law's taste leaves a lot to be desired. It would be just like her to pick out some god-awful casket with so many ruffles and ribbons that I'll look like a first-place show horse at the state fair."

Trey laughed out loud, then gave her a hug.

"Woman, if I was just a little bit older, I'd give you a run for the money."

"Sorry to disappoint you, cowboy, but you're not my type. Now show me your girl."

"She's asleep," Trey said.

"That's okay. I don't want to talk to her yet. I'm just curious about what kind of woman it takes to get under your skin."

Trey walked her down the hall, where they peeked into the room where Olivia was sleeping.

Ella glanced at Olivia, then turned her attention to Trey. She could tell by the look on his face that he was hooked. They moved back into the living room before she gave him her opinion.

"Well, all I can say is, she'd better be good to you, because I'd hate to have to whip someone who's been that hurt."

"Go easy on her, Ella. She's had a hell of a week."

Ella nodded as her expression softened.

"Yes, I heard all about it on the news." Then she

frowned. "Being rich and famous isn't always all it's cracked up to be, is it, boy?"

"No, ma'am, it's sure not."

"So, go do your thing. We'll be here when you get back."

He kissed her on the cheek.

"I owe you big-time."

"You can clean my gutters this fall."

He groaned.

Ella chuckled.

And then he was gone.

16

Trey got back to headquarters just as Chia and Sheets were coming out of Lieutenant Warren's office.

"What do we know about the fire?" Trey asked.

"Why . . . you needin' another arrest on your record?" David Sheets snapped, then swiped at a lock of his hair that had fallen into his eyes, messing up his comb-over.

"You need to cut that damn thing off," Chia said, and swiped it back in place on her way to her desk.

David's expression never wavered as he fired back at her, "Yeah, well, I'll cut mine when you cut yours, Chia Pet."

The reference to her thick, unruly curls went by the wayside as Chia poured herself some fresh coffee, then toasted her partner with a grin.

"The fondness between you two is touching," Trey

drawled, "but can anyone answer the question?"

"Yeah, we know who started it, for all the good it does."

"What?" Trey asked.

David grimaced. "Some drugged-out mother left her three kids, ages seven, four and two, all alone in the apartment. The four-year-old found a cigarette lighter. The rest is history."

"Damn, that's rough," Trey said. "How did you find out?"

"Where's my coffee cup?" David muttered, and moved toward his desk.

Chia sighed. It had been a rough morning for both of them.

"The seven-year-old was one of the survivors. She told, just before she died."

Trey sucked in a breath, then turned away. Sometimes saying nothing was the kindest comment of all. He sat down at his own desk, pulled a file out of the top drawer and turned on the computer. He saw Chia move closer.

"How's your girl?" she asked.

"Good. She was released from the hospital this morning."

Chia frowned. "I thought the Sealy house caught fire yesterday."

"It did."

"So the house is still livable, then?"

Trey sighed. He knew Chia. She wouldn't quit until she was satisfied she'd sucked all the info from him that she wanted.

"Actually, she's staying at my house for a few days. My neighbor, Ella, is staying with her during the day."

"So . . . Olivia Sealy is at your house."

"Yeah."

"Verrry interesting."

"Chia?"

"Yeah?"

"Shut up."

He heard a snort but kept his focus on the computer screen.

A couple of minutes passed before Chia came at him from another angle.

"So, what are you looking for?"

"I'm looking to see if Foster Lawrence's twin sisters were ever in the system."

"Any luck?"

"Not yet."

"Want some help? I'm better at that stuff than you are."

Trey grinned. "That's not saying much. Anybody's better at working computers than I am."

Chia rolled her eyes. "Give me the files. Tell me what you want."

"I want to find Lawrence's twin sisters. Their names were Laree and Sheree Lawrence. Identical twins. But there's no record of them in the files after the age of eighteen."

Chia nodded.

"What are we hoping to learn?" she asked as she logged on to her computer.

"I don't know. Maybe nothing, and then again, maybe finding someone important enough to Lawrence that he would get mixed up in kidnapping and murder."

Chia nodded and typed in a search engine. When Trey didn't immediately move away, she stopped and looked up.

"Don't you have something else to do . . . like charming heiresses or capturing bad guys?"

"You're starting to sound like your partner," Trey said.

Chia groaned. "Sorry. Just chalk it up to a really bad morning."

Trey thought about the seven-year-old child who'd died this morning.

"I can only imagine. So, anyway, thanks for the help," Trey said. "I've got an interview with another branch of the Sealy family. They just flew in from Italy. There's a chance that Mrs. Sealy might have some information we can use."

"If I come up with anything on the Lawrence twins, I'll call," Chia said.

"Thanks again," Trey said, and hurried out the door.

The Mansion on Turtle Creek was one of Dallas's finest restaurants. The adjoining hotel matched it in both service and style. Trey couldn't help noticing the quiet elegance and the studied manner of the employees as he strode through the lobby to the front desk.

"I'm here to see Mr. Terrence Sealy," he said, and

flashed his badge. "Would you ring his room and tell him that Detective Bonney is here?"

The desk clerk's expression never wavered as he calmly picked up a house phone.

"Mr. Sealy, this is Carlos at the front desk. Detective Bonney is here to see you."

When the call came, Terrence glanced at Carolyn and nodded. They'd been expecting the call.

"Send him up," Terrence said.

"Yes, sir, thank you, sir," the desk clerk said, then gave Trey the suite number and pointed in the direction of the elevators.

Trey nodded a thanks as he walked away. A couple of minutes later he exited, pausing long enough on the floor to ascertain which direction he needed to go, then turned to the right. His thoughts were on Baby Jane Doe, and the promise he'd made to her in the house at Lake Texoma. He needed a break in the case.

Moments later, he knocked on the door.

It swung inward almost instantly, which told him that they'd been waiting right inside for his arrival.

"Detective Trey Bonney, Dallas homicide," he said, and flashed his badge.

Terrence Sealy nodded cordially and shook Trey's hand.

"Do come in, Detective Bonney. This is my wife, Carolyn. Can we offer you something to drink? A coffee? Maybe some juice?"

"I'm good," Trey said, then turned to the woman. She was tall and thin to the point of skinny, but very well kept. Her shoulder-length hair was a faded ash-blond and turned under at the ends. Her makeup was skillfully applied, hiding the years life had put on her face. "Mrs. Sealy, it's a pleasure to meet you."

Carolyn smiled, and Trey was struck by the sadness in her smile.

"Please, have a seat," she said, then led the way to the sofa in the sitting room. As soon as they'd all been seated, Carolyn took the initiative. "Marcus tells us that you and Olivia are old friends."

Trey was a little taken aback, then realized he should have been prepared for this. He busied himself by taking out his notebook as he answered.

"Yes, ma'am. We went to high school together."

"We were so sorry to learn of her injuries, weren't we, Terry?"

Terrence Sealy's expression of dismay was obviously real. Trey could see the horror of what had happened to Livvie mirrored on their faces.

"I still can't believe all this is happening," Terrence said.

"Marcus also tells us that you're kindly providing a place for Olivia to recuperate until the repairs on their house are finished."

"Yes, ma'am. My next-door neighbor is looking after her while I'm at work."

"I can't wait to see her," Carolyn said.

Trey was beginning to realize that by taking Olivia home, he'd involved himself with the very family he was investigating. He would have to talk to his lieutenant about it, but for now, what was done was done.

"I'll give you my phone number and address before I leave," Trey said. "I know Livvie would love to see you."

Carolyn smiled. "She was only two when we left, but we correspond regularly."

Trey nodded, but it was time to get down to the business of why he was there.

"I hate to change the subject so abruptly, but I'm hoping you might have some information about Michael Sealy's personal life."

Carolyn's face paled, but her gaze never wavered.

"Neither Terry nor I knew he'd been having an affair until we arrived and learned that he'd fathered both Olivia and the other child."

"Brief as her life was," Trey muttered.

Carolyn tilted her chin a bit upward. It was her only concession to the anger she heard in the detective's voice.

"So, how can I help you?" she asked.

"Did you truly have no suspicions that Michael Sealy was having an affair?"

She never hesitated. "No, although learning of it now, there were a few signs back then that might have given it away had I pursued the issue."

"How so?" Trey asked.

"Once or twice I caught Kay crying," Carolyn said. "She was my best friend, and we were almost the same age."

"My wife is nearly twenty years younger than I," Terrence added, then wondered why he'd felt the need to say that.

Trey only nodded.

Carolyn reached for Terrence's hand and clutched it tightly, as if she needed the comfort of his touch to keep her focus.

"About those incidents," Trey said. "Did you ask her why she was crying?"

"Yes, both times, but she was vague. I just assumed they'd had a tiff and considered it none of my business."

"Did you ever see Michael with another woman . . . someone you didn't know?"

"No. I've thought about nothing else since I learned about the other child. I wish I did know something, but I don't."

Again Trey's hopes were dimmed. The weight of the unsolved murder was growing heavier and heavier to bear.

Then Terrence spoke up. "You know, Carolyn . . . there was that time when we saw Michael and that woman coming out of that office building downtown. Remember? It was right after Christmas, and you commented on the fur coat she was wearing and said someone must certainly have had a nice Christmas. I remember, because we'd just sold your fur coat to pay some bills." He added for Trey's sake, without apology, "We needed the money. We were going to move."

Trey's gaze shifted to Carolyn Sealy's face, watching as her eyebrows knitted in thought.

"No, I—oh! Yes, I do recall the incident, but didn't he say she was his insurance agent? And that was only a day or so after Kay had wrecked their new car, remember? The roads were icy, and we were all so relieved she hadn't been hurt."

"I remember that Kay wrecked a car," Terrence said. "But what if the woman wasn't an insurance agent? As I recall, Marcus kept all the family cars under one policy—his. There would have been no reason for Michael to be meeting with the agent, since the policies weren't in his name."

Trey's pulse kicked. "What did she look like?" he asked. "Do you remember if he mentioned her name?"

Carolyn frowned. "I think she was just above-average height. I remember because her head came to about Michael's shoulder. She had long dark hair, and I only remember that because it was just a few shades lighter than the mink she was wearing, but I'm terrible with names. If he ever introduced us, I don't remember."

"I think I do," Terrence said. "And don't ask me why something like this stuck in my mind for so many years, but it has."

"The name," Trey urged as he continued to make notes. "Do you remember her name?"

"The reason I remember it is because at first I thought he said her name was Larry, and I was appalled that someone would name their daughter Larry. Then he repeated the name, and I realized he was saying, Laree, with the emphasis on the last syllable. You know . . . La-*ree*."

Trey's hand stilled. "You're sure?"

Terrence shrugged. "As sure as I can be at the age of seventy-two."

"Son of a—" Trey caught himself before he finished what he'd been going to say. "Sorry. I didn't mean to say that aloud."

"You know who she might be?" Terrence asked.

"Maybe," Trey said. "Maybe. At any rate, I have to thank you for coming all this way. You just may have given me the link I've been looking for."

Terrence looked pleased.

"You will let us know if anything pans out?" he asked.

"The Sealy family will be the first to know," Trey said. "That I can promise you."

Carolyn stood. "Is there anything else?"

Trey quickly wrote down his phone number and address on a sheet of notepaper from his book and tore it out, then handed it to her.

"Livvie was asleep when I left her this morning, but Ella will answer the phone. If Livvie's awake, I know she'll be happy to hear from you."

"I notice you call her Livvie," Carolyn said.

"Yes, ma'am. I used to tease her and tell her that Olivia sounded too stuffy and proper for a girl who could finish off a banana split in under five minutes."

Terrence chuckled. "That's our girl."

"Detective, I'm thinking you like our Olivia very much, don't you?" Carolyn said.

"Yes, ma'am, I do."

"Good. She's given Marcus far too much of her life."

Trey shook their hands. "Thank you for your time. You've been most helpful."

"It's our pleasure," Terrence said as he followed Trey to the door. "I'm sure we'll be seeing you again," he added.

"Probably so," Trey said. "If I have any other questions, I'll call."

"Yes, of course," Terrence added.

Trey nodded to Carolyn, then quickly left. He was anxious to contact Chia and see if she'd come up with anything on the Lawrence twins. For the first time since he'd been handed the case, it was starting to make sense. If you got yourself in hot water, who else would you call but someone you could trust? And who better than a member of your own family? If Laree Lawrence had been the woman with whom Michael Sealy was having the affair, then it might explain Foster Lawrence's sudden dip into a life of crime. With this new information, he was determined to talk to Lawrence again.

Lawrence had, as promised, lawyered up. Trey's trip to jail was a bust, because Lawrence refused to talk to Trey without his lawyer present, and the lawyer was in court.

Foster had glared at Trey, then refused to look at him again, despite anything Trey had to say. By the time Trey left, he was pissed off with the system that had more rules to protect lawbreakers than those who kept the law, while on the other hand, Foster was convinced he was going back to prison, no matter what he did.

Trey had called Chia, only to find out that she and David had been called out on a new crime scene. A hitchhiker had been walking along Highway 75 near the Highway 635 junction, and as he'd passed an abandoned car, he'd noticed a strong odor coming from the trunk. He'd called the police from the first phone he'd come to, which led to the discovery of a body in the trunk, which had ended Chia's computer time.

With the day at an end, he gave up his frustration and headed home to Livvie. He hadn't talked to her since noon and hoped she and Ella had, at least, made friends. When he got there, it soon became obvious that he need not have worried. Livvie and Ella were at the kitchen table playing cards.

"Hey, how are my two favorite girls?" Trey asked as he walked into the room.

Ella sniffed and pretended to frown. "I've been suckered," she muttered.

Olivia grinned and pointed at the stack of kitchen matches to her right.

"I'm winning big-time," she said.

"What are you playing?" he asked.

"Poker," Ella said. "She said she didn't know how."
Trey grinned.

"Having a bit of beginner's luck, honey?"

"A bit?" Ella snapped. "If this was real money, she would already own my house."

"Only if you'd put it up for collateral," Olivia said,

unwilling to give an inch. "You could just quit."

"I don't quit."

"It's just matches," Olivia reminded her.

"No, it's the principle of the thing," Ella said.

"Should I go back out and come in again?" Trey asked.

Ella slapped her cards down on the table and got up, eyeing Olivia with a warning look.

"Don't think I'm letting this go," she warned.

Olivia reached across the table and turned up the hand that Ella had abandoned, then laid her own down with a flourish.

"I won again!" she crowed.

"No, you didn't," Ella snapped. "I already quit."

"Thought you didn't quit on anything," Olivia said.

Ella spluttered, then pointed at Olivia.

"Don't forget to take your medicine at seven."

"See you again tomorrow?" Olivia asked.

"Count on it," Ella said, and sailed out of the house without further comment.

Trey hurried to Olivia's side.

"Honey, I'm so sorry. I thought for sure that you and Ella would hit it off. Tomorrow I'll see if—"

"I love her," Olivia said. "She's the neatest person I've ever met."

"But you two were—"

Olivia arched an eyebrow and then began putting the matches back in the box.

"We're just alike," she said. "Neither one of us likes to lose. She'll be fine tomorrow."

"How do you know?" Trey asked.

"Because tomorrow I'll let her win."

Trey grinned. "Okay, then I'll just go tell her thank-you and let the rest of it ride."

Olivia waved him away as she continued to replace her winnings in the matchbox.

Trey hurried out of the house and then across the yard. He rang Ella's doorbell, expecting her to be furious with him. Instead, she answered the door with a grin.

"Hey, big guy . . . how come you're already over here? I would have thought you couldn't wait to put your arms around that sweetheart of yours."

Trey felt as if he'd just stepped into the twilight zone. He'd seen them fussing like two dogs over one bone, and now they were all smiles and laughter.

"I just came over to make sure you were okay," he said.

Ella frowned. "I'm fine. Why wouldn't I be?"

"Well, you seemed so upset, and I didn't want you to—"

Ella put her hand on his arm and shook her head. "Honey, don't worry. It was all just for show. I thought she needed a morale boost, so I was just letting her win. However, you don't mess around with poker, you know. Tomorrow I'll nail her hide to the floor."

Trey thought he was grinning, but he couldn't be sure.

"Okay, then, as long as everything is okay," he said.

"Right as rain, and for the record, she's a keeper."

"I'm going home now," Trey said, then kissed Ella on

the cheek, and headed back across the lawn.

When he got back inside his house, Olivia was pouring a can of pop over a glass of ice.

"Want one?" she asked.

"I need something stronger," he muttered.

"What did you say?" she asked.

"Nothing, honey, and yeah, I'll have a Pepsi. Only let me get it."

"I can pour pop into a glass," she said.

"I know, but maybe I want to baby you a little," Trey said as he took the can from her hand.

Olivia started to argue, then saw the need in his eyes.

"I'll just be in the living room with my head on a pillow and my feet up, waiting for you to baby me a little," she said, then winked at him as she walked out of the kitchen.

Trey's hand was shaking as he opened another can. He wasn't certain what was going to happen during the next few weeks, but he knew for sure he could hardly wait to see.

17

Trey grilled steaks. It was about the only thing he could cook and not mess up. He opened a plastic bag of ready-to-eat baby spinach and field greens and dumped them in a bowl, took the salad dressing out of the refrigerator and put them both on the table. He was looking for steak knives when the timer went off for the potatoes he had baking in the oven. He poured a couple of glasses of iced tea, put the plates and cutlery in place, and then stepped back to eye the table. Something was missing, but he couldn't think what.

At that point, Olivia, fresh from a shower, came into the kitchen. She looked at the table, whistled softly beneath her breath, then looked at Trey with new respect.

"I'm impressed."

He grinned.

She looked back at the table, then her forehead suddenly knitted.

"Do you have any steak sauce?"

"That's it!" Trey said, and went back to the refrigerator, got a bottle of ketchup and set it on the table. "Dinner is served."

Olivia arched an eyebrow. "That's steak sauce?"

"It is in this house," he said.

Olivia shook her head, dug into the pantry and came out a few moments later with a bottle of steak sauce that had never been opened.

"Where'd you get that?" Trey said as she set it on the table beside the ketchup.

"In the pantry," Olivia said.

Trey frowned. "I've lived here for more than ten years. You've been here less than twenty-four hours and you find stuff in my house I didn't know was there. What's that all about?"

"It's called being a woman," Olivia said. "Is it time to eat?"

"Definitely," Trey said, and pulled out a chair for her, then held her elbow as she sat down. "Is your shoulder hurting you much, honey?"

"Not bad," she said.

"Will you let me cut up your steak for you?"

"Yes, please, that would be great."

Trey cut the meat from a rib-eye into bite-size pieces and then put them on her plate, added a potato hot from the oven, and split and buttered it for her.

"Salad?" he asked.

"Absolutely," Olivia said.

Trey put some salad on her plate, then sat down, but instead of eating, he couldn't quit looking at Olivia.

"What?" she asked.

"I keep thinking this is a dream and any minute I'm going to wake up and you'll disappear."

"I'm not going anywhere," Olivia said.

Trey started to say something else, then picked up his fork and began to fix his own food.

For a few minutes they ate in silence, passing salt and pepper, opening the new bottle of steak sauce, getting napkins, nothing that required much thought. But they were both thinking hard and fast about the situation they found themselves in.

Olivia had asked for a second chance with Trey, not knowing that she would wind up in his home before the week was out, while Trey was torn between the joy of having Livvie so close and fear that something in the Baby Jane Doe case would ruin this relationship they were trying to renew.

Finally the meal was over. Olivia went to the living room to lie down on the sofa while Trey did the dishes. He brought her a dose of her painkillers and a glass of water when he was done.

He handed her the pills, which she gratefully took, then held the glass of water as she raised herself up enough to drink.

"Thank you," she said, and then winced as she lay back down.

"I should have shot the son of a bitch that night in the hospital and thought about it later."

Olivia reached for Trey's hand, then tugged him down onto the sofa beside her.

"You saved my life. It was enough."

He held her hand gently, eyeing the dark bruise where the IV needle had been, then the healing scrapes and bruises on her face.

"Ah, Livvie . . . what should I do with you? You turn me inside out with just a look, and you've been so hurt, and in so many ways."

"But, Trey, none of it was your fault. You just happened to be the one assigned to sort through the mess my family finds itself in."

Even though he wanted her there, Trey had yet to feel easy about her presence. If he had to venture a guess, he would say it had to do with trust.

"I know, but as a man, it's hard to see you suffering, know that I had my hands around the neck of the man who hurt you, and still left him breathing."

"My hero," Olivia said softly.

"I want to be," Trey said. "That and so much more."

"Just love me and forgive me," she said. "It will be enough."

He looked at her for a moment, then managed a small grin.

"We're really going to do this, aren't we, hon?"

She threaded her fingers through his.

"We're already doing it."

"And you're still gonna stay with me, no matter how this case turns out?"

She searched the shadows in his eyes, accepting his distrust as her just due.

"Yes, Trey. I'll stay with you—no matter what."

A self-conscious smile broke the seriousness on his face.

"Just so you know, having you to come home to was a damn fine thing."

Olivia grinned. "So, tough guy, just so you know, anticipating your arrival was damn fine for me, too."

He laughed.

Olivia shivered as the sound rolled through her and knew that she would remember this moment for the rest of her life.

It was a little after one in the morning and the third time Trey had gotten up to check on Livvie since she'd gone to bed. Every time he started to drift off to sleep, he saw her again as he'd seen her in the E.R., wounded, bloody and barely breathing. The horror of that memory pulled him out of bed and across the hall to see for sure that she was really there and really okay.

He'd barely slept the night before and knew he should go back to bed now and get what sleep he still could before the alarm went off at six. But he couldn't make himself move. Once he might have dreamed this would be their future, but it had been years since he'd let himself think of how much he'd cared and how much he'd hurt when it was over. Now, through a twist of fate, he'd been given another chance with her, and he wasn't going to let anything ruin it.

"Trey?"

He jerked. He hadn't realized she was awake until she spoke.

"Yes, it's me," he said, and moved to the side of her bed. "You could have something for pain again. Do you need it?"

"No."

"Drink of water?"

"No."

"Yeah . . . well, I'll just—"

"Would you lie down beside me?"

"I'm afraid that I'll—"

"Considering the fact that you've been in here at least twice since I went to bed, I'm guessing it's the only way we're going to get any sleep."

He sighed. "I didn't mean to bother you. I was just worried."

"So lie down beside me. You'll be close enough to tell if I'm in need of anything."

He grinned wryly. "I'm afraid if I get too close, you'll

know what *I'm* in need of, too."

"If you're willing to give me a couple of days, I'll see what can be done about that."

"Ah, Livvie, I'll give you the rest of my life. So, if you're sure you want to do this, here I come, ready or not."

Olivia didn't even have to move. Trey slid into the bed and then turned on his side so that he was facing her.

"You're not under the covers."

"I'm fine. You just close your sweet eyes and sleep good for me."

Olivia sighed, then closed her eyes. Oddly enough, she quickly went back to sleep.

Trey watched her, taking comfort in the steady rise and fall of her breasts. Even in the shadowed room, he could see the perfection of her profile, the sensuous curve of her lower lip, slightly parted in sleep. Her eyelashes were dusty shadows against her cheek, her hair dark silk against the pillows. He thought of her at two, sleeping like this, innocent and unaware of how quickly life could turn, and closed his eyes.

As a little girl, Olivia had seen the face of her parents' killer. And then a thought surfaced. Had she known there was another child? What if she'd seen her? Had she known they were sisters? Sweet Jesus, she wouldn't have even had the verbal skills to explain what was happening or what she'd seen.

Before, he'd known about her past, but only on the surface. She'd been a pretty girl who'd fallen for him as hard as he'd fallen for her. The fact that she'd been the victim of a horrendous crime had never entered into their relationship.

But they were grown-up now.

And he'd been thrust headfirst into her past as thoroughly as a man could be and not have been a part of it. He'd seen the bones in the suitcase, and it suddenly dawned on him how close she'd come to the same end. If fate—in the guise of Foster Lawrence—hadn't taken a lost little girl out of hell and dumped her in a mall . . . For the first time since he'd gotten mixed up in this mess, he could almost make himself feel grateful to Lawrence.

He hurt for the child she'd been. He ached for the woman she'd become. If it was the last thing he did, he was going to find the person responsible and make him . . . or her . . . pay.

She moaned in her sleep.

His eyes opened instantly.

She shifted slightly, then rolled over on her good side, pulled a pillow up against her chest to cushion her arm and scooted back against Trey.

He swallowed past the knot in his throat, gently slid his arm across her waist and pulled her closer until the full weight of her body was resting against him.

Only then did he close his eyes again.

Only then did he feel as if he was keeping her safe.

Only then.

Rose rolled over in her sleep, pulled the sheet up a

little higher on her shoulder against the blast of cool air from the window-unit air conditioner and dreamed of the day when the Sealy house would be renovated and she could go home.

Terrence couldn't sleep, and his restlessness had awakened Carolyn. It wasn't the first time they'd made love in the middle of the night in an effort to lay old ghosts to rest. They could have blamed their restlessness on jet lag, but it would have been a lie. The weight of the past was heavy on their hearts, and they were dealing with it as best they could.

Marcus sat in a chair near the window in his hotel room, staring blindly out into the night. The small circular courtyard of the hotel was lit against the dark, highlighting the clusters of shrubs and landscaping, but he wasn't seeing it. His mind's eye was taking him back through the years, and he was searching with the desperation of a parent who knows he has failed, trying to find the moment when everything had begun to go wrong.

Was it Amelia's death that had put Michael on a path to destruction? Had the loss of his mother when he was seventeen given him some kind of insecurity complex? How could his son have had two separate lives and his own father not know?

Marcus leaned forward, then buried his face in his hands. It was all his fault. If he hadn't always been chasing the almighty dollar, maybe he would have seen what was happening before it was too late. Then maybe Michael and Kay would never have been murdered and their baby stolen away in the night. And maybe— just maybe—the fate of Baby Jane Doe would never have been an issue, because she wouldn't even have been born.

Anna was curled up in her bed, sleeping the sleep of the innocent. The baby doll someone had had the wisdom to provide lay tucked up beneath her chin. Its wide, sightless eyes and small frozen smile seemed oddly obscene in a place where such sadness and confusion reigned, but its presence was, for Anna, a reassuring thing. She had always been determined. Even as a child, she'd been single-minded. In her mind, the last few years had never been. She was still the woman she'd been when Marcus Sealy had hired her as a nanny. She loved little Olivia with all her heart, but then there'd been a fire and they'd taken Anna away from all she knew. In doing so, they'd lost the baby. Anna had been terrified beyond words until that nurse had put the baby in her arms.

For now, all was well with her world.

Foster Lawrence was tormented. He felt as if he was caught in some damn loop in time, unable to escape the worst mistake of his life. His lawyer was pressuring him to cooperate with the authorities—to tell what he knew and save himself. And God knew he wanted to save himself. But he didn't have it in him to give up the one person standing between himself and freedom.

Olivia woke up in Trey's arms, and for one brief moment thought she was dreaming. Then he opened his eyes, and she knew what was happening was real. She saw the instant flare of desire that he quickly masked.

"Good morning, honey," he said softly, and kissed her cheek. "Did you sleep okay?"

"Remarkably well," Olivia said. "I think it was my bed partner."

He grinned. "I didn't sleep sound, but I sure slept happy."

Olivia laughed.

"I am so looking forward to the rest of my life."

The laugh died on Trey's face.

"Me too, Livvie. Me too."

"I need to get up," she said.

He sighed. "Sure, honey. Need some help?"

"Maybe," she said. "I'm sort of stiff first thing in the morning, but it gets better."

He rolled out of bed, then helped Olivia up. As soon as she was safely mobile, he headed for his own room to shower and shave. There was a day to begin and a case to solve before they could get on with the rest of their lives.

Sheree Collier leaned back in her chair and crossed her legs as she lit up a cigarette. Her family had been harping at her to quit for years. Too bad. This morning she'd just made her fifth big sale of the month and figured she had a right to celebrate. She took a long drag, pulled the smoke deep into her lungs, then exhaled through her nose. Her husband, Doug, hated when she did that. He said it wasn't ladylike—that it made her look like some cheap hooker. Sheree usually ignored him, but there were times when she hated him for the remark.

Still, today she was in too good a mood to hate anyone. She was great when it came to selling real estate and was intent on being Miami's Realtor of the year.

The phone rang in the outer office. Sheree glanced through the glass partition, watching as the office secretary answered. When the woman suddenly turned and held up two fingers at Sheree, she knew it was for her. She stubbed out the cigarette she'd been smoking, cleared her throat and punched the button on line two.

"Hello, this is Sheree."

"Mrs. Sheree Lawrence Collier?"

Sheree frowned. Something in the man's voice told her this had nothing to do with real estate.

"Yes, who's calling?"

"Mrs. Collier, my name is Detective Trey Bonney. I'm with the homicide division of the Dallas Police Department."

"If you're calling about my brother, I don't know a thing," she said shortly.

Trey's fingers tightened on the pen in his hand. He'd found her!

"So you *are* the sister of Foster Lawrence?"

"Yes, unfortunately."

"And you have a twin sister named Laree?"

Sheree gasped. "Has something happened to 'Ree? Oh God . . . I've been afraid of that for years. She just dropped off the face of the earth. We used to be so close, and I just knew something had happened to her. She would never have cut off all communication with me."

"Wait . . . wait," Trey said. "You misunderstand. I have no information regarding your sister, but I'm trying to locate her."

"Oh God," Sheree said, and grabbed a tissue from the box on her desk and began dabbing at her eyes. "You scared me half to death."

"I'm sorry," Trey said. "But am I understanding you correctly that you've had no contact with your sister?"

"No . . . uh, I mean, yes, you understand me right. 'Ree . . . Laree is my identical twin. We did everything together . . . always."

"How long has it been since you've seen her?"

Sheree's voice began to shake. Suddenly, being Realtor of the year didn't seem as important as it had a few minutes ago.

"Years . . . more than twenty, I guess. Maybe even twenty-five."

Crap. Another dead end.

"Where was she living at the time?"

"Why . . . in Dallas, of course. It's where we all grew up. Well, let me amend that. We grew up outside of Irving, which, as you know, is almost like a suburb

278

now. Our mother worked as manager at a motel on Highway 75 and waited tables at night in the motel coffee shop."

"What was your sister doing at the time she disappeared?"

"Actually, I had already moved away. My husband was in the air force, and he was stationed in California. I wrote to her regularly, but after a while, the letters began to come back marked 'Moved—Left No Forwarding Address,' so I gave up. It was awful—like losing a piece of myself."

"And your mother?"

"Oh, she died when we were freshmen in college. That's when Foster came to live with us. 'Ree and I were sharing an apartment at the time. Foster was only twelve. I worked days and went to night school. 'Ree worked nights and went to school during the day, so she was home with him more in the daytime. They got real close, you know."

Trey was taking notes as they talked, and it was all beginning to make sense. If Laree was the woman Michael Sealy had been seeing—and if she was the mother of the dead baby—it would explain how Foster wound up in the mess.

"So how old was Foster when you lost track of your sister?"

"Hmm, probably early twenties."

Trey scanned the files. The fit was getting tighter. Foster had gone to prison at the age of twenty-three.

"Wasn't long after that he got himself mixed up in

that kidnapping. I still can't believe he would do something that awful," Sheree said. "It wasn't like him. Really, it wasn't."

"Did you talk to your brother at any time during the trial?"

"No. My husband was ashamed for anyone to know we were kin. Looking back, I can see that wasn't right, but I let myself be swayed, and later, it was too late to make amends. He was already gone . . . shipped off to some federal prison in California."

"Did you know anything—anything at all—about your sister's private life at the time of her disappearance?"

Sheree thought back, vaguely remembering her sister raving about some rich man who was going to make her life perfect.

"Yeah, sort of. I think she was seeing this guy . . . some big shot, I guess. She said he was rich and was going to . . . you know . . . take her away from it all, so to speak."

"Did she ever mention his name?"

"No. Or at least if she did, I've long since forgotten it."

Trey had one more question to ask, but Sheree Collier beat him to the punch.

"You never did say why you were looking for Laree."

Trey hesitated. He didn't want to alienate the woman when he was going to need her further cooperation.

"It's a bit confusing, and right now, part of it is still theory."

"So?"

"As you know, your brother went to prison for his involvement in the kidnapping of a little girl named Olivia Sealy."

"Yes. But like I said, I'm sure he didn't do it."

"Yes, ma'am, but just hear me out. He was also the one who was responsible for returning her to her family."

"Oh! I didn't know that," Sheree said. "That makes me glad, but what does Laree have to do with any of this?"

"There's a possibility that your sister was the instigator of the crime, that she was having an affair with Michael Sealy, the little girl's father, and when he wouldn't leave his wife, she killed both Michael and Kay Sealy and stole Michael's child."

"I don't believe it! She wouldn't do something that awful!" Sheree cried.

"I can understand your feelings, but you also said you couldn't believe your brother would get mixed up in something like that."

"Yes, but I don't see—"

"What if his involvement was solely because of your sister? If she called in a panic about something, isn't it possible that he automatically went to her aid?"

There was a long moment of silence, then a sigh.

"Maybe . . . yes. Then are you saying you're looking for her for murdering those two people?"

"Not two. Three."

"But I thought you said—"

"Two weeks ago, a couple remodeling a house they'd just bought found a suitcase behind a wall. Inside that suitcase was the skeleton of a baby girl who was the same age as the child who was kidnapped. We've already determined that the dead baby and the kidnapped baby had the same father. What we don't know is which baby is which, or who killed the one left behind."

"Are you trying to tell me that two little girls, born to different women, looked so much alike that no one could tell them apart?"

"Not exactly. This is all theory."

"Then what do you want from me?"

"Since you don't know your sister's whereabouts I was wondering if you would consider letting us get a sample of your DNA. Since you were identical, we could compare yours to the DNA of both the dead baby and the one who is now grown. We would know if your sister had given birth to one of them. If she didn't, then you would be helping us clear her name."

"And if she did this horrible thing, I would be helping you to hang her," Sheree said.

"Lady, that little girl wasn't even two years old when she was hit in the back of the head, stuffed in a suitcase with a blanket and one sock and a wooden cross with the words 'Sleeping with angels' burned into it. If your sister did that, she deserves more than a hanging."

Sheree heard the anger in the detective's voice, and she couldn't blame him.

"I'll help," she said.

Trey sighed with relief.

"I can arrange for your DNA to be taken there."

"Is my brother back in jail?"

"Yes."

"In Dallas?"

"Yes, ma'am."

"Has he been charged with any crime?"

"Not yet, but he could be charged with withholding information or even as an accessory to that baby's death. We can't get him to talk."

Sheree suddenly felt old.

"I'll come there. I think I can catch a red-eye tonight and be there tomorrow," she said. "I want to talk to Foster. If he's protecting 'Ree from something that awful, then he needs to know it's okay to tell the truth."

"Thank you, Mrs. Collier. This is my phone number. Call me as soon as you get to Dallas and I'll arrange for you to visit your brother."

"All right," Sheree said, and hung up the phone.

For a few moments she stared down at the cigarette she'd stubbed out only minutes before and felt her stomach lurch. She jumped up from her desk and ran into the bathroom just in time to throw up. When she came back out, the secretary was standing anxiously by the door.

"Mrs. Collier, are you all right?"

Sheree's chin quivered. "No. I may never be all right again."

"Is there anything I can do?" the secretary asked.

"Book me a flight on the next plane leaving for Dallas

283

and cancel all my appointments for the next few days. I'll call you and let you know when I'll be coming back."

"Yes, ma'am . . . and without being too personal . . . I hope you haven't received bad news."

Sheree's chin quivered again, but she didn't let herself go.

"Honey, I appreciate your concern, but for the record, it was about as bad as news gets."

"Oh dear. Please know that you have my sympathies."

"I'm going to need a whole lot more than that," Sheree said, and then took her purse and walked out the door.

18

Ella was wearing red. She considered it a necessary power color. At eighty-one, she needed all the power she could get.

Olivia was wearing the same blue robe she'd come home in and felt somewhat envious of Ella's red slacks and blouse. She was tired of living in nightgowns and lounging robes, and was looking forward to a visit from Marcus, who was bringing her some of her clothes from home. He'd warned her they might smell of smoke, but she'd assured him she could take care of that. All she wanted was to dress normally again.

The physical therapist had come and gone, leaving

Olivia with a series of exercises she was to do daily, and had given a thumbs-up on using the pool in Trey's backyard. She had quickly called her grandfather back to remind him to pick up a swimsuit, as well.

Ella had been unusually quiet, fussing about the house, picking up clutter and running the vacuum. She'd even gone so far as to cut a large bouquet of purple crepe myrtle and put it in a vase on the dining table before she made herself scarce.

As soon as she hung up the phone, Olivia showered and put her robe back on, before going to look for Ella. She found her in the kitchen stirring up a batch of cookies.

"Can I help?" Olivia asked.

Ella eyed Olivia's slightly flushed cheeks and the way she was holding her arm, and pointed to a chair.

"You can sit yourself down, missy, before you fall down," she said.

Olivia arched an eyebrow.

"Do I look that bad?"

"I suspect you've looked better," Ella muttered as she measured almond flavoring into the dough.

Olivia laughed.

Ella grinned.

The doorbell rang.

"I can get that," Olivia said.

Ella pointed her wooden spoon and frowned.

"You stay set. I'm in charge here."

"It's probably Grampy."

Ella sniffed. "So? I'm not afraid of any old man."

Having said that, she strode out of the kitchen, still holding the long wooden spoon.

Olivia rolled her eyes, then got up and followed Ella to the door. She wasn't sure how her grandfather would react to being greeted by a hussy in red, and decided he might need some protection.

As it was, she need not have worried. By the looks of things, Marcus had charmed the frost right off of Ella's attitude. She was all smiles by the time Olivia got there.

"Here, you just give that suitcase to me. I'll put it in Olivia's room while you say hello to your girl," Ella said, then took the suitcase in one hand. Still carrying the wooden spoon in the other, she sailed past Olivia with a wink and a grin.

"Olivia, darling, it's so good to see you up and around," Marcus said as he crossed the room and took her in his arms.

Olivia closed her eyes, savoring the scent of his aftershave and the familiarity of his hug as he kissed the side of her cheek.

"How are you doing?" he asked. "Do you have everything you need?"

"I'm doing great," she said. "You're the one who's been displaced. Was the fire bad? Did it do much damage?"

"Let's sit," he said, and motioned toward the sofa.

She took his hand. "Let's sit in the kitchen," she said. "Ella is making cookies. I'm the official taster."

"Since when?" Ella asked as she reappeared in the hall.

"Since you told me to sit down before I fell down," Olivia countered.

Ella pursed her lips and gave Marcus a judgmental stare.

"She's spoiled, but I suppose you know that, since you're probably the one who did it."

"Not really spoiled," Marcus said. "Just well loved."

Olivia smirked. "She's just ticked because we were playing poker yesterday evening and I put her in bankruptcy."

Marcus looked somewhat startled by their bickering, then realized it was being done with a considerable amount of good will.

"Poker? You were playing poker?" he asked.

Ella sniffed. "There's nothing wrong with a good game of cards."

"I agree," Marcus said, and all but rubbed his hands together in anticipation. "I can't remember the last time I've played cards."

Ella smiled. "As soon as I finish those cookies, I suppose we could play a hand or two."

"I'd love that," Marcus said.

Ella's eyes almost glittered.

"Don't get your hopes up," Olivia warned her. "Grampy taught me all I know about cards."

"I let you win," Ella said. "He's on his own."

Olivia's mouth dropped. "You did no such thing. I won fair and square. You're just saying that to save face."

Ella pointed the wooden spoon at Olivia.

"Honey girl, I'm eighty-one years old. I have long since lost the need to save face, as you put it." Then she gave Marcus a long, considering look. "If we play, we're not playing with matches."

He nodded. "Done."

Olivia rolled her eyes. "What about the cookies?"

Ella took herself off into the kitchen.

They followed, took seats at the table, and suffered through the mouthwatering smell of hot cookies baking in the oven. When the last pan was out and the cookies cooling on a rack, Ella stacked a dozen on a plate, poured three glasses of sweet iced tea, whipped out a deck of cards from a kitchen drawer and carried everything to the table.

"I take no prisoners," she warned, and then shuffled the deck as slickly as any Las Vegas dealer could have done.

Marcus stuffed one whole cookie in his mouth and began to chew. When she shoved the deck to him to be cut, he did so without question.

"I like a woman with guts," Marcus said, and shoved the deck back at her, then took another cookie.

Olivia played two hands of poker, ate four of the still-warm cookies, finished her iced tea and excused herself for a nap.

The pair barely acknowledged her exit.

Olivia was still smiling as she drifted off to sleep.

There was a bounce to Trey's step as he came into the office. David Sheets nodded casually, then did a double take when he saw the smile on Trey's face. Chia pointed at him from across the room, then wiggled her eyebrows. Trey laughed out loud. Today was a good day. He'd spent the night with Olivia in his arms and awakened to the smile on her face. With the promise of many nights and mornings like that to come, he was on top of the world.

Besides that, finding Sheree Collier had gone a long way toward easing his frustrations over the mystery surrounding Baby Jane Doe.

"What's so great?" Sheets muttered as Trey sat down at his desk.

"Thanks to your partner there, we just may have a break in the Baby Jane Doe case," he said.

Chia gave a little whoop.

"She was on that list I gave you?"

Trey nodded. "Third call I made. Sheree Lawrence Collier lives in Miami, Florida."

"Fantastic. So do we know where Laree Lawrence is now?"

"No, and here's the kicker. Sheree hasn't seen or heard from her since Foster was arrested."

Lieutenant Warren walked up behind them as they were talking.

"Did I hear you right? You've got a connection between Michael Sealy and Laree Lawrence?"

"What I have is a connection between Foster and Laree, and what I know from her sister, Sheree, is that Laree had a rich boyfriend, who was supposedly going to make her a happy woman."

Warren frowned. "That still doesn't give us a connection we can take to court."

"Maybe not now, but that is subject to change," Trey said.

"How so?" Warren asked.

"Identical twins share the same DNA, and Sheree Lawrence Collier is on her way to Dallas. She's volunteered to give us a sample of her DNA. If it matches either Olivia Sealy or Baby Jane Doe, then we've got the other kidnapper. She has also offered to talk to her brother, Foster, in the hope of convincing him to tell what he knows."

Warren grinned and clapped Trey on the back.

"Good job."

"Congratulations go to Chia, too. She did all the Internet searches for me or I'd still be at it."

Warren gave an approving nod to Chia, who grinned happily.

"When is the sister arriving?" Warren asked.

Trey glanced at his watch.

"Unless her plane was delayed, she's already here. She booked a room at the Adam's Mark. She'll call when she gets settled. I'll take her to the crime lab for a DNA swab, then she's been cleared to visit her brother."

"Okay," Warren said. "Keep me in the loop. The sooner this is off our backs, the happier the commissioner is going to be. I'm having lunch with him today. I'll fill him in on what's happening."

Before Trey could answer, his cell phone rang. He looked at the caller ID.

"It's the Adam's Mark," he said, then answered, "Detective Bonney."

Sheree Collier's voice was a little shaky.

"Detective, it's me, Sheree Collier."

"Yes, ma'am. Are you ready for me to come get you?"

"As ready as I'll ever be," she said.

"Be there in about thirty minutes," he said.

"I'll be waiting in the lobby. I'm wearing a light blue dress."

Trey disconnected, then glanced at Chia and David.

"You guys want in on the interview when she goes to see her brother?"

"Absolutely," Chia said.

"Meet us at the jail in about an hour and a half."

"Count us there," Chia said as Trey left.

"Wonder why he's suddenly being so magnanimous?" David said.

Chia frowned at her partner.

"You know, I'm beginning to understand why Bonney likes to work alone."

"What?" David asked.

"You're jealous."

"I'm not," he muttered.

Chia nodded so fiercely that her curls began to bounce.

"You are. You're so freakin' jealous you can't stand yourself. More and more, you're acting like some bitchy girl. If you aren't careful, next you're gonna start having PMS."

Sheets' face turned a dark, angry red. He pointed at

Chia but couldn't think of anything to say that wouldn't get him in deeper than he already was. Frustrated, he just shook his head and walked away, leaving Chia with a grin on her face. She did a little two-step, then moved back to her desk.

Sheree Collier saw a tall, good-looking man stride into the hotel lobby. He was wearing blue jeans, a white sport shirt with small blue pinstripes and a brown jacket. She caught a glimpse of the badge he was wearing clipped to his belt and stood.

Trey saw the movement before he saw the woman, but as soon as he looked into her face, he recognized the Lawrence family resemblance. She was well dressed and well kept, and he would have been hard-pressed to guess her age if he hadn't had access to the files listing her birth date.

"Mrs. Collier?" he asked.

Sheree nodded as Trey shook her hand.

"You're doing a good thing," he said.

A crooked smile curled a corner of her lip.

"I've been telling myself that all the way here."

"I know this is rough for you."

Sheree sighed. "Let's just get it over with, shall we?"

Trey cupped her elbow. "I'm parked just outside. Are you ready to go?"

"Yes."

Minutes later, they were en route to the crime lab. The drive was less lengthy than the one he'd made when he'd first taken Marcus and Olivia Sealy for testing.

And when he pulled into the parking lot, he couldn't help but think of the chaos that had awaited them then, compared to the fact that today, no one seemed to care.

Part of it could be chalked up to the fact that the Sealys' involvement was old news, but also, no one in the crime lab knew there was any connection between his case and Sheree Collier, which meant there wouldn't have been a chance for any leaks.

"This won't take long," Trey said. "We'll go see your brother directly afterward."

Sheree nodded, and clutched at Trey's arm.

He could feel her trembling.

"Don't be nervous," he said. "I'll be with you all the way on this."

"I appreciate your kindness," she said. "But there's nothing you can say that will make selling out my family okay."

Trey frowned. "Why do you say that? You're not selling out your family. You're trying to keep Foster out of prison again."

"But in doing so, I'll be pointing the finger of guilt at my sister."

"You're pretty sure she's the mother of one of the children, aren't you?"

Sheree nodded.

"Why so?"

"Because after we talked yesterday, I started remembering other things."

"Like what?" Trey asked.

"Like, the fact that the few times I actually saw Laree

in the two years before Foster was arrested, there was a child in her house."

Trey's heart skipped a beat.

"A little girl?"

Sheree Collier nodded.

"What did she tell you about her?"

"Not much . . . only that she was baby-sitting for extra money."

"And you believed her?"

"She was my twin. We'd fooled plenty of other people in our youth, but never each other."

"I don't suppose you ever had a picture of them together?" Trey asked.

"No."

Trey thought, then came at it from another angle.

"If you saw a picture of the child, would you recognize her?"

"Maybe, if the child was the same age in the picture as the last time I'd seen her."

"How old would she have been?"

"Probably between a year and a half and two years old."

"I'll see what I can come up with," Trey said. "Now, let's get the test over with so you can go talk to your brother."

Sheree momentarily closed her eyes. She wasn't as convinced as the detective seemed to be that Foster would even want to see her.

"Hey, Lawrence, someone's here to see you," the

jailer said as he opened the cell door and pulled a pair of handcuffs from his belt. "Hold out your hands."

Foster stayed on his bunk.

"Is it my lawyer?" Foster asked.

"He's there, but there's a couple other people there, too."

"Like who?"

"I'm not your damn social secretary," the jailer said. "Either get up now or forget about it. However, if I was in the shit you're in, I wouldn't be passing up a chance to better my situation."

It was curiosity that got Foster off the bunk. He let himself be handcuffed, then escorted to the interrogation room. When he saw his lawyer through a window in the door, he shelved the attitude. Maybe there was some good news. God knew he could use some.

The jailer opened the door, put a hand in the middle of Foster's back and pushed him inside. When he was two steps into the room, Foster saw the cop who'd arrested him, plus another pair of cops, one male, one female. Before he could voice his complaints, a woman he hadn't seen suddenly stepped out from behind the detective. His frown deepened. He didn't know who she was, but he was in no mood for a party. Then she smiled.

Foster froze.

"Hello, Fossie . . . long time no see."

"Sis? Is that you?"

Sheree glanced at Trey. "Can I hug him?"

Foster was still handcuffed, and the jailer was there, too.

"Yeah, sure."

Sheree walked slowly toward the brother she'd denied, and when she was close enough to hear him breathing, she stopped.

"You're bald."

"No. I shaved it off."

"Oh."

There was another moment of uncomfortable silence between them; then Trey glanced at Chia and David, who got the message and moved toward the far corner of the room. At that point, the jailer stepped outside and closed the door.

Foster's lawyer stayed, but he, too, moved to one corner of the room, giving his client and his sister some privacy.

Trey shoved his hands in his pockets. Foster looked at him. Trey stared back.

"Fossie."

The old childhood nickname tugged at Foster's heart. He turned back to the woman, then leaned closer so that he was whispering.

"Sis?"

Sheree put her arms around him then and pulled him close.

Foster seemed to wilt as he laid his head on her shoulder.

"Oh, Fossie . . . it's been so long."

"Sis, which one are you?" he asked.

Sheree was taken aback. She and her sister had always been identical, but family could always tell them apart. Still, twenty-five years had elapsed since they'd seen one another and it stood to reason that he couldn't be sure which was which.

"It's me, Sheree," she said, and when she did, she saw quick disappointment in his eyes.

He nodded. "I wasn't sure. Funny, isn't it?"

"It's understandable. It's been a long time."

He nodded.

"Come sit with me," Sheree said.

Foster let himself be led to the table in the middle of the room. He sat; then Sheree pulled up a chair and sat beside him.

Foster eyed Trey, then her. At that point, he began to frown.

"Why are you here?" he asked.

Sheree sighed. "I can understand your surprise. It's been so long."

He smirked, but there was more pain than anger on his face.

"Yeah, I've been away. Where have you been?"

"I guess I've been away, too. Only I'm here now."

"Why?"

Sheree's eyes filled with tears, and for the first time since Trey had seen her, she looked every one of her sixty years.

"How did you get in so much trouble?" she asked.

Foster's eyes flickered, but he didn't answer.

"Foster. Was it 'Ree?"

His eyes widened. "I don't know what you're talking about."

"I think you do."

He leaned forward, lowering his voice again.

"Shut up, sis. You don't know what you're doing."

Tears spilled over onto her cheeks.

"Oh, Foster, I wish I didn't, but I'm afraid I do."

He looked away.

"How did you get mixed up in this? What did 'Ree ask you to do?"

He shuddered, but he stayed silent.

"Did you know about her baby?"

He jerked, as if she'd slapped him.

"She didn't have a baby."

"I didn't know it, either," Sheree said. "But I think we both know it now, don't we?"

He started to cry.

"What happened, Fossie? Talk to me."

Foster groaned. "Ah, God . . . it all started because of a wall. She called me to come fix a wall."

Trey's belly lurched. *Jesus Christ . . . the lake house.*

"What wall?" Sheree asked.

Foster slumped. He would have held this in forever against the cops, but not from her.

"Hell, I don't know . . . just some wall. Said she'd been partying with some friends at a lake house, and someone had gotten drunk and knocked a big hole in the wall. She said she'd get in trouble if she didn't get it fixed, so I loaded up my stuff and drove down from Amarillo."

Sheree looked up at Trey. "Foster was in construction."

Trey nodded.

Foster wouldn't acknowledge Trey's presence, but a part of him was relieved this was all coming out. He'd carried the weight of the secret too long as it was.

"So you went to fix the wall," Sheree said.

Foster nodded. "It was some house up at Lake Texoma. Remember when we used to go there for the Fourth of July?"

Sheree nodded.

"Anyway, I got there, and like she said, there was a big hole in the wall. She'd already cut a piece of Sheetrock and was trying to nail it in place, but she didn't know how to tape and bed, so I cleaned it up for her some, put the finishing on it, and told her that when it dried in a day or so, she could paint it and it would be good as new. I was loaded up and getting ready to leave when this little kid comes out of one of the rooms."

"What did 'Ree say?" she asked.

"I said, 'Who the hell is that?' And she says . . . 'My daughter.' I freaked. I said, 'What the hell do you mean, your daughter?' She laughed this sort of wild, crazy laugh, and the kid started crying, and then everything sort of fell apart."

"How so?" Sheree asked.

"She picked up the kid, like trying to make her quit crying and all . . . but the kid was hysterical. Kept screaming for her mama. 'Ree got a little crazy and started holding the kid too tight. I told her to quit, that she was hurting her, but she wouldn't let her go. I grabbed the kid out of her arms and then sort of slapped 'Ree in the face to calm her down."

"Did it work?"

Foster nodded. "Yeah. Then she got this real mad look on her face and told me to give her baby back. I asked her if she was going to be rough with the kid again. She said it was none of my business. I told her that I wasn't letting her go until she told me what was going on."

"What was the child doing all this time?" Trey asked.

Foster began to rock back and forth in the chair.

"She was crying. She cried herself to sleep in my arms," he said, then leaned forward on the table and hid his face in his arms.

"Then what?" Sheree asked.

"'Ree took her and laid her down. I followed her into the other room. That's when I saw the blood."

"What blood?" Trey asked.

"It was all over the bedroom floor. And there was some on the baby's pajamas. I asked her what happened here, and she said the kid had a nosebleed. Since I didn't see any marks on her, I made myself believe she was telling the truth. Then she told me to go. I wish to hell I had."

"If you were so concerned for the baby's safety, why did you ask for the money?" Trey asked.

Foster looked up; his skin was gray and pale.

"Damned if I know. A moment of stupidity. A moment of greed. Hell, I guess the devil had hold of me then."

Sheree was crying now, too. Foster looked back at her. His expression crumpled.

"I'm so sorry, sis. I knew better."

"I know," she said. "I know."

"Finish the story," Trey said.

"While we were arguing, the baby woke up again and got down from the bed. She was fooling around with an old portable television in the corner of the room and accidentally turned it on. At first we were startled by the sound, then I began to focus on what was being broadcast. It was all about the Sealy kidnapping. They flashed a picture of the missing kid on the screen, and I nearly had a heart attack. I confronted 'Ree. That's when she told me about the baby's father. She said he'd promised to take her away, then he dumped her. She said she made him pay for lying. She was going to make them all pay. That's when I thought she'd already made a ransom call. When I asked her, she said she didn't intend to ask for ransom because she had no intention of giving the kid back."

"Dear Lord," Sheree said. "What must 'Ree have been thinking?"

"She wasn't thinking," Foster said. "She was crazy. You could see it in her eyes." Then he sighed. "So I stayed. After a few days, I pulled the stunt about the ransom. Made the call myself. It was all pretty simple. They paid it. I had the kid with me. I gave her some stuff that put her to sleep, and I left her in the truck in a parking garage. I picked up the money, then I saw the cops on my tail. I lost them, then hid the money in the basement beneath a downtown restaurant where I used to work, went and got the kid from the truck and took her to the mall. I made sure she would be found. I didn't want anything to happen to her." He shuddered. "If I'd left her with 'Ree, I don't know what she would have done to her."

Sheree got out of her chair, put her arms around her brother and just held him where he sat. She cried for her sister, and for Foster, and for babies whose lives had been forever changed.

"Did you know 'Ree had a child with that man?"

Foster shook his head. "No. I swear to God, I never knew a thing about any of it until a few weeks ago. I get here, thinking I'm going to get my money and make a new start. Instead, I find out I'm wanted for questioning again, this time for a murder I didn't know anything about. *Then* I find out that the damn money I'd hidden had gone up in smoke years ago in some fire."

"Why didn't you tell the cops all this when you were arrested?" Sheree asked.

Foster looked at her as if she'd gone mad.

"She was my sister. I couldn't let anything bad happen to her."

Sheree grabbed Foster by the shoulders and shook him, as if he were a child who wouldn't listen.

"Foster! For God's sake, something bad had already happened! You had to know she wasn't right, or she would never have done anything so awful. Where did she go? Have you seen her since? Do you know where she is?"

Foster dropped his head.

"I haven't seen her since the day I stole the kid from the lake house. I heard her screaming at me as I drove away, but I never looked back. I couldn't bear to see her like that."

"And she never came forward at your trial or sent you word in any way?" Trey asked.

"No."

Trey cursed beneath his breath. Although they now knew who'd done the killings, they were no closer to bringing her to justice than they'd been the day the baby's remains were found.

"Why do you think she killed one of the babies?" Trey asked.

Foster looked up at him then.

"Hell if I know. I never knew there were two."

"There were, and we have to know which one she killed."

Foster flinched.

"What do you mean?" he asked.

"There's a possibility that the little girls might have looked enough alike that the wrong one went back to the Sealy family," Trey said.

Foster shook his head. "I don't know anything about that. I only saw the one kid. The one I let go at the mall."

Sheree looked at Trey.

"What's going to happen to Foster now?" she asked.

The lawyer spoke up.

"We'll file for an immediate release. He's already

served the time for his only crime."

"That's up to the D.A.," Trey said.

Sheree wiped her hands across her face, then stood and walked to the window.

Foster wouldn't look up.

And they were back where they'd begun, Trey thought. Until the tests came back on Sheree Collier, they would have no way of knowing which child had died and which one had been returned to Marcus Sealy.

Sheree Collier suddenly turned.

"Detective Bonney, why can't you trace Laree's whereabouts by her social security number?"

"That's how we found you, but all the activity on her number ended the same month that the kidnapping and murders occurred."

"Do you think she's dead?" she asked.

"I don't think anything," Trey said. "I operate in facts."

"Then where did she go? Where has she been? If she's still alive, she would have had to work to survive."

"She could have taken another identity," Foster said. "Guys in the joint did that a lot. It's easier than you think."

Sheree frowned. "Is that true, Detective?"

"Unfortunately, yes."

"Oh God, how will we ever find her? How will we ever know?"

"I don't know, ma'am," Trey said. "But thanks to you and your brother, we know a whole lot more than we did this time last week. At least now we know who to look for."

"But all these years have gone by. If she's gained weight or gone gray, she would look different. I color my hair the same color it was when I was younger and my own brother didn't even recognize me," Sheree said.

"We could use a picture of you as you are now, fool around with different hair color, add or subtract weight from the facial area, and maybe come up with a passable likeness."

"Why not?" Sheree asked. "I already feel as if I'm a traitor. Maybe if I let you bleed me dry, I won't have to face what I've done."

"No, sis," Foster said. "It wasn't you. It was us. We made the mistakes."

"Then why do I feel so awful?"

Foster couldn't answer. There was nothing left to say.

19

It was getting dark by the time Trey got home. Ella was in the yard watering the geraniums in the planters on either side of his doorstep. He grinned to himself as he saw her, dressed in her red pants and blouse. A perfect match for the red blooms she was watering.

"Hey, good looking," Trey said, as he came up the walk.

"Hello, yourself," Ella said, and turned off the water,

then rolled up the hose. "I made a casserole. It's warming in the oven. There's a banana cream pie in the fridge and salad stuff in the crisper. You're getting low on milk, and you're almost out of eggs. I started a list. It's on the cabinet."

"Lord, Ella, I didn't intend for you to take me to raise. I just didn't want Livvie to be by herself until she got a little stronger."

Ella's mouth pursed as she put her hands on her hips.

"I only did what I wanted to do. Besides, I haven't felt this useful in years. It's a nice feeling. Don't mess it up for me."

Trey grinned. "Okay. Point taken. Still, don't work so much, okay?"

"Whatever," Ella muttered. "Your sweetie is out back in the pool. Her grandfather was here, too."

"Marcus? Is he still here?"

"No. He left after I beat him playing poker."

The grin on Trey's face shifted. "You were playing poker?"

"Yes."

"For matches, right?"

"Lord, no. For money." She patted her pocket. "Won almost two hundred dollars off him. I left him enough to get home on, though. I'm not completely heartless."

"Crap," Trey muttered.

"What?"

"I'm a cop. You're gambling in my home. I think there's a problem somewhere in this, but I'm too damn tired to care."

Ella sniffed. "Don't get your britches in a wad. It won't happen again, but mostly because I don't think Marcus Sealy is a fool. I beat him once. He won't make the same mistake twice."

"For whatever reason, I thank you for the end to the gambling," Trey said.

"You're welcome. I'm going home now. It's almost time for my favorite show. Enjoy your evening. Tell Olivia that I'll see her tomorrow."

"Okay. Thanks again," Trey said, and hurried into his house as Ella crossed the lawn toward her home.

The house was filled with the homey scents of the food Ella had been cooking, as well as a faint odor of lemon furniture polish. There was an energy in the air that had been missing before Olivia's arrival, as if the house had come to life on its own. But Trey knew it was more than the people who'd been in it. It was the love growing between himself and Livvie that made the house feel like a home.

He closed the door behind him as he entered, quickly took off his jacket and hung it on a hook by the door, then slipped out of his shoulder holster, and put it in a drawer in his desk. He glanced out the kitchen window, saw Olivia in the pool floating in an oversize inner tube. He couldn't see much of the black bikini she was wearing, but it was enough to entice him to join her. A few minutes later, he came out of his room wearing his swimsuit and a grin.

Olivia heard the squeak of the storm door but

couldn't bring herself to open her eyes. Whatever it was, Ella would certainly let her know.

Then she heard water splash. Surely to God Ella hadn't fallen in! She turned just as a pair of long tan legs disappeared beneath the water. Seconds later, Trey came up right beside her. Water had slicked his thick, dark hair close to his head and was dripping off his lashes like tears. But there was nothing sad about his face. He was grinning from ear to ear. Olivia couldn't help but join him.

"Hey you," she said, and flipped water in his face.

"Hey yourself," he said, then pushed her inner tube to the side of the pool, where he could stand beside her.

Olivia told herself not to stare, but her brain wasn't listening. There was no way to ignore the broad span of Trey's arms and shoulders, or the flat six-pack of belly muscles. She'd wondered more than once how the boy's body had matured into a man's. Now she knew.

She was smiling as her gaze moved back up to Trey's face, but then she saw him frown and automatically reached toward her gunshot wound, trying to hide it.

Trey grabbed her hand, then turned it palm up to his mouth and kissed it—a long, lingering kiss warmed by his breath upon her skin. She stifled a moan.

She wanted him. As a seventeen-year-old girl, she'd known the boy intimately. She wanted to know the man even more.

"Trey . . ."

"Shh," he whispered, then turned her inner tube so her back was to him.

She felt his lips brush her neck, then the back of her ear; then his mouth trailed down her shoulder to the place where the bullet had gone in. He paused. She heard a sharp intake of breath; then Trey wrapped his arms around her and laid his face against the top of her head.

"Trey?"

"Not yet," he said.

His voice was trembling.

"I'm fine," she said softly.

"Jesus Christ, Livvie . . . I'm not, okay? Just let me hold you."

She leaned her head back against his chest and closed her eyes. Despite the trauma she'd suffered, she would never be sorry it had happened. Not when it had been the vehicle that brought Trey back into her life.

Trey swallowed past the knot in his throat as he tried to contain his emotions. The sight of that red, angry wound on her body had hit him like a slap to the face, and with it had come rage. He'd had his hands around that crazy bastard's neck. All he would have had to do was give it a twist. It would have ended Dennis Rawlins's reign of terror and saved the state of Texas the cost of housing the son of a bitch. But he hadn't done it—and he knew that he would regret the hesitation for as long as he lived.

Finally Trey moved. Olivia felt him shudder, then heard him take a slow, deep breath.

She leaned her head back until she was looking at him upside down; then she grinned.

"You look funny upside down."

"So do you," he countered, knowing she was teasing him to try to change the tenseness of the mood.

"Wanna race?" she asked.

"What I want has nothing to do with a swimming pool," he said.

Olivia's smile stilled; then she let her gaze slide from his face to his chest, then to the distorted shape of his body beneath the water.

"I thought you swam in the nude."

"Just say the word," he countered.

She didn't have the guts to call his bluff. When she finally looked up, Trey's eyes were dark, his face expressionless.

Trey's mind was in chaos. He wanted to make love to her, but she was in no shape for anything but a kiss. Then she surprised him with a question he wasn't expecting.

"Does what you're wanting from me have anything to do with a bed?"

Trey's nostrils flared.

"That is so not funny."

"You don't see me laughing, do you?"

"We can't do that . . . yet."

"Why? He shot my shoulder, not my ass."

Trey blinked. She'd surprised him.

"You know, Livvie, you've changed some since your high-school days."

"If you mean I'm not afraid to say what I'm thinking, then you're right. You've graciously allowed me a second chance with you. I want every-thing that comes with that, including making love with you."

"God, Livvie. You think I don't? But one of us has to hold on to a little sanity. Trust me, when you get well, you may be wishing you'd never started this fire again."

"I *am* well . . . well enough." Then she slid out of the inner tube and walked toward him. "See? I'm standing before you. On my own two feet. Shamelessly begging you."

"You don't have to beg," Trey said.

"I don't?"

The taunt pushed him over.

"Okay, woman. You win. Get your hot body out of my pool and into my house. I'll give you two minutes to get from the back door to my bed."

Olivia started climbing out of the pool. She reached for her towel as he slid his fingers beneath the back of the bra of her two-piece suit. It popped open and fell off her shoulders before she knew it was undone.

She turned, her hands automatically going to cover herself as her eyes widened in surprise. The passion on his face was startling, then exciting.

Her hands were on her breasts. Trey wanted them on him.

"One minute," Trey said.

She looked down at the bra lying on the concrete, then turned and headed for the back door. Seconds after she was inside, she heard the door slam, then the click of a lock. Before she knew it, he was right behind her.

She paused in the hall, uncertain which bedroom to go to.

"Time's up," Trey said, and scooped her into his arms and carried her into his bedroom. He stood her up long enough to pull the bottom part of her swimsuit off, then pulled back the covers and gently laid her down in the middle of his bed.

"Trey, we're getting everything all wet."

"Wet is good."

She shivered.

He pulled his trunks down, then stepped out of them, leaving them where they lay.

For a few moments Olivia stared her fill of his body and at the water droplets clinging to his skin and hair.

"Don't move," he said softly, and crawled into bed.

Breath caught in the back of her throat as he straddled her legs, then rocked back on his heels.

She started to reach for him, then winced.

"Dammit, Livvie . . . I told you not to move."

"Dammit back, Trey Bonney. I want to touch you and hold you. I want to know what it's like to be loved again."

He went down on his hands and knees, kneeling over her while keeping the weight of his body off her.

"Ah, sweetheart, I'll show you all that and more. Just close your eyes and enjoy the ride."

Olivia did as she was told.

At first she felt nothing except the give of the mattress

on either side of her body from the weight of his hands and knees.

Then something warm moved across the peaks of her breasts, and she knew it was his breath. He wasn't touching her, but she knew he was there. Her heart skipped a beat.

The warmth moved slowly from her breasts down past her rib cage, lingering at her belly button; then something wet swirled around the edge before dipping in.

She moaned. It was his tongue.

He moved lower, pausing at the juncture of her thighs. She felt the heat of his body and instinctively tried to open for him to come in. As she did, displaced water droplets from her own body shook free and rolled off her skin.

Again she heard him whisper.

"Olivia . . . don't move."

She was shivering now, wanting to touch him—to touch herself.

But there was no contact as he moved past her offering.

Now the heat from his breath was on her thighs, then her knees. When she suddenly felt his hands encircling her ankles, she stifled a scream.

"Easy," he whispered. "Let me."

He gripped her ankles, then loosened his touch enough to run his hands up to her knees, then back down to her ankles, skimming the surface of her skin just enough to remind her he was there.

Olivia shuddered.

"Trey . . . Trey."

"Shh."

She sighed and once again followed his directions.

He stroked her legs, slowly, intently. First up. Then down. Then up again. Then back down. Over and over, his fingers moved upon her skin, until she was lulled into a false sense of security.

Suddenly his fingers were encircling her ankles and he was pulling her legs apart.

She gasped. Finally.

But he didn't take her. Not yet. Not then.

"Have mercy," Olivia whispered.

"Is that what you want?" she heard him ask. "Do you want me to stop?"

"No. God, no."

She thought she heard him laugh, but the blood was hammering so hard against her eardrums that she could have been mistaken.

His hands were on her thighs now, rubbing up, then smoothing down, then sliding back up to the juncture without touching her where it ached.

Over and over. Up and then down.

Again he lulled her into a false sense of security. Just when her bones were beginning to turn to water, he pulled her legs up and gently bent her knees. Before she could think, his thumb was on her center.

She tried to arch toward it, but he wouldn't let her up. His voice was barely a whisper she had to strain to hear.

"I told you, Livvie, don't move. Don't move."

Then his fingers were on the nub, and he was rubbing. Up and then down. Around and around.

Olivia was holding her breath, but she didn't even know it until he told her to breathe, and when she did, lights popped behind her closed eyelids, like fireworks on the Fourth of July.

"Trey."

The panic in her voice was almost his undoing. He couldn't put his weight on any part of her body without fear of causing her pain, while he was nothing but one big ache.

He wanted in her so bad he couldn't think, yet somehow he managed to hold himself back.

And still he rubbed. Up and then down. Around and around.

The pressure was building fast, pushing downward to the pit of Olivia's belly, then farther down—all the way down to where his hand lay on her body, where her blood pulsed against his fingers in a hard and constant rhythm.

Olivia started to beg him; then speech became impossible. The fire he'd been fanning suddenly burst beneath his touch. Her chin came up, her head rolled back. Trey rose far enough up to press his mouth against her lips, catching the scream he'd heard coming.

He held her then, captured only by his mouth upon her lips and his hand upon her body, and when he felt the last trembling spasm sliding through her, he raised himself up on his hands, made a place for himself between her legs and moved in.

Olivia was immobile. He'd melted her as surely as if he'd set fire to her skin and then nailed her to the bed. He was in her now, pushing in, then pulling out. Completely satiated, weak and spent, she could do nothing but lie there.

He was bigger than she'd remembered—and so hard. Yet when he moved, it was like silk sliding within her. Just like in high school, they were still a perfect fit. He rocked her where she lay, in a rhythm perfect to the beating of her heart.

And when he came, she cried—for the loss of all those years they might have had together, and from the joy of loving him again.

One moment Trey had been sound asleep in the bed with Olivia curled up in his arms; the next he was sitting straight up in bed without knowing the reason why. He listened closely to the sounds of the house, trying to figure out if he'd heard something in his sleep that had awakened him, but everything was silent. He glanced at the clock. It was just after two in the morning.

Olivia rolled over, her expression confused and her voice raspy as she asked, "What's happening? Is something wrong?"

"No, baby, everything is just fine. Go back to sleep."

She closed her eyes as Trey got out of bed.

His wet swimsuit was on the floor where he'd left it. He picked it up, carried it into the bathroom and tossed it over the shower rod to dry. A pair of his shorts were hanging from a hook on the back of the bathroom door. He pulled them on and then headed out of his bedroom, intent on searching the house. Instinct had awakened him, and he wouldn't be satisfied until he knew everything was okay.

The house was quiet, as were the streets outside. Nothing had been disturbed. Still, he took his gun out of the drawer and did a quick check of the yard, making sure that all the screens were in place and the doors still locked. Once he was satisfied that all was well, he started back inside the house. That was when he noticed the lights were on at Ella's. He frowned. That was odd.

He pulled the front door shut and started across the yard. He was halfway across Ella's backyard when he saw the shadow of a man move between the light and the curtains on the windows. He frowned. Ella was a widow. Her only son lived in Florida. Then he remembered she'd been keeping company with some guy who owned a bunch of funeral homes. It would be embarrassing to think he was catching a thief and catch them together instead.

He paused and started to retrace his steps, when he saw the man raise an arm above his head. Trey stared in disbelief as something flew from his hand. When he heard the sound of breaking glass, followed by Ella crying out, he began to run.

He kicked in the back door with his bare foot and went in with his gun aimed. He caught a brief glimpse of Ella in her nightgown, tied up on the floor with the kitchen in shambles. He caught a glimpse of motion from the corner of his eye as a man came out from behind a door with a gun in his hand aimed right at Trey's head.

Trey spun and fired.

The man staggered, then dropped.

Trey kicked the gun to the other end of the room, then yanked an electric cord from the back of a toaster and tied him up before he could come to. He looked around for a phone, but the man had pulled it out of the wall.

Ella moaned.

He rushed to her side. She had a bruise on her face and a bloody lip, and when he untied her and helped her to her feet, she staggered.

"Easy, honey," Trey said, then picked her up and carried her to the window seat at her bay window. "What happened?" he asked. "Are you hurt anywhere else?"

"No. I'm just a little dizzy and a whole lot pissed," she said.

A little of the panic he'd been feeling dissipated. Ella being pissed was more normal than Ella being scared.

"He broke into my house. I thought I heard something and started to get up. Before I could get to the phone, he was in my bedroom trying to rob me. Said he wanted my cash."

"I pointed to my purse, and to the roll of money I'd

won off Marcus, but he didn't even touch it. He just kept talking crazy and swiping at his face, like there were spiderwebs or something he was trying to wipe off."

"Trey?"

Trey turned. Olivia was standing in the open doorway wearing a pair of sweatpants and an oversize T-shirt he recognized as his own.

"Stay with her," he said quickly. "I've got to find a phone."

"He pulled them all out of the walls," Ella said.

Olivia stared at the man on the floor, then gasped when she saw Ella's face.

"Oh no!" she cried, and hurried to Ella's side.

"I'm all right," the old woman muttered. "Just a little bunged up."

The man on the floor moaned. Trey flinched. He couldn't leave these two women alone with this creep, even if he was shot and tied up. From the way Ella had described his behavior, he would lay odds the man was higher than a kite.

"I changed my mind," Trey told Olivia. "Go back to our house and get my cell. It's on the hall table."

Olivia bolted, and was back far more quickly than Trey would have thought possible. She handed him the phone, then went to Ella's side.

Within minutes, police and ambulances were on the scene.

The man was taken into custody and transported to a hospital, while Ella was treated on-site. She argued about staying home, but Trey wouldn't listen. He told the EMTs to take her to the hospital and make sure she didn't have any internal injuries or a concussion.

Ella wanted to be mad, but she was too shaken up to argue. Instead, she pointed her finger at Olivia.

"You go back to the house and get in bed. You look pale."

Olivia wanted to laugh, but her eyes filled with tears. She leaned over and kissed Ella on the cheek as the EMTs were carrying her out of the house.

"You be good and get well."

Ella's mouth crumpled. "Now who's gonna take care of you?"

"When you come home, we'll take care of each other," Olivia said.

Ella managed a smile, but it was faint. Then Trey was pulling Olivia out of the way, and the ambulance soon sped away. A couple of detectives from robbery showed up. They recognized Trey on sight.

"Hey, Bonney! You live here?" one of them asked.

"No. Next door," Trey said.

"Can you fill us in?"

Trey nodded. "Yeah, just give me a minute to get Livvie back to the house."

"I can get myself there," Olivia said as Trey took her by the elbow.

"I know," he said as they started out the door. "But I need to know for myself that you're all right. I can't have both of my best girls out of commission."

Olivia sighed, then leaned against him as he walked

her back to the house. It wasn't until they were in his front yard that she realized her legs were shaking.

"I heard the gunshot," she said.

Trey kept on walking without missing a step.

"Yeah."

"I never heard the shot that hit me," she said. "But I got that same feeling of panic in my stomach."

"I'm sorry, honey. I'm sorry you were scared."

"It's okay. I'm just thankful Ella wasn't hurt worse."

"Me too."

"Trey?"

"Yeah?"

"How did you know?"

"Know what?"

"Know that he was there . . . that something was wrong?"

He paused in the halo of his porch light.

"I don't know. I just woke up and knew."

Olivia turned and slid her arms around his waist.

"You saved her life, Trey, just like you saved mine."

"Yeah, well, it was just—"

"You're a good man, Trey Bonney. It's going to be tough living up to someone like you."

"You don't have to live up to me, darlin'. Just live with me for the rest of my life."

"Was that a proposal?" she asked.

"Yes."

"Then I accept."

Trey tried to smile but couldn't quite get past the emotion welling up inside him.

"I have waited a long damn time to say those words to you, and you know what?"

"What?"

"Not once did I ever think you would tell me no. Isn't that strange?"

Olivia laid her head on Trey's chest and hugged him close.

"No, not strange, Trey. It just proves that your instincts are always right."

"Yeah . . . well, let's get you back to bed. I won't be long giving my statement. I need to get a little more sleep before I go back to work."

"Why? What's happening?" she asked.

It was the first time that Trey realized he hadn't told her about Sheree Collier or the meeting with Foster Lawrence. And it was just as well. No need reminding Olivia of the unanswered questions surrounding her identity until all the facts were out.

"Just more meetings and more questions to be answered about Baby Jane Doe."

Olivia nodded. "I'll be waiting for you," she said, and then disappeared back into the house.

Trey stood for a moment, taking to heart what she'd just said.

She would be waiting for him.

He couldn't think of anything better.

20

The events of the past two days and nights had Trey exhausted from lack of sleep. With Ella in the hospital for observation, he'd called Marcus to tell him what had happened and that Olivia would be by herself for the day.

Marcus had been horrified by the news about his new poker partner.

"Not Ella!" Marcus said. "Please tell me that she's going to be all right."

"She's already all right. Nothing broken. No stitches necessary. She has some bruises and scrapes, but she's basically in good shape."

"Praise the Lord," Marcus murmured. "As for Olivia, don't worry about her. Either I will be with her, or Terrence and Carolyn will come. They've been anxious to see her. If you don't mind having your house overrun with our family, that is."

"No, sir, not at all. I'm just sorry all this is happening. Also, I have a favor to ask."

"Ask away," Marcus said.

"When you come, could you possibly bring some pictures of Olivia before her parents were killed?"

"Yes, of course, but why?"

Trey quickly filled Marcus in on everything that had happened with Sheree Collier, and the fact that she'd seen a baby with Laree off and on for the two years prior to the kidnapping.

"So she might be able to give us a positive identification?" Marcus asked.

"Between that and her DNA, before long, we should be able to answer the question of which baby is which."

"Tell Olivia that one of us, or all of us, will be there shortly."

"Remember, I have a pool at the house. It's small, but it's a great way to pass the time. Livvie will be in it part of the day doing therapy on her shoulder."

"Trey."

"Yes?"

"I feel the need to tell you again how sorry I am that I so misjudged you."

"Forget it. That was a long time ago."

"Still, I don't like it that I was so narrow-minded. I thought myself better than that. You've shamed me by your generosity and your ability to forgive. Don't think I'm unaware of that, or of the fine man you've so obviously become."

Trey didn't say so, but he took heart that Marcus approved of him now. It wouldn't have changed his determination to marry Olivia, but it definitely made things easier for them to pursue a relationship.

"Then, I'll say thank you, and we won't have to speak of it again," Trey said.

"Done," Marcus said, then glanced at his watch. "I'm going to call Carolyn right now. Terrence can take her to your house. I had promised Anna Walden that I'd bring her to see Olivia. The people at the home said she's confused about where Olivia is, and I thought a brief visit might help. If it was for any other reason, I'd just put her off, but I hate to confuse her any more than she already is."

"No problem," Trey said. "Livvie's been concerned about her. She'll be glad to see her, I'm sure," Trey said. "Oh . . . and I heard about the poker game."

Marcus chuckled. "I lost."

"Yeah, I heard that, too."

"She told me I was too old for her," Marcus said. "Can you beat that?"

Trey laughed out loud.

Olivia came into the room just then and smiled to herself. She had always loved the sound of his laugh.

When Trey saw her, he waved her over.

"Marcus . . . wait a minute. Livvie just woke up. I'll let you talk to her while I finish getting ready for work. Hope to see you this evening."

He handed Olivia the phone, kissed his own thumb, then put it square in the middle of her lips and winked.

Olivia was so muddled by the unexpected gesture that she forgot her grandfather was on the line.

"Trey, I—"

He put a finger up to his lips to remind her to be cautious of what she said, then grinned. She blushed and put the phone up to her ear.

"Grampy?"

"Good morning, darling. How are you feeling?"

"How am I feeling? Oh . . . I feel fine."

Trey was looking at her, undressing her with his

eyes. She made a face at him, then pointed a finger at him to leave. Satisfied that he'd gotten under her skin, which was his intention, he grinned, then walked away.

Unaware of the byplay, Marcus continued his explanation.

"I had a phone call from the home where Anna is staying. They said she's been looking all over the place for you, so I thought it might help her if she came for a quick visit. Are you up to that?"

"Oh, Grampy, yes! I've been so worried about her. I would love to see her."

"Good. I told Trey that Terrence and Carolyn have been anxious to see you, so I'll send them your way first, and Anna and I will come along later."

Olivia's heart lifted. All her family together. It would be great.

"That sounds perfect. I'll be looking for them," she said.

"We'll see you later, then."

"Okay. Bye, Grampy."

"Goodbye, dear."

She hung up, then went in search of Trey.

When he heard her footsteps, he turned. His smile was quick, his voice low and husky when he said, "Good morning, Livvie."

She walked up to him.

"Good morning yourself. Did you get any more rest after we went back to bed?"

"Yeah, some. Enough to get by, anyway." He slid a

hand beneath her hair at the back of her neck, then pulled her close.

She lifted her chin.

He lowered his head.

Their lips met—hers opening slightly. She tasted minty, like his toothpaste, and he got hard just thinking about how they'd made love. When they finally parted, Trey made a low, growling sound, then frowned, reluctant to let her go.

"First time I ever knew toothpaste could be sexy."

Olivia grinned. "Anything that has to do with you is sexy to me."

"Keep talking like that, woman, and I'll be late for work."

Suddenly Olivia's smile felt wrong. She was experiencing so much joy when so many things had gone wrong.

"Speaking of work . . ."

Trey stifled a frown. He'd been dreading having to tell her about the new developments, but he knew it had to be done. Now she'd even given him an opening.

"What about it?"

"I've been so out of the loop. What's been happening since Dennis Rawlins was arrested and put away?"

"A couple of pretty important things, actually."

"Like what?" she asked, and sat down on the corner of his mattress.

Trey sat down beside her. "We know that Foster Lawrence got mixed up in the kidnapping because of one of his sisters."

Olivia gasped. "His sister? Is she the person who killed my parents?"

"Probably, but we don't have any solid proof of it. All we have is Lawrence's version. He says he didn't arrive on the scene until after the kidnapping had occurred. I believe him. To make a long story short, his sister's name is Laree Lawrence, and she called him to come fix a hole in a wall. He was doing that when a baby girl came out of the other room."

"That would be me," Olivia said.

Trey didn't comment.

Then it dawned on Olivia what Trey had said before.

"He was fixing a hole in— Oh my God . . . the baby in the suitcase?"

He nodded.

"Who was the baby? Why did she kill her?"

Trey took her hands, then held them gently, wanting her to know that he was always with her, no matter what.

"We also found out some more information about Foster Lawrence. Laree was an identical twin. We found her twin, Sheree Lawrence Collier, in Miami. She's been in Dallas since yesterday. She gave us a DNA sample and was the one who finally got Lawrence to talk."

Olivia frowned. "Why would you want a DNA sample from her when she wasn't involved in the crime?"

"As I said before, we believe Laree killed your parents, but she also had a baby the same age as the one that Michael and Kay had. We know that Michael was the father of both girls. And as you know, one of the babies was killed. What we have been needing all along was some way to prove which was which. It's difficult to believe two half sisters would look that much alike, and your grandfather is positive that you're you." He grinned and poked the end of her nose. "And I know for sure that you're the you I fell in love with, and the one I don't ever intend to lose again."

Olivia's lips trembled, but she wouldn't let herself cry.

"Yeah. We know that for sure, don't we, Trey?"

"Damn straight. So Sheree gave a DNA sample, which can help us prove which baby was which, be cause identical twins share identical DNA."

"Oh."

"And there's another plus."

"I can't believe any part of it is a plus, but . . . go on."

Trey made a face, then kissed Olivia's cheek.

"Sorry, baby . . . I was speaking from the standpoint of a detective trying to solve a crime."

"I know, and I'm the one who's sorry. I keep feeling so damn sorry for myself, when I should be thanking the good Lord that I'm still alive. It's just as likely that I could have been the one in the suitcase."

"Exactly."

"So . . . the other plus? Remember?"

"Yeah. Sheree saw her sister several times over the two years before the kidnapping, and each time, she had a little girl, the same little girl, who she kept claiming she was baby-sitting. Only now we know different. So here's the deal. Sheree Collier's DNA will confirm, once and for all, which of the babies is which."

"Does she know where her sister is now?"

"No."

"Okay," Olivia said. "I can see where this is still a positive thing."

But Trey heard the fear in her voice. "It's scary news, I know. But you have to keep remembering that neither Marcus nor I cares which way it turns out. You're still the girl we love."

She nodded, then leaned against him, letting his arms enfold her and give her the momentary confidence she so desperately needed.

A short while later, Trey left for work. Olivia waved goodbye as if everything were perfect; then, as soon as she was alone, she began to shake. Her whole world was teetering on the blood of a stranger. She couldn't bear to think of being the child of a killer. Even if Michael Sealy had been her father, her Grampy would never be able to look at her the same again and not remember that her mother had killed his son.

"God, please don't let it happen."

By noon, Trey's house was filled with guests. Ella had been released from the hospital, brought home by ambulance, and was holding court on a lounge chair by Trey's pool.

Terrence and Carolyn were there, too, suitably shocked by Olivia's healing gunshot wound and equally taken by Trey's next-door neighbor, who had plenty of stories to tell about Trey, the hero of the hour.

". . . and then he kicked in the door and came in shooting. I've never been so glad to see anyone in my entire life," she said.

"My word!" Carolyn exclaimed, eyeing Olivia with renewed interest. "And you say you've known him since high school?"

"Not exactly. I knew him in high school. Then we . . . uh . . . lost touch with each other until recently. He was assigned to the case of Baby Jane Doe, which, of course, led back to me."

Carolyn smiled and put both hands on her heart.

"How romantic. Childhood sweethearts find each other again."

Terrence smiled benevolently.

"My wife. Ever the romantic."

"And why not, I ask? What's wrong with happy ever after?"

"That's been my philosophy," Ella said, and winked at Olivia. "I think I'm going to like having her for a neighbor."

Olivia blushed, but she was happy—happier than she'd ever been in her life.

"How about some lunch?" she asked.

Carolyn jumped up. "I'll fix it. Just show me where everything is."

"Follow me," Olivia said, and when Ella would have gotten up, she pointed at her and frowned sternly. "You can come in, but you're not going to do anything."

"Allow me," Terrence said, and offered Ella his arm, which she took gratefully.

They moved into the kitchen, where Ella was seated at the table despite her complaints. Olivia and Carolyn were fixing sandwiches when they heard a knock at the door.

"I'll get it," Terrence said.

Olivia looked up, her hands messy from the tomatoes she was slicing. "That's probably Grampy and Anna."

"Better make a couple more sandwiches, then," Carolyn said.

Olivia nodded and sliced another tomato. She was rinsing off her hands when Marcus and Anna came into the kitchen. Anna was cuddling a doll in her arms, but otherwise looked healthy and fit. Her hair had been washed and fixed, and she was wearing a nice pair of beige slacks and a loose cotton blouse in a pink and beige print.

Olivia felt sad for the confusion on Anna's face, but when she said Anna's name, some of the confusion lifted.

"Grampy! I'm so glad to see you and thank you for bringing Anna to visit." Then she put a hand on Anna's arm and moved directly in front of her. "Anna . . . it's so good to see you again."

Anna blinked. She knew that voice. She looked closer at the woman in blue, then smiled, because she knew that face, too.

"Olivia? Are you my Olivia?"

Olivia put her arms around Anna's shoulders and just held her close.

"Yes, darling. I'm your Olivia. Come and sit down here beside Ella. She's a new friend of mine."

Anna frowned a bit.

"Can she make meat loaf like Rose?"

"No one makes meat loaf like Rose," Olivia said. "But Ella can play cards. She's very good at poker."

Ella grinned, then patted the chair beside her. She'd been briefed about the woman's declining mental health and felt empathy. She was all too familiar with the effects of declining years.

"I like to play cards, too," Anna said.

Ella smiled. "Then we will. What do you like to play?"

Anna frowned. "I think I like to play hearts."

Olivia put her arm around Anna's shoulder and tried not to look at the plastic baby doll she was clutching so tight.

"We can play after we eat. Would you like to eat with us, Anna?"

"Yes, please," she said.

"Sandwiches are ready," Carolyn said.

"Great!" Terrence said. "I'm starving." Then he smiled, a little bit embarrassed. "I suppose I'm not really *starving,* but I *am* hungry."

Everybody laughed, which lightened the mood. Even Marcus found the grace to chuckle. He put his arm around Olivia as they began seating themselves around the kitchen table and whispered in her ear, "How are you holding up?"

Olivia resisted the urge to roll her eyes.

"I'm fine, Grampy. I'll just be so glad when all this has been settled."

"Trey told you about finding Foster Lawrence's sister?"

"Yes."

"He asked me to bring some old photo albums for the woman to look at. They're in the living room."

Olivia nodded.

"Don't worry about any of that now," she said. "Let's just eat."

Marcus hugged her, then helped her into a chair. Carolyn busied herself carrying the last of the food to the table, then they all began to eat.

"I think we need to bless the food," Anna said.

They all stopped.

"Yes, of course," Marcus said quickly.

"I'll do it," Anna said, and laid the doll she was holding in her lap.

Nobody said a word as they all bowed their heads.

For a few moments Anna was silent. Then she leaned forward and closed her eyes.

"Thank you for the food. Thank you for the friends. Thank you for helping me find my baby, amen."

"Amen," Marcus echoed.

The meal began with some awkward moments, but the uneasiness soon disappeared as they began to eat. When they were done with their sandwiches, Olivia went to the pantry and got the cookies Ella had baked the day before, while Carolyn began refilling the glasses of sweet iced tea.

Marcus began praising the cookies, and Carolyn was teasing him about the cookie crumbs at the corner of his mouth, when they heard the front door open, then shut.

Carolyn stopped speaking in the middle of a word. There was a long stretch of silence, then Olivia spoke.

"It's probably Trey."

Marcus got up to see, just the same.

Moments later, he was back with Trey, but Trey wasn't alone.

"Hey," Trey said. "Looks like we're just in time."

Olivia got up and greeted him with a quick kiss to the cheek.

"We have some sandwiches left over in the fridge. Are you hungry?"

Trey hesitated. He hadn't expected to bring Sheree Collier to a family reunion when he'd stopped to check on Olivia, but it was too late to do anything about it now. He turned and looked at Sheree, who was obviously uncomfortable.

"Everyone, this is Sheree Collier. Mrs. Collier, would you like something to eat?"

"No, but thank you," she said quickly, well aware that at least some of these people were part of the family her sister had decimated.

Everyone nodded politely at Sheree, but tension was high.

Marcus's expression was drawn, but, ever the gentleman, he offered Sheree his chair.

"Mrs. Collier, won't you please sit? At least have a cold drink and some of these cookies. They're delicious."

Unaware of the underlying tension, Ella beamed.

"I made them myself," she said.

Sheree smiled stiffly, gave each person in the room a quick glance, then sat down. She took a cookie and nibbled at it while Carolyn went to fix a glass of iced tea.

Trey turned to Marcus.

"Did you bring those pictures?" he asked.

"Yes, they're in the living room."

"I'll get them," Trey said, and hurried from the room.

When he came back, Terrence was helping Carolyn clear the table, and Sheree Collier was sipping tea and trying to look inconspicuous, but it was impossible, considering the unusual connection they all shared.

"I found my baby," Anna said, and beamed.

Sheree glanced at the odd, heavyset woman, then at the doll she was holding, and quickly looked away. Olivia felt like crying. Her poor Anna was gone. There was nothing left but a shell of the person she'd been.

Trey laid the album down in front of Sheree, then looked up.

"I think you all know why Mrs. Collier is here, and you need to understand that she is in no way guilty for what amounts to a tragedy in her family, as well. But if her presence is going to make you uncomfortable, she and I can go into the other room to look at these photos."

"I have no problem with you staying," Marcus said.

Terrence and Carolyn didn't answer, only nodded, which Trey took for agreement with Marcus. Carolyn kept staring intently at Sheree Collier, as if trying to see the woman from so long ago in her face. Finally she looked up at Trey, then shook her head.

He understood that she'd been unable to identify the woman she'd seen with Michael. It had been a long shot. They still had the pictures, though, and the outcome of the DNA test.

Suddenly Sheree gasped as she looked, for the first time, straight into the eyes of the child her sister had taken, the child who had become a woman. Trey looked questioningly from the older woman to the younger.

"I'm fine," Olivia said, catching his gaze.

Sheree looked away, opened the first album and began scanning the pages. Marcus sat down beside her and began putting names to faces.

"That's my wife, Amelia, with our son, Michael. He was seventeen when she died. You don't want to look at all this. Let me turn to the pages where Olivia came into our family."

Sheree blinked back a quick blur of tears.

"Thank you," she said softly. Her hands were trembling as she laid them in her lap.

Anna got up from her chair and started out of the room.

"Where are you going?" Marcus asked.

"To put the baby to sleep," Anna said.

Ella got up. "I'll go with her," she said. "We're unnecessary here, anyway."

"Thank you, Ella," Trey said.

Sheree didn't pay any attention to their exit. She was busy scanning the pictures on the pages before her.

"Who's that?" she asked, pointing.

"That's Michael and his wife, Kay. That's Olivia, but she's all wrapped up. That's right after she was born. They were bringing her home from the hospital."

Sheree nodded. She stared at Michael's face for a long time, then at Kay. Finally she pointed to Kay.

"You know . . . she looks enough like my sister and I did at that age to be part of our family."

"Really?" Trey asked.

"Yes. We were all a little above average height, with dark wavy hair. Also, her face is shaped the same, and she had a turned-up nose. Odd."

Marcus frowned but remained silent.

Sheree looked through several more pages of pictures before her expression changed as she pointed to a picture in the middle of a page.

It was of Michael and Olivia, obviously taken at Easter. She was holding a small decorated basket of colored eggs. There was a smear of chocolate on her face and another one on the front of her dress, but they were laughing and looking straight into the camera.

"Oh my God," Sheree muttered.

Trey moved closer.

"What?"

"That little girl."

"What about her?" Marcus asked.

"It's the same one that Laree had at her home."

"It can't be," Marcus said. "That's Olivia before the kidnapping. She never had a nanny or a baby-sitter. She never went to day care. Kay hardly let her out of her sight."

Sheree frowned. "I know what I saw. That's the same little girl."

Trey felt sick. They'd considered the possibility that both of Michael's daughters might have resembled each other, but it had been too far-fetched to assume they would have been difficult to tell apart. Marcus's certainty that he'd recognized the child who'd been returned to him was the cornerstone of Olivia's entire identity.

"You're mistaken," Marcus argued.

"I know what I saw," Sheree said, and looked up at Trey, who shoved a hand through his hair in frustration.

"Look, there's no need to argue. We've already considered this possibility," he said.

"What possibility?" Marcus asked.

Olivia shrank back against the wall and put her hands over her ears. She didn't have to listen to know what was going to be said.

"That the two girls looked alike."

Marcus paled. "That's impossible. They had different mothers."

"Who Sheree has already stated looked alike." Then he added, "The little girl in that picture sure looks like your son, doesn't she?"

"Oh yes," Marcus said. "We noticed that from the start."

"So why couldn't both girls look like him?"

Marcus opened his mouth to argue, but then realization hit and he looked away, unwilling to admit the truth of it.

Trey glanced at Olivia. She looked as if she'd seen a ghost.

Sheree frowned and pointed at the picture. "Are you saying that the baby I saw isn't her?"

"I'm suggesting the possibility. You say she is, but Marcus is equally sure that the baby in this picture could never be the one you saw with your sister for the better part of two years."

"Dear God," Sheree said. "How will we ever know the truth?"

"Your DNA," Trey said. "It will be the deciding factor."

"Let me look some more," Sheree said. "Maybe I was mistaken. Maybe I just saw what I thought I was supposed to see."

"By all means. We want you to be sure," Trey said.

Sheree began going through more of the pages. It soon became apparent to her that a large gap of time had occurred before pictures were added again.

"These are all after Michael's and Kay's deaths, aren't they?" she asked. Tears were pouring freely down her face now. "I'm so sorry," she said. "So very, very sorry."

Marcus put a hand on her arm. "You didn't do it. You

have nothing for which to apologize."

But she just shook her head and kept turning the pages until, once again, she stopped. This time, when she pointed to a picture, she was shaking.

"Oh my God!" Sheree said.

Trey moved in for a closer look.

"Who is that?" he asked.

"Why, that's the nanny, Anna. That picture was taken a few months after she came to work for us," Marcus said.

Sheree gasped, then stood abruptly.

"She worked for you? That's not possible!"

The horror on Sheree's face was there for all to see, but it was Trey who understood first.

"Who is she, Sheree?" he asked.

"Laree. It's Laree. Oh dear God, that's my sister."

Olivia moaned as she sank to the floor, then covered her head with both arms, as if shielding herself from an oncoming blow.

Marcus's face paled instantly, then slowly turned a dark, angry red.

"I hired the woman who killed my son?"

Sheree was shaking, but there was a resolve in her voice that hadn't been there before.

"I don't know what she did, but that's my sister, Laree. Please, you have to tell me where she is. I have to see her."

"You were sitting across the table from her just a few minutes ago," Trey said.

Sheree frowned. "I'm sorry, but—"

"She was the one holding the doll."

Now she was the one in shock.

"It can't be. We're twins. I would know my own sister."

When she started to get up, Trey stopped her.

"Stay put. This is all happening too fast."

Olivia staggered to her feet and walked into Trey's arms.

He held her close, afraid for her in a way he couldn't control.

"Livvie . . . sweetheart . . . look at me."

Olivia moaned.

He took her hands away from her face and said it again. "Look at me."

Finally she did.

"Between us, none of this matters. Nothing changes."

She nodded.

"Say it," he said.

She drew a slow, shuddering breath, but it was the look in his eyes that got her through it.

"None of this matters. Nothing changes."

"Yes," he said softly, then held her close while he took his cell phone out of his pocket and dialed a number. When he got an answer, he began to talk fast.

"Chia . . . I need you and Sheets to get to my house ASAP. The Baby Jane Doe case is coming together and I need some disinterested parties."

Chia wasn't the kind to ask a lot of questions. "Be there in fifteen," she said.

"Make it ten."

"Lights and sirens all the way," she said.

Trey took a breath, then dropped the phone back in his pocket and put his arm around Olivia as he turned around.

"We're all going to go into the living room now. We're going to sit down, and you're not going to mention a thing about what's just been said. I'll do the talking, and you'll all just sit." Then he pointed to Sheree. "Can you handle that?"

She was crying openly now, but she nodded.

"Marcus? I need you not to react in any way. If I'm ever going to get anything out of her, she can't be upset."

Marcus was shaking. The fury on his face was evident.

"She lived in my house. She put her hands on my grandchild—and I let her," he said.

"We can't be sure which one died," Trey said. "Now, I don't know about you, but I want to know the truth of this damn mess. So, are you going to be quiet?"

Finally Marcus agreed.

"Yes."

"I'll hold you to your word," Trey said.

Terrence got up then and went to Marcus. For the first time since the night of their fight, he touched him.

"Marcus, we're here for you. Let us bear some of this pain."

When Terrence put his hand on Marcus's back, Marcus shuddered, but he didn't pull away. Carolyn took Marcus's hand, and together, they went into the living room and quietly took their seats.

Ella looked up as they all came in. She was in the act of opening her mouth when Trey frowned and shook his head. A little unnerved, she stayed in the chair next to Anna, who was calmly rocking the "baby" in her lap.

Olivia followed Trey into the room. She was afraid to look at Anna, but when she got closer, found she couldn't look away. This was the woman who'd killed her parents? The woman who'd murdered a baby? It seemed impossible, but then all she had to do was look at the shock on Sheree Collier's face to know that the woman hadn't lied. Not about something as horrible as this.

Once Trey was satisfied that everyone was settled, he moved a footstool next to Anna's rocker and sat down. For a few moments, the silence that held them seemed too heavy to bear. Then Trey leaned forward.

"Anna?"

She looked up, vaguely recognizing the face of the man, and smiled. "You love Olivia," she said.

Olivia bit her lip to keep from crying.

"Yes, I do. I love her very much."

"Love is good," Anna said, and held the doll a little closer.

"Who loves you, Anna?"

She frowned. "Why . . . Olivia loves me. She's always loved me." Then she leaned closer, whispering, "Always. Since the day she was born."

Olivia covered her face. She couldn't look at the woman anymore and even deal with the possibility that she was her mother—that she'd killed Michael and Kay's daughter and kept her. But it didn't make sense that she would have killed her own child.

If Olivia had believed her legs would work, she would have gotten up and walked out of the room. Instead, she was held captive by her fear and the weight of a madwoman's words.

"So which one is your baby, Anna?"

Anna frowned. She looked at the "baby" in her arms and then at Olivia. Her forehead furrowed, and she began to shake her head in denial.

"Not fair. Not fair."

Trey's stomach knotted. He was getting sicker for Olivia by the minute, but he couldn't quit now.

"What's not fair?"

Anna frowned again. Her lower lip pouted, and then she suddenly shoved the doll out of her lap.

"Doesn't want me or the baby. Not fair. Not fair."

"Who doesn't want you, Anna? Who doesn't want your baby?"

Anna's fingers curled into fists as they lay in her lap, and for a bit, she didn't answer.

Trey glanced at Sheree. He was about to take a big chance on Anna clamming up completely, but it was a risk he had to take.

"Laree."

Anna reeled as if she'd been struck. Her eyes filled with tears, and then she shook her head in denial.

"She's dead."

"Who's dead?"

"Laree. Nobody wanted her . . . or her baby." Then she chuckled. "But they wanted Anna. Anna was somebody special. She got her baby and the place where she belonged."

"God in heaven," Marcus muttered.

Trey gave him a warning glance.

Terrence put his arm around Marcus's shoulder as Carolyn clutched his hand.

"Who didn't want Laree?" Trey asked.

"Michael. Michael lied. You're not supposed to lie."

"That's right, Anna. You're not supposed to lie."

The sound of police sirens suddenly pierced the uneasy silence in the room. Trey looked pointedly at Ella, who was the only one personally unaffected by the revelations.

"Are you up to being my welcome committee?"

"Absolutely," she said. "I'll wait for them outside and bring them in."

"Thanks," Trey said.

Anna frowned and looked down at the doll she'd pushed aside.

"Too many babies. Michael wanted Laree once. Then she had that stupid baby."

Trey grunted as if he'd been punched in the gut. He was afraid to continue, but he had to go on.

"If Laree didn't want her own baby, why did she take the other one?"

"What other baby?" Anna muttered.

"The one that was in Michael's house."

"That's my baby. My baby deserved to be special."

Once again, Trey was stunned. What had she just said? Had she substituted her child for the real Sealy heir?

Olivia was sobbing quietly now. Trey heard her from across the room, yet he didn't dare go to her for fear that Anna would stop talking. And there was so much that needed to be said.

"Your baby was special," Trey said.

"Yes. Special."

"Then which baby did you put in the suitcase? Which baby did you hide behind the wall?"

Anna reeled in the chair as if Trey had just punched her square in the jaw. Her fingers curled on the arms of the chair as the doll she'd been holding fell to the floor. In a sad twist of irony, she rocked on its head, breaking it open.

It cracked like a shot.

Anna cried out in dismay and tried to reach down, but Trey wouldn't let her move.

"Which one?" Trey asked, pushing harder now. "Which one did you kill?"

Anna put her hands over her ears and then screamed.

"The wrong one was with Michael. I gave them mine."

At that point, she slid to the floor in a faint.

21

Chia and Sheets came running into the house as Anna slid onto the floor.

"What the hell?" Chia asked, and reached for her cell. "Is she sick? Do you need an ambulance? What happened to her?"

Trey pointed.

"That's our missing twin. She needs to be arrested, and I don't want to be the arresting officer of record when I'm going to marry the woman who may be her daughter."

Chia's mouth dropped.

"What in hell are you—"

"It's a long ugly story," Trey said, and then felt for Anna's pulse. It was strong and steady. "She just fainted, but we're going to have a hell of a time taking her to trial. She's out of her mind, and I would be, too, if I was in her shoes. Just take care of her," he said, and moved toward Olivia as fast as he could go.

She was in the corner of the room with her hands over her ears and her eyes squeezed shut. The keening sound coming up her throat was as scary to him as the night she'd been shot.

"Livvie . . ."

She wouldn't look at him, and she wouldn't stop moaning.

"Livvie . . . sweetheart," he begged, and then picked

her up and carried her out of the room.

He took her to her room, kicking the door shut behind him as he went, then sat down on the bed and held her in his lap and began to rock her where they sat.

"I know, baby, I know," he said softly, and rubbed his chin against the crown of her hair as she clung to him in shock. "It's going to be okay. You're my sweet-heart . . . my love . . . we're in this together, remember? You for me and me for you. Just like when we were kids."

The horrible sound she'd been making stopped. She was shaking, but she was finally quiet. He knew that somewhere inside the hell in her mind, she was listening to the sound of his voice.

"You're my best girl. Always were. Always will be. There isn't anyone or anything that can change that. You know that, Livvie. Trust your heart. Trust in me. I love you, baby. So much. So much."

And still he rocked. He felt her shaking subside, then felt her go limp.

"You're all right, Livvie. Do you hear me? You're all right."

"I hear you," she said.

A wave of relief swept through Trey so fast that it took his breath away. For a few moments he didn't trust himself to speak. He leaned back far enough that he could look into her face. He saw a terrible sadness in her eyes, but the woman he knew and loved was back.

"I need to talk to your grandfather for a minute. Will you be all right until I get back?"

She nodded.

"I won't be long."

"Go," she said. "Do whatever you have to do to make this go away."

"I'm doing my best."

"That's all I ask," she said.

When he laid her on the bed, she rolled over onto her side and curled into a ball. He recognized the defense. She was making herself as small a target as possible so as not to be hurt anymore.

"Love you, baby," he said again.

She shuddered, then closed her eyes. "I don't deserve you, but I thank God that you're here."

He had to be satisfied with that as he hurried from the room.

An ambulance had come and gone, taking Anna away.

Marcus was all but prostrate, and Ella was tending to him as if she'd done it all her life.

But it was Terrence and Carolyn who'd stepped into the breach and taken charge.

"Talk to me," Trey said.

Terrence moved a distance away to spare Marcus the pain of having to relive this again.

"They arrested the woman and tried to read her rights to her, but we all agreed she didn't hear or understand them. The paramedics have taken her to Dallas Memorial. The other two detectives took Mrs. Collier with them to the hospital. They said to tell you they'd be in touch."

Trey nodded, then glanced at Marcus.

"Does he need a doctor?"

"I don't think so. He just needs time."

"Who could have known?" Carolyn said as she walked up behind her husband and then slipped her hand along his elbow. "If we hadn't been in Italy when all this started happening, I'm sure we would have recognized Anna as the woman Michael had introduced us to."

"But we *were* in Italy," Terrence said. "And nothing can be changed. Nothing can be taken back. God knows I've lived with the truth of that fact all my life."

Carolyn laid her head on Terrence's shoulder as she turned to Trey.

"What's going to happen to Anna?" Carolyn asked.

"Probably wind up in a hospital for the criminally insane."

"We don't really know which baby she killed, do we?" she asked.

"No."

"But we will?"

"When the DNA test Sheree submitted to comes back, we'll know, although we will also take one from Anna . . . Laree . . . to make the result irrefutable."

"Is Olivia all right?"

"No, but she will be."

"I'm so sorry," Carolyn said. "But I must tell you that we're blessed to have you in the family."

"Thank you," Trey said. "But the blessing is all mine."

"Trey!"

It was Marcus, and the command in his voice was unmistakable. Trey turned around, acknowledging the demand without taking offense.

"Yes?"

Marcus stood up.

"Whatever truth has been revealed today, you need to know that we are grateful."

"Yes, sir," Trey said.

"I thought I told you to call me Marcus."

Trey sighed. "That you did."

Marcus reached for Trey's hand and started to shake it, then embraced him instead. The hug was brief, and he quickly dropped his arms and stepped away.

"Thank you. I had decided that my son's killer would never be found, that I would go to my grave without an answer." His voice was raspy and thick with emotion.

"But there are still questions, aren't there?" Trey asked.

Marcus's features tightened as he wiped a hand across his eyes.

"She's still my granddaughter. It doesn't matter. Whatever the truth, it won't change what's between us."

"Even if the woman who gave her life is the one who killed your son?" Trey asked.

Marcus swayed on his feet, but his gaze never left Trey's face.

"Even then."

"She's in her bedroom," Trey said. "She'd probably

like to hear that from you."

Marcus nodded, then walked out of the room.

"God in heaven," Trey muttered, and then stuffed his hands in his pockets. That was when he realized Ella was gone.

"Where's Ella? Is she ill? Hell, with all that's happened here, she—"

"I'm fine," Ella said as she came hobbling out of the kitchen. "Open your hand," she ordered.

He obeyed without thought.

She dropped a couple of painkillers in his palm, then handed him a glass of water.

"Take them. If you don't already have a headache, you will."

Trey downed the pills and the water, then set the glass aside and put his arms around the tiny woman.

"I'm not liking the fact that my best girls are too damn fragile to hug properly."

"We're only bent, not broken," she said, and hugged him back.

"Thank God," Trey muttered. "And thank you. For everything."

"Hey, since you went and saved my life, it's the least I can do."

"Shut up, Ella. Just shut up," he muttered.

She grinned.

"My hero."

Trey groaned. Some hero. He'd just destroyed the best part of Olivia's world and was praying to God that she would be able to forgive him.

• • •

After another week, Olivia's shoulder was almost well. Only now and then did it twinge, usually when she was trying to lift more than she should.

Foster Lawrence had been released from jail and, at his sister Sheree's invitation, had finally gotten that trip to Florida. He was going back home to live with her.

Rose had come to see Olivia right after Anna's arrest, full of concern and shock. Olivia hadn't been able to talk about it, and she sensed Rose was miffed about being left out of the loop, but she couldn't let herself care. It took everything she had to cope with her own doubts and fears.

Ella's presence next door, as well as her wise and often caustic wisdom, made getting through the days easier. And there was the sight of Trey's car coming up the driveway each evening to get her through the nights.

There was a distance between her grandfather and herself that was all her doing. He'd tried to talk to her about what had happened, but Olivia didn't believe him. She didn't know how he could ever look at her again without remembering Anna's revelations, because she had yet to conquer the disgust at seeing her own face in the mirror.

For days she'd searched her features, looking for something—anything—that would match the face of the young woman Anna had been with her own face.

She looked, but she couldn't see past the haunted expression in her own eyes. She didn't know what she would do if the worst were found to be true.

Trey was her strength—her rock—her love. It was only through him that she was able to cope. She held on to his faith in her and tried to let that be enough.

And then one day the phone rang.

She answered.

"Hello?"

"It's me. I want you to come down to the station."

"Now, Trey? But I—"

"I'm sending a car for you. It should be there in about five minutes. Marcus is on his way, too."

Suddenly she knew.

"The tests. They're back, aren't they?"

"Yes."

"Tell me what—"

"Don't argue. I'll explain when you get here. I've got to go. They're bringing Anna in from the hospital now."

"What for? I don't want to see her."

"You will. Please. Just trust me on this."

"Yes. Okay."

"Thank you, baby. See you in a few."

She hung up, then realized she was still in her swimsuit from her daily therapy. She ran down the hall to the bedroom and threw on some clothes. She was stepping into her shoes when there was a knock on the door.

It was her ride, and it was the longest thirty minutes she'd ever spent in her life.

Marcus came into the precinct only moments after

Olivia's arrival. Trey was waiting for them at the front desk.

"Come with me," he said.

Marcus's chin jutted. He'd been as hesitant and defiant as Olivia had been, unwilling to look at Anna Walden's face again. But Trey had been adamant, and Marcus had finally agreed to come, if only to hear the final verdict.

"This is ridiculous," Marcus muttered.

"The whole damn thing has been a nightmare for me, too," Trey said. "So bear with me."

Olivia slid her hand in the bend of Trey's elbow and gave it a squeeze.

"I'm with you," she said.

Trey paused, then stopped and kissed her.

"I know, honey. Forgive me if I was rude."

They rounded a corner, and she saw a half-dozen people standing in front of a window. When she joined them, she saw Anna in a room alone, sitting at a table. Trey shifted her focus by introducing her.

"Marcus . . . Olivia, this is my lieutenant, Harold Warren. And you remember Detective Rodriguez and Detective Sheets."

They nodded.

"The others are from the D.A.'s office. We'll do the introductions to everyone else later. For now, we're going in. They'll be able to see and hear everything that's going on inside that room, but we won't see them, understand?"

"Yes," Marcus said, and took Olivia by the hand.

Olivia wanted to ask questions, but before she could speak, they were being led inside.

"Have a seat," Trey said. "Anywhere."

Marcus dragged a couple of chairs as far away from Anna Walden as he could get; then he and Olivia sat down, while Trey opened a file and laid it on the table in front of Anna.

She sat with her head down and her hands lying loosely in her lap. A bit of drool was hanging from the corner of her lower lip, and when it finally dropped, she seemed oblivious.

But Trey knew something they didn't.

"Laree, the tests are back."

Anna didn't move—didn't blink.

"She doesn't know who Laree is," Olivia said.

Trey didn't argue, but he also didn't agree.

"Look at the tests, Laree. You mothered one of the babies, and we know it, so you may as well acknowledge that much. You also killed one of them. You led us to believe that it was your baby who was returned to Marcus Sealy—that you did it because you were angry that the wrong baby was going to inherit the Sealy fortune. But you were wrong, weren't you? And you know what else? I think your subconscious already knew it."

Marcus's gaze was riveted on Trey's back, and on the shudder he suddenly saw rippling through Anna Walden's frame.

"This test is, without fail, proof that you are the mother."

Anna raised her head and looked straight at Olivia.

357

The wild, crazy stare was still in her eyes.

"My baby. My beautiful, beautiful baby."

Olivia felt as if she was going to throw up, but Trey had told her to trust him, and so she stayed.

Trey pointed at Olivia. "She's beautiful, all right, but she's not your baby."

Olivia moaned. The relief was so great that she felt the room starting to spin. Her grandfather's hand caught her wrist, steadying her where she sat.

Anna frowned.

"My baby."

"Save the crazy part for someone who buys it," he said.

Anna blinked, then swayed, but her expression never changed.

"My baby. He hurt me. I hurt him. I took his baby and made it go away."

"Oh, you killed a baby. There's no mistaking that," Trey said, and then shoved the DNA report right in front of her. "Look! I dare you! Look at the proof of what you did!"

Anna looked up at Trey's face, then laughed an empty, eerie laugh. She looked at Marcus and frowned.

"Stupid thumbs. Everyone should only have two thumbs—not three. You messed it up."

Trey pointed at the paper.

"That's right. They both had two thumbs on one hand. And the babies were both the same size, and they had the same thick dark curls and the same upturned noses. What happened? How did you get them confused?"

"I know my baby," she muttered. "A mother knows her baby. Shut up. You're wrong. You're wrong."

"Then read the report and tell me I'm lying."

"Where's my baby?" Anna said in a high, singsong voice. "I can't find my baby."

Trey slapped the table with the flat of his hand. By now, he was shouting.

"That's because you stuffed her in a fucking suitcase and plastered her up in a wall. What the hell made you do something so evil? Tell me, Laree! Why did you kill your own child?"

Her mouth began to tremble; then the features on her face looked as if they were going to melt. Everything sagged as she began to take short, anxious breaths.

"It's a lie. It's a lie!"

"Read the damn report!"

She flinched, but she couldn't look away. Olivia watched in disbelief as the crazy part of Anna/Laree disappeared. She saw anger. She saw fear. Then she saw something else. At that point, Anna Walden came undone.

"This is wrong," she said, repeatedly jabbing at the paper with her forefinger.

"No. What you did was wrong, but the tests don't lie."

"You fixed it. You made them read this way."

"No. Sheree's tests came back the same thing as yours. The baby we found in that suitcase is the one you gave birth to. You killed Michael and Kay Sealy. You stole their baby, then you killed your own. Now you tell

359

me how in the hell that was going to work for you? Tell me, dammit. I need to understand!"

Anna reeled backward, as if the force of his fury was physically painful.

She picked up the test result and read it again, and she started to cry. At first only a few quiet tears, then deeper sobs.

"There has to be a mistake," she said. "I took the kid, and I wasn't going to give her back. But Foster messed everything up. I was going to keep Olivia and in a few days give Sophie back to them. They looked enough alike that nobody would know the difference, and my Sophie would be in her rightful place as heir to the Sealy money."

"What happened?" Trey asked.

"The babies were playing together. Just sitting on the floor in a patch of sunlight, laughing and poking each other in the nose, then the chin, then laughing and doing it all over again."

Anna covered her face against the memories, but they wouldn't go away.

"I left them alone for just a minute to fix them something to eat. I wasn't cruel. They were hungry."

"What happened?" Trey asked.

"I heard one of them crying. When I went in there, they were both naked, standing in the middle of a pile of clothes. For a moment, I couldn't tell them apart. Then Olivia bent down and picked up her blanket, and I knew. My Sophie grabbed at the blanket, but Olivia wouldn't let it go. I hit her. She fell backward against the corner of the fireplace. I heard the pop, like the sound a ripe watermelon makes when you split it. She didn't move again. I hadn't meant for it to happen that way, but it was too late to take back. She was so still. So I dressed her in the clothes she'd come in and then left her on the bed. I wasn't sure what to do with her body, but I didn't want her to be found."

Trey wouldn't let himself look at Olivia. He had to stay focused.

"But you killed the wrong one, Laree. You killed your own baby."

"No. She grabbed the blanket Olivia came with."

"That doesn't mean a damn thing, but this test does. You killed your own child. Foster came along, and before you knew it, he had asked for a ransom, which messed your plans up considerably. Then he goes and gives the surviving baby back without any concern for your feelings."

"It doesn't matter," she said. "Sophie was where she belonged, no matter how it happened."

Trey pointed at Olivia.

"Only she's not Sophie."

"She is. When Marcus hired me, she quit crying. She was my baby."

"She quit crying because she was all cried out," Marcus said.

Anna began to tremble. She looked at Olivia.

"You're my baby. Tell them, darling. Tell them you're mine."

Olivia stood up and walked out of the room.

Anna got up and tried to follow, but Trey stopped her, then turned her toward the mirror on the other side of the room, where a half-dozen people on the other side were watching the drama unfolding in mute horror.

"Look at yourself, Laree. Look good and hard. You murdered Michael and Kay Sealy out of nothing more than jealousy and revenge, but that wasn't your worst mistake. You really screwed up when you took their daughter. What kind of woman is it who can't tell her own child from another? What kind of mother does what you did?"

Anna tried to cover her face, but Trey wouldn't let go of her arms. She closed her eyes, but the truth was still there, pushing at her, reminding her of that tiny body lying crumpled in the suitcase she'd found in a closet. It was the hell that had been hovering at the back of her sanity, pulling her under. She wanted to go back to that place in her mind where the truth had been deeply hidden.

Shadows beckoned to her. She imagined she felt tiny fingers pulling at her from the inside out, then heard a tiny voice screaming at her from afar.

"Here's the kicker, Laree. There's one more thing that the coroner discovered. One thing we didn't catch the first time out."

She couldn't bring herself to look and didn't have the guts to ask.

Trey shook her—hard.

"Open your goddamn eyes and look at yourself!"

Laree looked.

"You know that baby you stuffed in that suitcase . . . the one you buried behind that wall? Well, she wasn't dead. There were tiny scratch marks on the inside of the suitcase and residue of the lining beneath her fingernails."

Outside, Olivia cupped her hands over her mouth, stifling a moan of disbelief. Chia Rodriguez slipped an arm around Olivia's waist without speaking.

Marcus bowed his head, then stared at the floor.

But it was Anna, looking up into the mirror at the reflection of Trey's face behind her, who had to face the hell of what she'd done.

"You're lying."

"Not about that. Never about anything like that."

Anna moaned; then she started to scream, tearing at her hair and clawing at her face as she fell to the floor.

Trey looked at her there, then motioned at Marcus. Together, they walked out of the room.

Olivia was waiting for him just outside the door. Her face was streaked with tears, and the look in her eyes was one of desperation.

"Please, tell me this is finally over."

"Almost," Trey said, and together, they walked away.

Dawn came in four shades of pink, dragging with it a burst of sunshine that gave promise of a beautiful day.

It had been a month since the revelation. Olivia considered it the day she'd been reborn. Her identity was no longer a mystery, and her faith in herself had been renewed.

Grampy had resigned himself to the fact that she wasn't leaving Trey's house, although the renovations to the Sealy estate were almost done. He and Rose had both moved back home, happy to be there despite the hammering on the roof.

Laree/Anna had not been able to live with the hell of what she'd done. Less than a month after her incarceration in a prison for the criminally insane, she was found hanging from a bathroom showerhead. She had taken a coward's route out of her guilt by committing suicide, and there was no one at her funeral to mourn for the loss.

But it was Trey who set the clock on Olivia's world, and it was Trey who had stayed fast beside her when she'd been at her worst. With only a couple of months to go to the date they'd set for their wedding, there was still one thing Trey had vowed must be done. Something about keeping a promise he'd made to a baby called Jane Doe.

"Livvie, honey, are you ready?" Trey asked as he poked his head into the bedroom.

"Almost," she said. "I still can't reach far enough up to fasten the hook on the back of my dress."

"That's what I'm here for," Trey said, and lifted her hair aside, then fastened the dress. "All done." When she turned back around, his eyes darkened. "And so beautiful."

"Thank you, darling," Olivia said, then laid a hand on the front of his suit coat. "I'm only going to say this once, but don't think I will ever forget it."

"Say what?" he asked.

"If you are as faithful to me for the rest of our lives as you were to the promise you made to Sophie, then I will consider myself blessed."

The unexpected compliment brought tears to his eyes.

"Someone had to care," he muttered.

"She's blessed that it was you. Now let's go put her to rest. She certainly deserves it."

Epilogue

Through the years, they made an annual pilgrimage to the family plot in a small cemetery outside of Dallas where the baby had been buried, to the hillside where Marcus Sealy's wife and parents, his son and daughter-in-law, as well as a brother and sister, then finally Marcus, had been laid to rest.

And always Trey would kneel down by the baby's marker to pull away any errant strands of grass that had missed the lawn mower's blades, while Olivia would place a small spray of pink roses on the ground.

Then they would stand back to look, with their arms around each other, and read to themselves the words carved into the stone. It was the only thing they could do to offer proof to the world that for a brief moment in time a tiny girl with dark curls, an upturned nose and a giggle always waiting to come out had lived.

Olivia had grown accustomed to the sadness she felt

...at having had a sister she couldn't remember. But she made it a point to pay the visit just the same, so she wouldn't forget.

Just as she'd done every year before, she laid the spray of pink roses on the grave as Trey pulled at the grass. As they stepped back to view their handiwork, their gazes fell on the words carved in the stone above the birth and death dates.

Sophie Sealy
Sleeping with angels

"Rest in peace, little girl," Trey said, then put his arm around Olivia's shoulders and pulled her close against him. He could smell the lilac scent of her shampoo and the sharp hint of frost in the air. Another year almost gone. Time moved too fast.

They locked hands as they started back to the car. Then something—some sound—caught Trey's attention. He stopped and turned around.

"What is it?" Olivia asked.

A frown came and went, then he shrugged it off.

"I thought I heard something, but I guess I was wrong."

They moved on to their car. Then, from somewhere off in the distance, so if they'd listened just a little bit longer they might have heard it, came a baby's soft giggle, and then the sound of little feet running quickly through the leaves upon the ground.